Revel Barker started writing for newspa
and worked for two weeklies and an ev
Riding, then joined the *Daily Mirror* as a staff reporter before his
21st birthday. He specialised in investigations and feature writing,
then became defence correspondent and foreign editor of the
*Sunday Mirror* before retiring as managing editor with Mirror
Group newspapers.
He is now a publisher of (mainly) journalism-related books and
lives on an island in the Mediterranean.

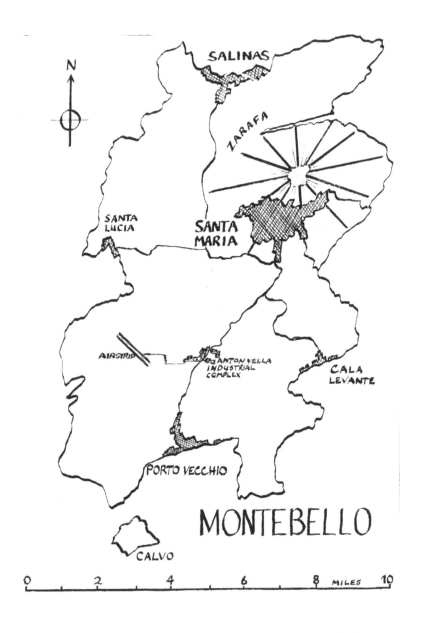

MONTEBELLO

Map: David Carrington

# The Mayor of Montebello

## Revel Barker

P

Palatino Publishing

First published in 2012 by Palatino Publishing

Copyright © Revel Barker, 2012

By the same author:

> *The Hitler Scoop*
>
> *Round Up The Usual Suspects* (editor)
>
> *Field of Vision*
>
> *Crying All The Way To The Bank: Liberace v. Cassandra and the Daily Mirror (Famous Trials)*

ISBN: 978-1-907841-08-8

Palatino Publishing 66 Florence Road Brighton BN1 6DJ United Kingdom

palatinobooks@gmail.com

This book is dedicated to those few good friends
(they know who they are)
who provided inspiration and encouragement
in the writing of it.

# One

Everybody who knew him, which it transpired was most of the island population, would have described Giuseppe Benedetto as a good guy, an essentially honest man, straight as a die.

Even after the bank hold-up.

A basically simple man, a fisherman by calling, he passed his mornings from sunrise in the sheltered inshore waters trolling for barracuda, bass, bream, lampuga, and *piesce san pietro*, which the British extolled as John Dory. Before lunchtime he would be at his brother's stall in the *Souk*, helping to sell his catch. In the early afternoon he would potter around his smallholding overlooking the *porte vecchio*, hoe the hard biscuit-coloured earth and feed his livestock, then snatch a short siesta before heading to La Spada, the predominantly fishermen's pub on the harbour, for a few glasses of local wine before heading home to cook his own supper of fish or home-produced rabbit, chicken, or eggs, usually with pasta. In common with all men on Montebello he considered himself an excellent cook of plain food.

Most of the year he lived alone, but during the English school vacations he would be joined by his girlfriend, a teacher from Liverpool called Audrey, who he'd met after she'd read a travel article in the *Guardian* and come out on a fortnight's exploratory holiday with a friend. They'd met Giuseppe at the bar of La Spada on their first night, persuaded him to take them fishing, and later asked him to give them a conducted tour of the island. That hadn't taken long but Audrey had immediately become enchanted by both the fisherman and his island. Before the end of her first week she shared a siesta with him and for most of the second week she abandoned her travelling companion and spent the nights at

Giuseppe's farmhouse, returning alone several times a year for every school break thereafter.

At the outset of each visit she would buy him something from the gift shop at John Lennon Airport; maybe something connected with The Beatles, a taste in music they shared, or a souvenir from Liverpool Football Club.

She would also exchange a couple of hundred pounds into thousands of Italian lire (the exchange rate was slightly more than 2,400 lire to the pound) – perhaps as an insurance against the relationship going wrong and needing to finish her holiday by booking in to the Porto Hotel, but also because she always tried to persuade Giuseppe to let her treat him to a restaurant dinner (which his Montebellan macho pride refused to allow). So instead, while he was out fishing, she'd sometimes take his little red Mini Moke – bearing the GB sticker she'd bought for a joke, also at the airport, because it represented his initials – into town and buy pork, lamb or beef for dinner, and sometimes a few small knick-knacks or modern cooking utensils for his farmhouse.

Giuseppe's home was as basic and as simple as its owner: two ground floor rooms which had originally housed animals had been converted into a living room and large kitchen; upstairs had become a bedroom and a bathroom. The wide front door, painted blue generations ago, had suffered from scorching sunshine and scouring from red sand blown all the way from Libya by the strong and humid southerly winds known as the *ostro* and the *scirocco*; an ancient key sat permanently in the rusty lock, on the outside, for crime was virtually unknown on Montebello.

After six or seven years of Audrey's visits the house contained an extensive library of sixties music, the 'Merseybeat' collection being augmented by The Searchers, Cilla Black, Billy J Kramer And The Dakotas, and Gerry And The Pacemakers, and a unique assortment of Liverpool soccer souvenirs – unique, at least, on an island where most of the men supported Juventus, Inter, or Manchester United at long distance. It also contained, in a drawer reserved for her personal use in the bedroom, a few thousand, then a few hundred thousand, Italian lire because Audrey never really saw the point in taking the currency back home.

Their situation – accruing pop records, Beatles artefacts, soccer souvenirs and cash – might have lasted interminably, as it appeared set to do. But at the end of one of the visits, after he had driven her to the airport and returned home to retrieve her laundry from the washing line on his roof, he folded it neatly and placed it in Audrey's drawer, where he noticed, not for the first time, the biscuit tin in which she kept her unspent cash. He opened the box and counted the contents.

There was almost one million lire inside it.

But Giuseppe was an honest man. The cash was as safe in his keeping as it would be in the APS – the Apostleship of Prayer Savings Bank.

He was, however, a proud man and, in the nature of most moderately successful fishermen, sometimes prone to boasting. He shared with his more intimate associates in the Spada bar the knowledge of his girlfriend's stash as proof, as he saw it, of her trust and her love for him.

His friends were also honest men. Lino, the baker, might ask tourists three times the going rate for cheese or pea *pastizzi*; Salvu the taxi driver would always overcharge visitors; Spiro, the electrician, might use cheap two-core wire instead of three-core cable when rewiring a foreigner's house; but they would never cheat or steal from each other.

Instead, they introduced Giuseppe to something called five-card poker, a game he had heard of, but never played. And two nights a week, thereafter, the four men met at Giuseppe's house – because the other three all had wives at home – and after steaming bowls of *spaghetti alio olio* the kitchen table was cleared and a stack of Liverpudlian LPs put on the record player to entertain them quietly but rhythmically in the background. His friends frequently complimented him on the speed with which he had picked up the fundamentals of the game. And when he ran short of cash, as he often did, he could always take a temporary advance from the seemingly bottomless pot in the drawer upstairs.

It wasn't until Audrey's postcard arrived with details of the itinerary of her forthcoming visit, so that he could meet her at the airport as usual, that Giuseppe thought of checking the money in the biscuit tin. As he counted, he started to break into a sweat. He laid out the banknotes several times, in different order, but whichever way he checked the balance, it was 800,000 lire short.

What could he do? He had never formally borrowed money in his life. He realised that *la donna Fortuna* didn't look upon him sufficiently kindly for there to be any chance of winning back the money playing cards. He didn't understand mortgages and didn't know any friends who could loan him anything like that amount in cash.

There was only one thing for it.

He had to rob a bank.

Giuseppe had seen the movies on television: he knew what to do.

He returned to Audrey's drawer and found a pair of nylon stockings. He pulled one over his head and looked in the mirror to confirm that it squashed the basic features of his face into an unrecognisable form. He already looked like a bank robber, he thought.

And – no simpleton, Giuseppe – he reckoned that his target bank should be on the far side of the island, farthest away from his home village, where he thought there'd be less chance of meeting anybody who would know him. There was a bank north of the mountain, at Salinas, where earlier generations had carved out salt pans in the rocks on the shore.

The planning all seemed so easy; he couldn't understand why Hollywood made so much fuss. It would be a sin, he knew, but he had no doubt that the village priest would absolve him – and not even suggest restitution because, first of all, it was an act of desperation by a poor man and the bishop had said that it was not, for example, sinful for a hungry man to steal bread; second he didn't have the wherewithal to repay it; and third, even if he had, there would be no way he could do it anonymously. In any case, hadn't he heard that the bank's profits were counted in hundreds of billions? He didn't know what a billion was, but they'd hardly miss a few hundred thousand...

He drove nearly ten miles north in the blazing morning sunshine, via the capital (and only) city of Santa Maria, skirting the terraced foothills of the long-extinct volcano alongside the olive groves and orchards introduced by the Romans to the beautiful mountain that had given the island its name, through the area where there were more brightly painted donkey carts than cars, until he had travelled almost as far as it was possible to drive from his home.

Parking directly outside the bank, he lifted his shotgun from the back seat and pulled the stocking mask over his face before heading straight for the *Guarda Finanza* constable who was courteously about to open the door for him. The officer did a double-take when, too late, he noticed the mask. Giuseppe didn't speak, but gestured with the business end of the shotgun that he should lead him inside.

There were two cashiers behind the counter, but no customers. Giuseppe approached one of the bank clerks and told him: 'Give me some money.'

But the bank employee took his time responding and allowed his gaze to wander up from the red shirt to the red face that looked like a sun-dried tomato beneath the nylon denier, then sucked his teeth and said: 'Oh, fuck off, Giuse.'

The policeman, however, had a different view. 'It's me he's pointing the gun at. Give him the money!'

This produced a shrug from the cashier, who wasn't used to being told what to do, and who now asked: 'How much do you want?'

'Eight hundred thousand.'

The notes were slowly counted out.

'Put it in a bag, please.'

The cashier looked about him then, with a sigh and another shrug, he reached under the counter, produced a brown paper bag, removed his lunch – four *pastizzi* – from it and replaced it with the banknotes.

Giuseppe said: 'Thank-you,' then walked backwards to the door, still pointing his gun at the policeman. He ran the couple of paces across the pavement, placed the bag on the front passenger seat with the shotgun on top so that it wouldn't blow away, put the key in the ignition and sped off, as fast as his little red Moke with the GB sticker on the back would carry him.

As he drew up outside his own front door two *carabinieri*, a captain and a sergeant, emerged from the side of the house.

'How goes it, Giuse?'

'So-and-so, *capitano*…'

The captain nodded towards the gun. 'Where've you been?'

'Hunting.'

'What's in the bag?'

'My lunch, *capitano*.'

The captain picked up the grease-stained packet. 'Give us a *pastizza*, Giuse, I'm famished…'

# *Two*

Orazio Verdi didn't usually countenance interruptions when he was putting his bi-weekly (Tuesdays and Fridays) editions of *La Gazzetta* to bed, but when the caller announced himself as the *commandante* of *carabinieri*, the young reporter who had answered the phone decided it would be wisest to transfer him immediately to the boss's desk.

'It's Cesare! We have a bank robbery. Hold your front page!' he yelled down the phone.

Then he dictated the details – in English, because he could, and he knew from experience that the editor would be taking a note in his native language in copperplate Pitman's shorthand.

'Thanks, Cesare,' he said when the colonel had finished relaying the details. 'One thing… don't charge him, don't even name him, until the newspaper hits the streets, eh?'

'Everybody will know his name by tonight, in any case.'

'Yes. But…' He didn't need to explain the complications of local criminal law to the colonel, who obviously understood them better than most people.

'No problems. *Ciao.*'

Orazio Verdi wasn't the editor's real name, but his *pseudonimo* – what the English would call a nom de plume. The identity on his British passport showed that he was Horatio Greene; the other name was a near-Italian equivalent more suitable, he thought, when writing articles that were critical of local government on an island in the middle of the Mediterranean.

Now he summoned his small staff around him. He told Dino, the chief sub-editor, to downsize the planned front page lead story on olive subsidies to a single column and clear the rest of the front. He sent one reporter with a photographer to interview the two bank cashiers and another to speak to the officer who had been on the door. A third was despatched to La Spada, the fishermen's pub, to see what snippets he could pick up there.

While he briefed them the journalists caught each other's eyes. Any minute now, they were thinking, he's going to say 'This is how we used to do things in Fleet Street.' But the editor returned silently to his keyboard, rapidly transcribing his shorthand notes into copy and automatically translating it into Italian for his newspaper.

The adrenalin was flowing. This is what he was best at – what he'd spent most of his life at – knocking out fairly instant hard news stories for Page One.

*Madonna!* It was just like the old days. This was how he used to do things in The Street!

The reason the editor didn't want the bank robber to be named, or officially arrested, was that English criminal law restricted the amount of information that could be reported once an indictment had been made. And, through a quirk of history, possibly influenced by native island lethargy, it was English law that pertained on this otherwise Sicilian island.

In its history Montebello had been invaded and ruled by tribes that nobody had heard of – the Sicani, Siculi, Elymni – and by Carthaginians, Greeks and Phoenicians, followed by Romans, assorted Sicilians and Italians, Jews, Vandals, Saracens, Normans, Spaniards and British. Some of them, like the Vandals, had done little more than vandalise the island; others had introduced culture, arts, craft, industry and farming. Different invaders had made their distinguishing marks. The Romans left hillside terraces, roads and agriculture; the Arabs left place-names, including *Souk* for the market place and a tradition of flat-roofed biblical architecture; the British left red telephone kiosks and pillar boxes and blue lamps over the doors of police stations; modern-day native Montebellans left litter – empty bottles, fast-food wrappers and cigarette packets – all over the place, guaranteeing permanent employment for an army of street cleaners.

Part of the island history was also recorded in the paintwork of doors and windows; it signified the original ownership of the buildings and, although it might be touched-up from time to time, by convention the colour was never changed. White meant Norman, blue meant Greek, pink Phoenician, red Spanish, yellow Jewish, green British. You could provoke an argument with a local householder, just by remarking on the colour of his shutters.

You could also tell a lot about the wealth of the owner – at least, of the original owner. Successful merchants, bishops' family members, land owners, and even some priests, added open stone balconies to their houses; less well-off families built enclosed wooden galleries; poorer people had simple windows overlooking the streets.

It was only in the last two hundred years that things had started to get complicated. In 1798 Napoleon's navy, looking for a safe harbour on its way to Egypt, had occupied the island without local resistance but the normally compliant islanders had objected when French troops started pillaging first the churches and then their homes. The local elders despatched one of their most competent fishermen, the now greatly revered Anton Vella, to locate Nelson's Mediterranean fleet and ask for help and in 1800 a frigate commanded by Captain Matthew Ireland RN arrived in the harbour and drove the invaders out.

The British then ruled Montebello until the end of the First World War when they handed the island over to their Italian allies. In the meantime they had built schools, a hospital and even a small Anglican church. But they hadn't revoked the Napoleonic laws of inheritance, nor even introduced English as the official language. They had, however, imposed English criminal law and an English courts system. During the Second World War the island had been first Italian, then British again, and afterwards Italian again, and temporary host to a Nato (mainly Anglo-American) base. It had occurred to nobody to change the rule of law.

As a lieutenant in the Fleet Air Arm in the summer of 1943, Greene's father had played a short but significant role in the island's colourful heritage.

He had taken off from an aircraft carrier somewhere south-west of Malta in search of a downed Messerschmitt pilot, located the aircraft in the sea, and dropped a rubber dinghy. Almost immediately afterwards the clouds had closed in so that he couldn't see where the sun was, and at the same time both his radio and his compass failed to work. He circled, searching for the carrier or for anywhere safe to land and, with his reserve fuel tank starting to approach the empty mark, suddenly spotted the island that he recognised from his charts as being Montebello – enemy territory.

Jimmy Greene flew slowly over the island looking for a place to land, while waggling the wings of his Swordfish biplane, hoping to signify that he was in difficulty and not presenting a threat. He identified an air strip and flew over again, this time noticing that many of the streets of honey-coloured houses appeared to be displaying a large number of what seemed to be white sheets.

He landed safely, cut the engine and sat in the cockpit, still trying to make contact on his radio, and within a few moments found himself surrounded by Italian military vehicles. He removed his belt and service revolver and climbed out, to meet what was obviously a senior officer wearing the white-plumed trilby hat of the *Alpini* regiment. He walked towards him, exchanged a salute… and the Italian drew his sword, presented it to Greene and said, in English, 'Please accept our surrender.'

When the Italian electricians repaired his radio he was able to report that he had single-handedly captured a battalion of 700 soldiers. The responding message, one day later, was that the carrier had no capacity for hundreds of prisoners of war; that he was being promoted to lieutenant-commander to put him on the same rank as the local commandant; and that he should continue to rule the garrison pending further orders.

While being entertained with delicious fresh food and unlimited quantities of good wine in the Italian officers' mess he learnt that the troops on the ground had interpreted the unusual movement of his wings as signalling the start of an Allied incursion, probably prior to the invasion of Sicily itself. But since the *Alpini* had little or no sympathy with either Mussolini or the fascists they were perfectly happy to accept the unintentional turn of events philosophically.

He had stayed there, later assisted by a company of the Coldstream Guards, as de facto military governor until the end of hostilities in 1945. Then he returned to London and to his pre-war job as a reporter on the *Daily Express*, married the news editor's daughter, and the only child of that union – christened Horatio in honour of his naval experience – had followed in his professional footsteps, first as a reporter on the *Yorkshire Post* in Leeds, then in Fleet Street on the *Daily Mail* where he occasionally worked in direct competition with his father.

The family had taken all its annual holidays on Montebello, which Jimmy Greene had already started to consider as his second home. Horatio had often remarked that if it hadn't been for the many opportunities for foreign travel that his job provided, he might never have been anywhere else. But in the late nineteen-eighties when his marriage broke up and his employers offered what appeared to be an exceptionally generous round of voluntary redundancy packages for editorial staff, Horatio, fluent in Italian from childhood, decided he would take the money and retire there.

At first he had supplemented his pay-off with occasional bouts of freelance writing – travel articles for magazines and the broadsheets, news stories for the tabloids about Brits getting into trouble while on holiday and interviews with various celebrities, footballers and criminals who had fled to the island in the hope of finding sanctuary from the British press. Years earlier, at a party at the *castello* – several cocktail parties and a few dinners were always arranged in his father's honour on their visits – he'd met Hannibal Spiteri, publisher and editor of *La Gazzetta*, who, after he'd been living there a few years, offered to hand over the editorship to him.

Horatio had asked for roughly twice as much salary as the publisher wanted to pay, eventually settling on a lower amount, but tied to a sliding scale increasing in line with circulation and company profits. He had also asked for, and received, the publisher's guarantee of editorial independence; political opposition in the island's governance was ineffectual, he had explained, so the newspaper needed to do the job for them.

Within a couple of years, following what he described as 'the *Daily Mail* formula', he had improved the paper to the extent that he was earning more or less the amount he had originally demanded and the publisher was more than content to pay it.

His editorship had not, however, got off to the most auspicious start. The morning that the first coverage of the monthly local council meeting had appeared under his editorship, he'd been summoned across *viale* Anton Vella to the *municipio* and the mahogany-lined office of Silvio Morano, the mayor, who complained angrily that not only was the newspaper too critical of council action (or inaction) he had been misquoted and quoted 'out of context' in the paper's report of the proceedings.

Horatio had naturally said that he would pursue the complaint with the reporter who had covered the meeting, and report back. And the mayor said that, yes, he should definitely do that, because he could always withdraw the newspaper's licence to publish (every activity on Montebello seemed to require a licence, and an annual fee) – and see how Hannibal Spiteri would like that, as the first consequence of handing over editorial control to somebody from England, even one with such an illustrious forebear.

As he left the office Horatio noticed that among the many photographs on the wall was one of the mayor's father, who had held the position before him, shaking hands with *Governatore Giacomo Greene*…

Aldo, his chief reporter, readily admitted that he had 'misquoted' the mayor, but denied that any of his account had been inaccurate or out of context.

'You can't quote him directly,' he said, 'because the man speaks gibberish. The best you can do is report what he thinks he is trying to say.'

He produced a blue covered spiral-bound notebook from a jacket pocket. 'This is an example of what he actually said' – and he read a paragraph from his shorthand notes. Then he opened the paper to the report of the meeting: '...And this is what I quoted him as having said,' reading his account out loud.

'You're right,' Horatio told him. 'Gibberish. Fluent claptrap. I congratulate you on your translation.'

He telephoned the mayor. 'We have a problem. Most people don't talk in complete or grammatical sentences, so a good – and kind-spirited – reporter usually writes what the speaker intended to say, rather than directly quoting the way he said it. It's up to you. We can report what you say, or we can report what you mean. If I were you, I'd leave it to the reporter to make you look good, and coherent.'

'No,' said the mayor. 'I have, haven't I, been in public, you know, community, municipal, service for two, I mean 20, decades, years, and I always say, you should know this, to mean what I say.'

'So what you are saying is...?'

'I insist that you correctly report exactly and whatever I say,' the mayor told him.

'Your wish, Mr Mayor,' Horatio told him, 'is my command.'

So the following month, acting on the editor's explicit instruction, Aldo typed up the mayoral speeches and comments exactly as they had been delivered, with hardly any finished sentences, incomprehensible grammar, every um, er, and ah, every repeated word or phrase and with virtually no paragraphs.

What appeared was a full page of solid and effectively unreadable type, with hardly any paragraph breaks. Horatio had thought of clearing the schemed advertisement off the page, then thought better of it and turned the dense column of type over onto a second page.

The ink was hardly dry when Manuel, the mayor's clerk, came on the phone asking for the editor: 'The mayor sends his compliments and asks you to come and see him.'

'He sends his compliments?'

'I added that bit,' said Manuel. 'But he wants you to come, right now.'

'I'm very busy. Please give the mayor my compliments and tell him he can come and see me, if he so wishes.'

He stood, walked to the window, and watched as mayor Morano, a copy of the latest edition of *La Gazzetta* under his arm, waited for a gap in the traffic then scurried across Anton Vella Street. He opened the door in readiness and the mayor, slightly breathless after having climbed the stairs, stormed in and threw the newspaper onto the editor's desk.

'What is the meaning of this nonsense?'

'You think it's nonsense?' asked Horatio. 'I think you're right. Unfortunately for both of us, it's exactly what you said at the council meeting. And, what's even worse, everything is in context.'

'It's ridiculous.'

'I read every word,' Horatio told him. 'And I'd agree that it's ridiculous. It's also totally illiterate, and from my point of view it's terrible journalism, but our mutual consolation will be that anybody who looks at that page will automatically turn to the next one. Nobody will read it. Thank goodness there's an advertisement in the corner for *Preparation-H*, a haemorrhoid ointment, to brighten the page up a bit.'

Clearly a compromise, a truce, was essential and it eventually came from the mayor. He conceded that he had been 'perhaps too critical' of the reporting in *La Gazzetta*. He agreed that his speeches were generally more coherent in the newspaper than they were in Aldo's notebook, and he promised not to complain again.

For his part, the editor promised that he would instruct Aldo always to present the mayor's speeches in the best possible literary and grammatical style. While his newspaper reserved its democratic right to criticise the council, he said, he would equally make sure of praise where it was due. Horatio wasn't quite finished; he told the mayor that the newspaper needed to know – and where appropriate to announce – what he was going to say, before he said it. That way, with the speech and the council decision being reported in the next edition, the mayor would be getting

14

what the editor described as 'two bites of the cherry' in terms of publicity.

They shook hands on it, establishing, if not a deep friendship, at least an enduring professional relationship.

Later that day Horatio invited Franco di Giorgio, president of the Campanello public relations and advertising agency, to dinner and told him he needed to know what was going on in the commercial world in Montebello, before it happened. Di Giorgio represented virtually every business concern on the island. If the newspaper was going to report the firm's clients' activities, he also expected them to advertise in the newspaper – with the agency of course collecting its usual 15 per cent of the rack advertising rate.

'Never dismiss the importance of advertising,' he told his editorial staff. 'Advertising is information; it tells readers what's on at the cinema and where the best deals of the day are at the supermarkets. Without advertising, we wouldn't know that Guinness was good for you or that Persil washes whitest. And it pays our wages.

'News is a different commodity. You tell people what's going to happen, before it happens, then you tell them it's happened, after it happens. That way, the readers begin to rely on the paper.

'At least, that's the way it works in Fleet Street.'

# Three

*In England the cuckoo's song is said to be the first harbinger of spring. In Montebello it's the cuckoo mentality of the authorities that heralds the start of summer...*

Horatio, typing away as Orazio Verdi, realised that he'd need to check with Aldo or Dino whether *cuculo* actually meant crazy in Italian, as it did in English; he suspected that it might not.

*For example, they dredge the harbour at the end of June, piling effluent on the road at the entrance to the port. They create a traffic lane system to the ferry terminal that can have been designed only by a cretin who has never driven a car towards the port, and plastic bollards are hit by cars and strewn all over the road.*

*They close major thoroughfares for roadworks from Porto Vecchio to the city centre without anything as helpful as a diversion sign – all projects, presumably, that could not have been tackled in winter. They announce the demolition of the classical façade of the Principessa Elisabetta hotel, due to start, apparently, in August.*

*They start to resurface roads in Sta Lucia, carefully leaving the iron manhole covers protruding above the fresh tarmac by at least ten centimetres. Yet throughout winter they didn't even touch the pot-holed surfaces of tourist routes to the main resorts.*

*The airlines run more than two hours late, the ferry leaves when it feels like it, and passengers are stranded because sometimes the ticket machine doesn't work.*

*Meanwhile returning tourists, eager to spend money, search in vain for long-remembered cash machines at the harbour, the airport or in the Anton Vella industrial estate (all places where one could park while collecting cash).*

*The marina looks like a scrapyard. The ferry terminal looks like a suburb of Beirut. The Hilton hotel development appears to have been abandoned.*

*Porto Vecchio has obviously become a no-go area for the construction industry.*

*Short of putting up signs saying Tourists Go Home, it's difficult to conceive how the island could be made less appealing to visitors. Yet tourism is our biggest industry. Small wonder that it is declining, year on year.*

*And the mayor says that things on the island are nothing like as bad as the overwhelming majority of normally laid-back residents – and this newspaper – think they are, proving, if nothing else, how closely some politicians are in tune with the electorate. Or not.*

*So what is the cause of this spurt of disruptive activity as the tourist season (as we used to know it) kicks in?*

*Oh… could it possibly be because there's an election coming up soon?*

He was interrupted by the ringing telephone. The mayor told him it was a beautiful morning and he was about to celebrate it by opening a bottle. Would the editor care to join him?

Horatio fancied a drink. In the old Fleet Street days he'd have been in the back bar of the Harrow by now, sharing a half-bottle of bubbly with his feature-writing chums Vince Mulchrone and Bill Greaves, then a second half-bottle, and often a third (for some reason, nobody ever suggested buying full bottles). And only then the day, and the day's drinking, would start in earnest.

He pushed away his keyboard, lifted a jacket from the wardrobe and crossed the *viale* Anton Vella to the *municipio*. He walked through the back door into the mayor's chamber. After two years in the editor's job it had become a well-worn path for him.

They shook hands, and as he concentrated on pulling the cork the mayor asked, as he frequently did: 'And what are you – or the esteemed *signor* Orazio Verdi – criticising my administration for, this week?'

'The list is already too long to recite, and he's not finished yet. You can read all about it in the paper. *Il signor* Verdi is assuming that this sudden spurt of activity is not unrelated to the fact that there's an election in the offing. Even if it won't be taking place before next spring.'

'Ah, yes; the election…' said the mayor, as if he hadn't given the subject much thought. Then he asked: 'You going to the *castello* tonight?'

Horatio said that he would be sending a reporter, because the *contessa* was merely looking for sponsors for the opera and the newspaper would obviously cover the meeting as a fund-raising event. He wouldn't personally be a sponsor but *La Gazzetta* would support the opera in terms of publicity – 'Donating cash would be pointless because then they'd need to spend it on advertising, so it amounts to the same thing.'

'You don't like opera?'

'I don't like the noise it makes; I wouldn't like it even with the sound turned off. It's usually crap acting – you get better performances at the amateur dramatics. And every opera has only one decent tune. You wait too long to hear it and by the time it comes it's too late to leave the theatre and go for dinner.'

Nevertheless, the mayor told him, he personally was required to attend by virtue of his position. '*Noblesse oblige,*' he said. And, with the aforementioned election looming, it did no harm to be photographed alongside the aristocracy.

'Aristocracy?'

'The nobility. Isn't that what you'd call a count or countess in England?'

'Nobility, maybe, for a count,' Horatio told him. 'But they wouldn't be classed as aristocracy in England.'

'What's the difference?'

'Tradition… history.'

And Horatio told him that Montebello's so-called nobility had neither quality. The title dated back no further than 1946 when King Umberto – who had previously ceded sovereignty to Mussolini – was leaving Italy for the last time. As he boarded the aircraft at Ciampino airport he suddenly remembered that there were loose ends that needed tying up. He called his chancellor out of the crowd of treasury officials who had come to see him off. 'The accounts,' he said, pointing to the staff. 'Make sure those people do the accounts.'

Amid the roar of the aircraft engines the chancellor apparently misunderstood the message. The Italian word for accounts is the same as for counts, *conti*. The official returned to the palace and immediately ennobled those members of staff who had been at the airport, as *conti*.

'Did you never wonder why they are called the count and countess of Ciampino? The contessa has got breeding but the count's dad was a royal bean-counter, ennobled only because he'd gone to wave goodbye to the king.'

'How is it that you know more about Italian history than I, an Italian, do?'

'I read books.'

'Ah, yes,' said the mayor, refilling their glasses. 'You read books. That's what I wanted to talk to you about.'

He said his nephew, Sandro, didn't read anything – 'I think the last time he opened a book was to colour in the pictures.' The mayor's sister had sent the boy to Sapienza university in Rome to study law and public administration, but he had quit and come back to Montebello before the end of the first year. He still lived at home and spent most of his time playing with the computer and frittering away his future inheritance in night clubs. He was virtually unemployable, lacking even the social graces to get a job as a waiter.

'Why didn't you find him something? There must be hundreds of jobs in the government that don't require any talent whatsoever.'

'He doesn't want one. He has a career plan. Either he's going to win the lottery or inherit my wine business; he doesn't care much which happens first. But if he takes over the winery it'll be bankrupt within a year, you'll see. Now my sister has decided that when I retire Sandro should take over from me as mayor.

'Do you think you could arrange that?' asked the editor. 'Appoint your own successor?'

'Oh yes. I have a strong and loyal following. They hate it, you know, when you attack me. The people would vote for whoever I nominated.'

'Astonishing.'

'Not really. There are people out there…' he waved beyond each of the four corners of the room, 'who owe me favours. Jobs I've created, sinecures I've awarded, licences I granted, building permissions I allowed in non-development areas…'

'*La Gazzetta* should be exposing all this, you know.'

'No it shouldn't. It's merely oiling the wheels of local government. It's how things work. But…' the mayor was ignoring the interruption, '…young Sandro is virtually illiterate. Not even the best efforts by you and Aldo could make him appear intelligent.'

'You have a solution in your hands, then. Don't resign. I mean, it's not as if you're doing a bad job.'

'But I am not doing a good one, as your *signor* Verdi reminds me, twice every week. In any case, I have had enough. And my winery is suffering from my neglect – by the way, this new *bianco* is not bad, is it? Let's open another… When my father came to the same conclusion he handed over to me, so now I need to hand over to somebody else.'

'But if not to your nephew, then whom?'

That, said the mayor, was what he wanted to talk to Horatio about.

He'd had a *lampo di genio*, a brainwave: instead of constantly carping and criticising the council and the mayor, why didn't Horatio take on the job himself?

The editor nearly choked on his white wine.

'Ridiculous,' he said, wiping his mouth on a handkerchief. Then he grinned: 'Of all your mad ideas, that is the maddest.'

But the mayor insisted that there was real – he had to wrestle with his limited vocabulary to find the word – *sinergia*, synergy, in his suggestion. 'You want to know what the mayor is thinking; you'd be thinking it. You want to know what he's saying; you'd be saying it. You want to know what the council is doing; you'd be doing it.

You want the mayor to speak in grammatical sentences; you'd be writing them. You want…'

'OK,' said Horatio. 'But even if it were realistic, they wouldn't vote for a foreigner as mayor.'

'I tell you. They will vote for whoever I tell them; plus, presumably you'd also have the support of the newspaper.'

'I wouldn't want to spend every day arguing with Montebellans…'

'You do that every day, in any case. Only this way, there'd be some point to doing it. In any case, you don't need to decide here and now. Go away and think about it. But let's finish this bottle, first…'

When he returned to his desk there was a note from Dino, his chief sub-editor. Horatio would need to re-jig his intro. 'Cuckoo' didn't work in Italian for describing crazy ideas.

# Four

Because it was the favoured watering hole of local journalists, the Greenes, father and son, had naturally gravitated towards the Ireland pub on their regular holiday visits, and Horatio still frequented the place to drink with his editorial staff after work. Having a drink to 'unwind' was another tradition he had imported from Fleet Street.

Named in honour of Matthew Ireland, the Royal Navy captain who had kicked out the French, it had a copy of what was presumed to be his portrait in place of honour behind the bar. It was a long narrow room with benches and tables along the side walls, and stools in the gangway between them that allowed just enough space for movement and for Carmena, the 81-year-old owner with the trademark wrinkled stockings, to serve drinks.

The walls were painted in a colour that might once have been magnolia – Navy cream, was how Jimmy Greene described it, suspecting the paint to have been appropriated by the gallon from naval stores. Certainly, he said, the ceiling fan had been liberated from below decks on one of His Majesty's ships and he would occasionally recall how one of the Royal Marines he'd served with would jump into the revolving blades and stop the fan with his closely shaved head. The pub, being named after a seafaring hero, had been a popular place for serving seamen at the end of and immediately after the war; it was more than likely, he thought, that they had helped furnish and decorate it.

And the nicotine stained walls – not repainted in 100 years, Carmena boasted – reflected that tradition. There were framed poster-sized illustrations of the British Home and Atlantic Fleet off Southend in 1909, and in the Spithead Review of 1911, with naval warships stretched as far as the eye (or the illustrator) could see; a chart depicting flags of all nations; a *Daily Express* map of the world showing the colonies in fading red; pictures of three British coronations – Edward VII, George VI and Elizabeth II; and a photograph of a Fleet Air Arm Swordfish biplane (although not, said Jimmy Greene, actually the specific aircraft with which he had single-handedly 'captured' the island). There was also the mandatory picture of Pope John Paul II.

British and Irish tourists, failing to grasp the original point of the pub's name, had returned to the island and contributed further adornments – an Irish tricolour flag, a mirror with a harp etched into the glass, and a welcome sign saying *Céad Míle Fáilte*. Carmena, never one to disappoint or disillusion her paying customers, had responded to the compliment by stocking Guinness. Montebello thereafter had its first 'Irish pub'.

Jimmy Greene had always called it 'the noisy pub'. At one time British ex-pat residents had tended to sit along one wall and the locals along the opposite side; nowadays, with both communities having become more or less bi-lingual, people sat where they liked and shouted their conversations from one table to the other. The result of this, when the bar was busiest, was often almost deafening, but then it created an opportunity where two people, sitting side by side, could enjoy a tête-à-tête without much likelihood of being overheard by the other customers

But it was early evening when Horatio entered the bar with Aldo and there was only one other customer, a builder and developer called Portelli, who had that day's edition of *La Gazzetta* open on the table in front of him. He raised his eyebrows and nodded towards Carmela who brought two bottles of *birra Moretti* and two pint glasses (another Fleet Street tradition) across as they sat down beside him and flicked off the crown corks on the table's metal rim. Carmena returned to the counter to add two ticks to Portelli's tab.

'So mayor Morano has started his campaigning, you reckon? And he thinks the voters are so naïve that he can do nothing for four years, then make himself look busy for one last year, and we'll re-elect him.'

'You always do,' said Aldo. 'Works every time.'

'The man is useless. He does nothing for the island. He can't. *Non ha coglioni*… he has no balls. He's been mayor for 19 years and what has he done? I'll tell you. In 19 years he has repaired 24 pieces of road. And when I say repaired, I don't mean that he has rebuilt them. Only resurfaced them. And I mean parts of roads, not entire roads.'

Aldo surreptitiously slid a notebook and pencil out of his pocket and made a note to be checked later. It was an interesting statistic, if true, and he thought Portelli would know the facts.

'We don't build roads, here,' said Horatio. 'We lay tarmac. Underneath the tarmac there'll be an ancient cart track, never intended for anything heavier than a horse and cart. That's why they keep crumbling. If there's a dip in the road, when they resurface it there'll still be a dip, only a few inches higher. And it'll be this weird water-soluble tarmac that will need relaying again in a few years time, thus guaranteeing permanent employment for you folk.'

He took a mouthful of beer, then continued: 'You know, at school we were taught twice about road-building – during history lessons. First, we learnt how the Romans made roads. Then, with the invention of tarmacadam, we were taught how the Victorians did it, digging foundations and laying increasingly smaller layers of crushed stone, as aggregate, and then the tarmac on top to bind it. So every English schoolboy knows more about road building than the department of transport does, here.'

'The only good thing,' said Aldo, 'is that they'll finish the ferry terminal before the election. I go down there often and I've never seen anybody actually working on it.'

'Nine years, they've been building it,' said Portelli. 'But yes – it'll be finished just before the election so the mayor can be photographed cutting a ribbon. And his picture in *La Gazzetta*.' He was still smarting from the fact that his firm hadn't been awarded the contract for the new terminal. It had gone to the mayor's cousin. 'It's corruption, plain and simple,' declared the builder. 'The man has to go. The problem is that, apart from this newspaper,' he stabbed a finger at Orazio Verdi's editorialising, 'nobody ever criticises the bastard.'

'Not even you,' said Aldo. 'You say you suffer from his corruption, but you don't say or do anything. It's the same with everybody. They keep quiet because they, or maybe their family members, want favours from him, now or in the future. They don't want to upset him.'

Manuel, the council clerk, parted the fly netting across the entrance and walked in, closely followed by Spiro, the electrician.

Horatio raised a finger and drew a circle in the air to signal to Carmena an order for drinks all round.

'We're plotting to overthrow your mayor,' Portelli told them. 'He's corrupt and he's starting to campaign again for re-election, and he's got to go, this time.'

'He's useless.' Spiro agreed. 'He's got no balls. None of them has.'

Wiping the froth from his lips, Manuel told them it might not be necessary to overthrow his boss. The mayor had been talking about spending more time among his vines. He might not seek re-election this time.

'Great!' said Portelli. 'Then we need to find another candidate.'

'He rather fancies handing over to his nephew,' said the clerk.

'Sandro? That good-for-nothing! Who'd vote for that idiot? Nobody even knows him. He's a *quaquaraquà*.'

Horatio laughed. It was one of his favourite Sicilian expressions and meant a person had no value. The *quack* part of the word referred to the sound a duck makes.

'If he's photographed alongside his uncle, cutting ribbons and opening roads, he might get credit, or some acclaim, by association…'

'No way!' declared Portelli. 'We need somebody new.'

As the bar started to fill, other customers readily joined in the discussion, offering ideas for nominees for the next mayor. Most of the council members, it was generally agreed, were unsuitable: none of them had any *coglioni*. The majority of local businessmen who were considered were dismissed on the grounds that they all had vested interests.

It was Spiro the electrician who suddenly announced that he had the answer. The solution was staring them all in the face, he said. 'There is only one choice: *il signore redattore* – the editor!'

Horatio smiled, modestly, waving a hand dismissively. 'I already have a job.' But consensus in the Ireland bar was that he would be the ideal – indeed, the only – acceptable candidate. As Horatio stood and asked for his tab, Portelli grabbed his arm.

'It isn't a stupid idea you know. What are you doing for dinner? Let's go somewhere and talk about it. I'm serious.'

Horatio had no plans for dining that night, so the two men left the bar together.

They chose Giosetta's, not only because the food was reliably good but because it had alcoves where men, or lovers, could talk discreetly. A waitress put a plate of *bruschetta* and a bottle of olive oil on the table. Horatio unscrewed the cap, sniffed the contents, then called her back and asked her to change it.

'You sent a bottle of wine back last week. Now you're sending the oil back?'

'It's gone. It's greasy and smells like linseed. Show it to Giosetta.'

The owner appeared at the table quickly, apologised, and replaced the bottle of oil with a new one, opening it and pouring a measure into a sherry glass, inhaling its aroma then offering it for Horatio to sample. He sipped it like fine brandy, tasted green salad leaves, a hint of tomato and an aftertaste of light pepper and nodded his approval. She told Portelli: 'He has a good nose, your friend.'

'I'd rather be an oil expert than a wine bore,' said Horatio. 'Wine tasting is mostly snobbery; olive oil is much more down to earth.'

Portelli asked whether he'd ever thought about growing his own olives on the empty land behind his house. 'There are few things more pleasant for a gentleman than to sit in contemplation under his own olive trees.'

When Horatio said he thought, agreeable as it might be, that the process took too long and the harvesting was too labour intensive, the developer said that he could easily acquire five-year-old mature trees for him, and that his neighbours would tend them and organise the harvesting, and add them to their own crop in return for a modest share of the production. He said he would organise it.

But to return to the important issue at hand, there were several reasons why the editor would be the ideal choice for mayor, he said. Foremost, he had the interests of the island at heart. He was fair. He was independent. He knew what was wrong with the place and he knew how to put it right. He was opposed to corrupt methods. Portelli had been counting the reasons on his fingers but quickly gave up. He knew the people and what they needed and wanted. But most of all, said the developer, the editor could not be bribed; he could clean up corruption.

'Sounds good. Whoever it is you're describing, I'd vote for him myself. But... forgive the question... I don't wish to appear rude, but... what's in it for you?

'Building licences, government tenders, contracts.'

'Ah. I see.'

'Don't get me wrong. I can get licences, whoever is in charge. But I want the contracts and the tenders to be awarded on *condizioni di parità* – a level playing field. The big difference, for me, between you and Morano is that you don't have any cousins in competition with my business.'

For his own part, Portelli added, he could promise the votes of his entire family – fourteen, at least. Maybe 18.

Horatio smiled at that offer. 'So I'd need only... what? – Another 18,000?'

'They'd soon come. Spiro has about a dozen.'

'Thirty. Well, we're going in the right direction, but – '

'The rest will follow. They're all sheep. After all, if they'll vote for that idiot Morano they'll vote for anybody.'

'And that's intended to be taken as some sort of compliment, is it?'

It was raining as they left the restaurant. 'The island may have its faults,' said Horatio. 'But it tends to rain only at night. How civilised is that?'

# *Five*

When, slightly later than usual, Horatio walked in through the newsroom, Aldo followed him into his office, closing the door behind him. 'So… have you reached any conclusion? Are you going to become our next mayor?'

'What I have concluded is that this island doesn't really need a newspaper. News travels far faster than we can possibly deliver it. When I stopped at Café Jubilee for my morning heart-starter more than a dozen people came up to shake my hand, and congratulate me for standing as the next mayor.'

'And you said…?'

'That they were premature; that I hadn't made that decision.'

On his way from the café to the newspaper he had called in at the council clerk's office where, not surprisingly, he had been greeted with the same question and had given the same answer. But he had suggested what he thought was a better solution – that the clerk, Manuel, should stand for mayor himself.

After all, Horatio argued, nobody knew better how the council was run, and how it should be run; the clerk knew what the people wanted from their elected representatives because he read all the incoming correspondence and took their phone calls; he knew what needed doing and how to do it; and as far as keeping the council members in control was concerned he knew, as Horatio put it, 'where all the bodies are buried'.

When Manuel responded that as a government official he was not allowed to take an active part in local politics, Horatio told him he could take leave of absence; in the unlikely event that he wasn't elected he would obviously be offered his job back. Manuel explained that it was not an option for him, since it would involve broken service and affect his pension.

'I can't even campaign for a candidate in an election,' the clerk said. 'But of course behind the scenes I would give you all the help you needed if you were the candidate, and I'd obviously help in every way, after you won, to make everything work properly and efficiently.'

Horatio said he didn't think that he could spare the time to do the job, but the clerk countered that argument by asking how much of the day he thought mayor Morano devoted to it. 'He is the mayor in the mornings and a wine-producer after lunch; you can be mayor in the mornings and editor in the afternoons…'

'So…?' said Aldo.

'So, make yourself useful and pour me a drink.'

The reporter took two glasses from the cabinet – another Fleet Street tradition (drinking solo was deemed to be a sin) – and paused, grinning, with his hand at the door of the fridge. 'Would Mr Mayor wish to declare this refrigerator open?'

Horatio watched as Franco, the public relations guy, took a Havana cigar from the leather container he produced from his jacket pocket and, rolling it between his fingers, held it first against his right ear, then beneath his nose. He examined its colour, then produced a guillotine cutter from another pocket and applied it to the sealed end, exactly one-sixteenth of an inch in, and sliced it cleanly. Then he took a long-stemmed cedar match, struck it, waited for a couple of seconds while the sulphur burned off, and held it half an inch from the factory-cut end of the cigar, which he revolved slowly as he drew the air through it. He turned the glowing end towards his face, confirming that it was burning evenly. Only when he had completed this ritual, and savoured the first draft of tobacco behind his teeth, and expelled a mouthful of smoke, did he speak.

'The first question is why do you want to be mayor of Montebello?'

'I don't.'

'It's a rhetorical question. You may never be asked it. But you need to know the answer. It's because you feel you can make a difference, that you can make a positive contribution to the community. Personally, I don't think you have a choice in the matter. The process has already gone too far. You can hardly criticise another person who takes the job if you were not prepared to do it yourself.'

'Oh, great. Thanks a bunch.'

It had been Aldo's suggestion for Horatio to speak to the PR guru, who 'knows the market and has the demographics'. It made sense.

Franco listed the opposition – only the possibilities at this stage because no other candidate had thrown his hat into the ring. There were two coalitions, left and right; no single party had sufficient supporters to field a candidate on its own.

'There's a saying back home,' said Horatio, nodding, 'that if two Englishmen were shipwrecked and cast ashore on a deserted island, the first thing they'd do would be form a club. My belief is that if two Italians were marooned, they'd immediately form two political parties.'

On one side were the socialists, republicans, communists, democrats, democratic socialists, progressives, liberals, eco-socialists and the greens; on the other, the Christian democrats, nationalists, liberal-conservatives and the neo-fascists. Horatio, said Franco, would of course be independent of parties and coalitions.

'Yes; for the first time uniting them all, in their opposition to a *straniero*, a foreigner.'

'That's your strength. They are unable to unite, on anything. They can't even unite in opposition. They don't even agree inside their own political parties... All you need is a manifesto.'

Franco listed a number of headings and of policies. 'Health... you obviously want better and more facilities at the general hospital, so that fewer people need to take the ferry to Sicily for treatment, or to be flown by police helicopter in an emergency... employment: you want more industry attracted to this island to create jobs, so young people don't need to emigrate to find work... tourism: a better projection of the benefits, including the relative cheapness of accommodation and the choice of decent restaurants and attractive beaches, far better than many on the mainland. Education: higher standards, especially in the teaching of English, for people in the tourist industry and youngsters who want to go abroad to learn or to work. Transport: more and better roads and a more frequent and definitely more punctual ferry service, and a bus service to all the villages… Law and order: a shorter time-span between people being arrested and their appearance in court…'

He made notes as he spoke, and as Horatio signalled his agreement to the suggestions, occasionally interrupting to make contributions of his own.

'And corruption…' he said.

Di Giorgio studied his cigar for a few moments. 'Corruption?'

'I know it's nothing like as serious, or as obvious, as the rest of Sicily, and probably not even as widespread – definitely not as blatant – as it was in parts of the UK in the 60s and early 70s, but it exists. And people know it exists. And they don't like it.'

'That's not quite true. As you say, it's comparatively low-key. But it's wrong to say the people don't like it. They use it.'

'They know that the planning authority is corrupt, because they see people with money get permission to build in designated non-development areas. They believe that the courts are corrupt because they see people walk free who they know should be sent to jail.'

'It's often more a matter of perception,' said di Giorgio. 'If somebody gets planning permission, and somebody else doesn't, the person who is refused assumes that bribes have been paid by the other guy; if an accused person doesn't go to jail, it's always possible that they didn't deserve imprisonment in any case. Perhaps there has been a bribe along the way, too; perhaps there hasn't.'

'And there's also nepotism, what I call the brother-in-law syndrome, where family members are shown favouritism, whether in licences, permissions or even court cases. Everybody knows it goes on.'

'You're a newspaperman, I'm a marketing man. Beware of the idea that everybody knows anything. You know that they don't.

But everybody thinks, or everybody suspects... it's not the same as everybody knowing. You need to consider, first, that the relative or friend might simply be the best person, or the most deserving, or offer the best tender, for the job.'

'If the best person for the job gets it after paying a bribe – even though he might get it anyway – that's still corruption. But, yes, I know what you mean. Oppositions always say that governments are corrupt, but when you ask for evidence – as we have done at *La Gazzetta* – all we get is that everybody knows...'

'Yes, any form of payment is corruption, literally. But paying a *pizzo* is something of a tradition here, *fari vagnari a pizzu*, wetting somebody's beak. Truth is, they'd rather do it than not do it. It's endemic. It's built into the basic cost of living – certainly into the basic cost of developments.'

'But it shouldn't be. Why should local government officers – and, worse, magistrates – get gifts or bribes for doing their job, one that they're very well paid to do anyway? And for making decisions that they were going to make anyway?'

Di Giorgio took a long contemplative draught on his Havana. He agreed, he said, with what the editor was saying. But if your garage sent you a calendar for Christmas, wasn't that both a reward for doing business and an inducement to use the same place next year? If a tradesman gave a good customer a discount for prompt payment, or quoted a price without VAT in return for settling the bill by cash, wasn't that a form of corruption? Did Horatio want to stop that sort of thing happening? And did he think that he could?

Maybe not, said Horatio. But he had heard of an instance where a planning officer actually asked for the gift of an apartment, in a block of eight that were proposed to be built, in return for recommending planning permission. His newspaper had tried investigating the story, but got nowhere with it.

Eventually di Giorgio agreed with Horatio that taking a stand against official corruption – payment to government employees – should be part of the manifesto. He said that the wording should stipulate that such payments were not only illegal, but unfair. He said that the people who didn't pay bribes – or didn't offer the highest bribes – would certainly consider them to be unfair, so would agree with him, and maybe even vote for him, which was what mattered.

Horatio asked how the commune would pay for all the new projects he wanted to promise that he would introduce, if elected.

'Don't worry about funding,' Franco told him. 'These days there are grants available, for absolutely everything.'

He said he would 'type up some notes' and send them round to Horatio in the morning.

'One other thing,' he said finally. 'I don't wish to appear offensive, but get your hair cut and trim your beard. You will be photographed a lot, and you want to get the women's votes.'

'Some notes' turned out to be an excellent basis for a manifesto for the mayor's job. He called in the chief sub and chief reporter – both of whom had declared their total commitment to support, if Horatio decided to go for it. 'We're going to do this,' he said, having come straight to the office from the hairdresser's. 'Take this, run off a couple of copies, and knock it into shape.'

Alone in his office he opened the wardrobe where he kept a couple of jackets and some clean shirts and studied himself in the full length mirror on the inside of the door. Not a vain man, he didn't usually bother too much about his appearance but thought he generally looked fairly smart – certainly in contrast with the majority of locals who usually dressed either for the fields or for the beach, even when conducting business. He was one of the few men on the island – Franco di Giorgio was another – who owned more than one suit and who wore shoes rather than sandals, and trousers instead of shorts, at least when he was working. Now he examined himself in the mirror and thought about 'the women's vote'.

He'd never thought of himself as a ladies man. But he considered that, in the general scheme of things, he probably wouldn't be described as bad looking. Not overweight; at six feet (give or take half an inch) he was one of the tallest people on the island; and although he'd just turned 50 there was no evidence yet of middle-age spread, in spite of the fact that his only exercise – apart from swimming in his pool for refreshment from the heat in summer – was walking from his house to the car, or from his office to the coffee shop. He never sat in direct sunlight if he could avoid it but the reflected rays from his patio and from pavements and buildings over the years had given him a near-permanent and healthy looking light tan.

Did the combination of all that make him attractive to the floating female voter? He had no way of knowing, but he wanted to get them on the basis of policies rather than looks. He was no film star, but he thought the hairdresser had not done a bad job.


What emerged over succeeding days from the three-way editorial discussions based on Franco's notes was a final document, *Time For A Change*: 'This time, before they tell you what they'll do, ask them to show you what they've done.' It was run across a double-page spread in *La Gazzetta* to announce Horatio's candidacy.

Reaction from some of the parties was immediate, and Horatio insisted that any copy from any political party, and any critical letters from readers, must be treated fairly in his newspaper. The communists had been first to respond – protesting that, after two generations of the Morano family as mayor, the island appeared to be now set on yet another dynasty – because Horatio's father had been governor of Montebello, he presumably thought that he was entitled to succeed to the top job. The nationalists said that they'd already had plenty of experience of governance foisted upon them by a foreign power; they didn't need another foreign ex-colonialist telling them how to run their island.

Horatio didn't respond personally to these opposition attacks. But Aldo spent a morning with mayor Morano and returned to the office with notes for a signed article declaring why the editor would be getting the vote of the outgoing incumbent. The mayor also took the opportunity to attack most of the other candidates as they, in turn, announced their candidacies.

The labour man, the mayor wrote, wanted more jobs – 'but not for himself; he's never been anything other than a party official and has never done a real day's work in his life.' He dealt with the communists and nationalists in a single paragraph, generously pointing out that *Commandante* Greene had been the most benign, progressive and popular ruler in the history of Montebello and that it was 'entirely due to his accidental intervention' that the island – uniquely in the Mediterranean theatre – had been saved from being bombed during the war.

Dino handed the copy back to Aldo. 'Change *accidental* to *timely*,' he said. 'We are the victors, here. We write the history.'

The election, the following spring, was a landslide victory for Horatio. From developer Portelli's 18 family votes and Spiro the electrician's 12, he had somehow amassed more than 20,000. Horatio Greene was now the mayor of Montebello.

The following day's edition of *La Gazzetta* was printed later than usual in order to carry the news of what sub-editor Dino, when writing the headline, to Horatio's amusement described as a *shock risultato*.

'More than half the people may have voted for you,' he argued, 'but they must be amazed that so many of their neighbours did the same. Surely, that's how they would have reported it in Fleet Street.'

# Six

There was a one-week overlap of jurisdiction during which the island of Montebello officially had two 'joint' mayors. It gave the outgoing official an opportunity to shred any compromising documents, commented Aldo, cynically; but in practice it allowed the incoming incumbent time to get his feet under the table.

First thing on the agenda was a photo-call, at which mayor Morano ceremonially removed his *tricolore* sash of green, white and red and placed it over the shoulder of new *sindaco* Greene. There was the clichéd picture of the two mayors shaking hands, and of the new one seated in the centre of a team photo of the entire council, the *consiglio comunale*. The photographer from *La Gazzetta* would wire copies to newspapers in Sicily and in Italy who would ignore them on the basis that Montebello was too distant, too insignificant.

Aldo also insisted on telephoning news stories to the London papers. 'An English mayor in the Mediterranean,' he said. 'That has to be a news story.' Horatio agreed. The newspaper operated a 'linage pool' for any stories that the staff sold to foreign publications. The editor usually referred to it as 'the Ireland fund', since the cash, when it eventually arrived, was mainly spent there, across the bar.

Aldo listed the story lines he had planned for the different titles: FORMER MAILMAN ELECTED MAYOR, for the *Daily Mail*. WAR HERO'S SON… for the *Daily Express*. TRUE BRIT IS BOSS ON SUNSHINE ISLE… for the *Daily Mirror*, *Sun* and *Star*, and ENGLISHMAN ELECTED MAYOR OF MEDITERRANEAN ISLAND for *The Times*, *Guardian* and *Independent*.

'You're getting the drift of things,' the editor told his chief reporter. And they both laughed and said, in unison: 'Yes, that's the way they do things in Fleet Street.'

After the photo session Sophia, the mayor's (and temporarily the joint mayors') secretary, came with Manuel to discuss the appointments schedule. She had marked what she described as the 'big' meetings with an asterisk.

All sorts of people and organisations had to be met. The magistrature, the chamber of commerce and the chamber of advocates; the tourism operators and the farmers' union; the fire brigade chief, the hospital director and the airport manager. First among them, she suggested, should be the bishop's chaplain, followed by the chief of police and the magistrates' clerk, for by virtue of his office the mayor was now also chairman of magistrates. The chaplain would want to organise the traditional service of blessing for the new mayor, she said.

Horatio said he didn't think that anybody's chaplain 'came high in the batting order'. He realised that they might not fully understand the analogy, but they both nodded in agreement.

Sophia, a 25-year-old long-legged honey blonde with pouting lips and – unusually on an island where most people's were brown or hazel – piercing blue eyes, pouted further and pointed out that the chaplain was a monsignor…

'The chief of police is a colonel and the magistrates' clerk is a doctor of law. I am not sure of the order of precedence, there. But the court clerk works for me, so he can drop whatever he is doing and come over here now. I'll see the chief of police at his convenience, sometime today, and we'll slot the chaplain in somewhere…'

Horatio had often claimed that, as a reporter on regional and national newspapers, he had 'spent more time in English courts than your average lawyer'. The criminal justice system on Montebello was, uniquely for an Italian region, still mainly based on English practice but there were important differences that he needed Vincenzo – the magistrates' clerk who came over from the court house immediately after being summoned – to explain to him in detail.

The chairman of magistrates, provided that he had a qualified lawyer in attendance acting as clerk, could sit alone for sentencing, or he could be accompanied by one or two magistrates who were lawyers when hearing a trial for certain offences. Montebello was the only place in Italy that had trial by a jury of peers – elsewhere, important cases were heard by a panel of judges. On Montebello, the chairman could preside alone at a trial by jury; he handled the major cases, usually sitting one day a week, while the other magistrates, the qualified lawyers, looked after the minor offences.

He asked Vincenzo how many cases were currently outstanding, and awaiting a hearing.

'Just over two thousand.'

'*Madonna!* How did you allow that to happen?'

The court clerk wasn't prepared to take the blame. 'You must understand,' he said, 'that the court sits only in the mornings, four days a week. Many of the cases are petty, anyway – car parking appeals and suchlike.'

'If a motorist is prepared to argue against a parking ticket, and wait for a hearing, and turn up in court to find that his case isn't being heard that week... he must think he has been wrongly ticketed, and that he has a good case, eh?'

'I suppose so.'

'So... let's assume that the majority of the appellants are in the right... can't we just give them all an amnesty, and clear what you say is a large number from the list?'

'You're the chairman; you can grant an amnesty to anybody you like. Of course, if you don't collect the parking fines, this may affect the income that the council receives from them.'

Horatio pressed the button on his telephone console to call Manuel. 'How much income did the council receive last year from parking fines?'

'I'd need to look it up, but my memory is that the council received nothing.'

'Make a note for me to meet the director of traffic wardens in the next few days.'

He asked about 'the big cases'. He remembered that *La Gazzetta* had covered a number of arrests for sex cases, some involving children, that he didn't recall ever coming to court.

Vincenzo said that the police and the prosecution service 'were not always ready to proceed', when the previous chairman had called them forward, and there were some that had what he described as 'difficulties in procedure'.

Asked to explain, the clerk at first hesitated, then sighed and said: 'I suppose you might call it family complications. Everybody is related to somebody in the system.'

It was Horatio's turn to sigh. 'Get your secretary to bring over a print-out of outstanding cases, then you can sit in Manuel's office with some coloured pens and mark all the car-parking appeals in, say, green, and every case that's been outstanding more than six months in red. Then we'll make a start on the red ones. We'll sit all day for a week, or longer, if necessary, and get the backlog cleared.'

Fleet Street journalists didn't work set hours or clock on and off for shifts – they reported the news when there was news to report and, when there was none, they went out to look for some; then when they'd found it and written it they went for a drink. The production staff, copy editors and designers, made the pages when they had stories to fill them. As Horatio sometimes said, by some miracle there was always exactly the right amount of news to fill a paper – no edition ever came out with blank pages. *La Gazzetta* worked in the same way. Horatio could see that his plan of working as mayor in the mornings and editor in the afternoons might take some time to introduce and adjust. For a few weeks he could foresee that he'd be available at the newspaper only in the evenings or through the night.

For his first, formal, meeting with the new mayor the police chief turned up at the council office in full dress uniform – red striped trousers, lots of silver braid on the tunic and even the *lucerna*, the two-pointed Napoleonic hat – looking like the lead performer in a

Gilbert and Sullivan operetta. He marched in to the mayor's office, stood at attention and briskly saluted Horatio who shook his hand and told him to take a seat and relax. Cesare was a handsome man, tall and dark with a neatly clipped black moustache and a shiny near-bald head. There was a saying in Sicily: *Nun tèniri amicizia cu li sbirri ca cci perdi lu vinu e li sicarri* – don't maintain a friendship with cops because you'll lose your wine and your cigars. But the two men were old friends; the newspaper enjoyed a good working relationship with the *carabinieri* and the cop paid for his drinks and carried his own smokes.

The local police detachment was described as a heliborne unit. It ran a small fleet of helicopters, ostensibly to deter the mafia infiltrating the island from Sicily and to patrol offshore to watch for smuggling. The aircraft were also available to fly emergency medical cases to 'the mainland' for treatment.

Cesare produced a packet of Marlboro from a tunic pocket and looked around the office. Horatio also looked round, then stood and walked over to remove a No Smoking sign from the wall before accepting the offer of a cigarette.

'As you know, there's very little crime on this island,' Cesare told the mayor. 'At least, not what people would consider to be serious crime. Occasionally it is necessary that somebody is murdered. That is unavoidable in a Sicilian community. But generally we are almost crime-free. You know, for example, that we've never had a car stolen on Montebello.'

'That's because there's nowhere to go with it… But I'd like to think that it's the high visibility of your police presence that deters crime,' said Horatio.

'I'd like to think that, too. It justifies our being here. Without us, there could be anarchy. And of course organised crime.'

'And yet there are more than two thousand cases waiting to come to court… So what we've got is disorganised crime…'

'That's because my corps is more efficient than your courts. We catch them faster than you can sentence them. But, as I say, they are mainly minor offences.'

Horatio told him that the magistrates clerk had said the police were sometimes 'not ready to proceed' when more important cases were due for trial.

That was nonsense, Cesare responded firmly. 'Most times, the magistrates don't want to try them.'

'Why not?'

'It's difficult to give a specific answer that covers everything. But most likely it will be because somebody – a magistrate, maybe even the mayor, maybe the clerk to the court – is related to the accused person, or involved somehow in business with them.'

Horatio said he wanted to make a start on clearing up the backlog of long-outstanding cases, especially the major ones. He remembered one in which two men were accused of raping – 'defiling' was the definition in the actual charge – a 13-year-old girl, and even of making a video recording of each other in the act.

'Thirteen? The girl is 20, now: a young woman. That's how long the case has been awaiting trial.'

'And at the initial hearing, I seem to recall, the men were confined to house arrest, but my reporters frequently see them drinking in the harbour, at La Spada...'

That may be so, said Cesare. But his men didn't usually go into that bar.

'The police allow a bar to be a no-go area?'

'Not at all. There's never any trouble down there. But the owner doesn't object to his customers smoking in the bar which, since your predecessor made a deal with the Greens for votes, is now of course illegal. And my officers have more important things to do than book people for smoking. Do you want me to arrest the men for breaking curfew?'

'No,' said Horatio. 'I want them in court, next week.'

He pressed the button on his telephone console again and asked Manuel how the court clerk was doing with his list of pending cases.

'He's waiting to bring it in to you.'

'Tell him to come in.'

Vincenzo was told to take a seat while the mayor and the police chief studied the red and green markings. Horatio took out his own pen and, ticking off ten cases, asked whether the prosecution was in a position to proceed on all of them. Cesare said he was pretty confident that all of them were ready for trial.

He told the clerk to get in touch with the lawyers and call them to court. 'We'll sit all week, if necessary. Two weeks, if necessary. We'll make a start to get the decks cleared.'

As Vincenzo stood to leave, Horatio told him: 'Make me another list. All the accused people to whom you are personally related or with whom you have any business dealings.'

'Business dealings?' The court clerk appeared perplexed.

'Your builder, electrician, plumber, gardener, local shop-keeper, car mechanic… your butcher, your baker, your candlestick maker… anybody who might be an embarrassment to you if they appeared in your courtroom… Anybody who might think, however misguidedly, that they could expect special treatment because they have personal dealings with you.'

And then, as an afterthought, he added: 'Your office is going to be busy. Much busier than before. You'll need more help. Perhaps you could offer a job to Sandro, mayor Morano's nephew…'

'On the basis, you mean, that he's a good-for-nothing law school drop-out…?'

'On the basis that he used to have pretensions of sitting in this chair. Give him a fancy title like special assistant, or associate clerk. He can help with the clerical work. If, after say a three-month trial, he turns out to be no good, you can fire him.'

'I think you'll do well in this job,' Cesare told him, before taking his leave with another crisp salute.

The meeting with the bishop's chaplain was fairly brief. The monsignor explained that following an election it was traditional for the church to bless the new mayor at a special service in the cathedral.

'The bishop feels I need his blessing in order to do the job?'

'Ah… no. Not in this case. His excellency normally blesses the new mayor, of course. But in this instance, because he cannot bless you personally, he will bless the position of mayor, instead.'

'And he cannot bless me personally, because…'

'Of course… you understand… that as a divorced English protestant…'

'Your priests bless houses, don't they? And they even bless cats and dogs – presumably, though, only Catholic cats and dogs…? And dogs that have had only one bitch?'

'Oh yes. And if you were taking your car to Sicily on the ferry, and you gave your priest a few thousand lire he would bless your car, too.'

Manuel, sitting in on the meeting, grinned widely and stamped his feet with glee. 'I guess that shows you where protestants come, in the batting order…'

# *Seven*

The multi-coloured marble tiles in the entrance to the council offices were still wet from being mopped when Horatio arrived to start work – on only the second day after his election. He stopped to talk to the cleaners who sat in the foyer drinking coffee and waiting for their shift to end. Almost all of them said they had voted for him because he had promised 'change', although one of the women confessed she had voted for the Christian Democrats because she always had done, and another said she never voted at all because 'all politicians are corrupt'.

Totally unembarrassed by being in the presence of the mayor they asked what he planned to do and told him what they wanted to be done. One of the cleaners, with a daughter at school, said she wanted higher standards of teaching both English and Italian because the best-paid jobs in Europe appeared to be as translators in Brussels, and the pupils were not being equipped for them. Another wanted more, and better, child-care facilities for working mothers, and a third cleaner wanted to know why tomatoes – 'the most tasty in all Italy and grown here in their millions' – were so expensive on the island.

One of the women handed him a cup of instant coffee and another brought him a hard-backed chair and they went on to quiz him about his private life. They knew he was divorced, so, did he have a girlfriend (he didn't); how often did he revisit England (usually once a year, briefly); did he have children (two twin daughters); was his father, the *commandante*, still alive (he wasn't).

Horatio had planned to have a bit of time alone making notes at his desk before the rest of the staff turned up, but he enjoyed talking to the women; it was a bit like the old days when, on rare occasions as a reporter, he had met actual readers of the newspapers that employed him; journalists chained to their desks or 'work-stations' in Fleet Street never met the people they were writing for. Once at his desk, he made a note of the points the women had raised with him.

He would have arrived earlier but, on leaving home he had seen one of Portelli's trucks outside and walked round the back of his house, through the palm trees and the small orchard, and found two men pacing out the boundaries of his field which ran down to the rocks and the sea at Cala Levante. They told him their boss had instructed them to take its measurements for planting olive trees – they thought it was big enough to take about 250, but maybe more.

'But the soil isn't that good. All I ever seem to harvest is stones.'

'We'll bring a machine,' one of the men said, 'and plough it properly for you, and remove most of the stones. Maybe make you some paths or walls with them.'

He turned a page on his pad and made a note to call and ask Portelli how much 250 olive trees would cost, and how much he would charge for rotavating his field.

Manuel was the first staff member to arrive. He put his head round Horatio's door and told him: 'Something that Sophia didn't mention yesterday is that you need to do an assessment of all the *assessori*, the executives who make up the *giunta comunale*, who are personal appointments by the mayor and who – in theory at least – serve only for his term of office and resign when a new mayor is elected. Or, obviously, you can keep them on.'

'How many people?'

'Thirty-eight.'

'*Madonna!* And they're only the executives?'

Manuel came in and sat down. 'Well, the government employs about 40 per cent of the population, and they all need bosses.'

'So, 60 per cent of the people are earning wages and paying taxes to pay the salaries of the other 40 per cent...'

'More than that, because some of the 60 per cent will be on government work – contractors building roads or buildings. As for paying taxes, well, I don't know. But about half of them are working to support the other half. It isn't what you'd call tax-efficient, here, but fortunately most of their wages come from central government, some from Sicily, some from Rome, some from Brussels. But in terms of employment they're all answerable to you.'

He quoted from memory – local police, education, arts and culture, finance and treasury, health, welfare, childcare, the elderly, transport, environment, planning, agriculture, fisheries, ports, the airport, customs, tax collection, judiciary, employment, licensing, tourism, information, communications, telecoms, industry, commerce, water, electricity, land registry, civil registration, statistics, waste management, cleansing… there were others that he couldn't recall off the top of his head.

Legally, they were now all serving three months notice, he said.

Horatio, commenting that there appeared to be more government employees on Montebello than had been needed to run the entire empire of ancient Rome, asked him to contact all of them and ask them whether they wanted to keep their jobs. If they were planning to retire, he needed to know in order to find a successor. If they wanted to stay in place, they should write him a one-page note, saying so – and telling him why they deserved to keep their jobs. 'Meanwhile, I'll ask mayor Morano which of them was any good.'

'He'll tell you that they all were good; they were his personal appointments. They thought they all had jobs for life.'

'Nevertheless, I'll try to sort out everything within a week, it's only fair. But I want to get the law courts properly organised first. That's my priority. Justice delayed is justice denied.'

Manuel, recognising an old Sicilian proverb, took the register of outstanding court cases from a nearby table, placed it in front of the mayor and left him to it.

Horatio was working on the list of pending trials, and remarking to himself how many 'personal contacts' the court clerk had honestly admitted to having – he had even included his cleaning lady on the list – when Manuel knocked on the door and came back in.

'Just thought I'd tell you... you asked me to contact the traffic wardens' boss to tell him about the amnesty for parking-fine appellants. Well, I didn't need to. He has phoned me. One of your reporters had rung to ask him for a quote about it and he's furious. He wants to see you.'

The mayor smiled. 'He would. I think you and I should take a walk round to his office and see him. Say about 10.30 this morning?'

Manuel said they should make it 11.15. He said he thought it would be 'more interesting' at that time.

Around eleven Horatio told his clerk that they both deserved a break from paperwork and took him to the Café Jubilee for coffee. As the two men sipped *macchiato*, Manuel opened his briefcase and passed a sheet of paper across to his boss. 'Sorry; more paperwork,' he said. 'But well worth a quick look.' It was a breakdown of salaries in the traffic department.

Just before 11.30 they walked unannounced into the traffic warden headquarters. The clerk led the way to the executive's office, told the two pretty young secretaries why they were there and waited while the director was informed that he had visitors. The man didn't stand up when they walked in; he didn't even remove the cigar from his mouth as he embarked on his complaints.

First, he objected to hearing from a newspaper, rather than from the mayor's office, about the amnesty. But Manuel told him that he had tried, as a matter of courtesy, to inform him about it the previous afternoon — but nobody had answered the phone.'

Then the director said that the traffic division was one of the very few revenue-earning government departments and that an amnesty of such a size would vastly reduce its income, which was unacceptable.

'Yes,' said Horatio; 'that's what we're here to talk about. The revenue, where does it go? We passed two clerical offices on the way in. Both empty. Where are the clerks?'

The man looked at his watch. 'At lunch.'

'The sign on the door says this office opens at 8.15, and they've gone for lunch? And they'll be back at... when, exactly?'

The executive shrugged and said that, in summer, because of the temperature, it was normal – as the mayor surely knew – for government employees to work only in the mornings. It was impossible for anybody to work efficiently in the intense Mediterranean afternoon heat.

'I've always said,' Horatio told him, 'that the greatest invention of the entire Mediterranean was not the pyramids, nor even the discovery of astronomy or the invention of mathematics, but the siesta. But that was of course before the invention of air-conditioning. All your offices are air-conditioned. I see no reason why people shouldn't be able to work, nowadays, after lunch. And another thing, about one third of your salaries list is for overtime. How does that happen?'

'People get parking tickets over the weekends. They all need to be processed.'

'The problem,' said Horatio, 'is that this revenue-earning department isn't producing any revenue except for itself. Overtime payments stop now.'

'You can't do that!'

Manuel shook his head, grimly. 'Oh, he can.'

'The staff won't stand for it...'

Manuel grinned at Horatio. 'What'll they do? A traffic wardens' strike? You could be the most popular mayor in all Italy. And it's still only your first week.'

'There you have it,' said Horatio, turning to leave. 'No more overtime, no afternoons off, no new recruitment. Starting this afternoon. Get them all back to their desks.'

'One thing,' said Manuel, who was responsible for the paperwork, '... have you done your formal letter of resignation yet?'

'No; not yet.'

'Do so,' Horatio told him. 'And it will be accepted.'

As they left the building Horatio turned to look again at the secretaries. 'Pretty girls,' he said.

'He has twice as many secretaries as you.'

'Very smart office, didn't you think?'

'Smarter than yours, anyway.'

'And the motorists of Montebello are paying for all that. The cigars and the cedar panelling. By the way, did you really call him yesterday about the amnesty?'

'I lied. But it was a safe lie; I knew there'd be nobody in the offices after lunch.'

'Just as you knew there'd be no clerks in the office after 11 this morning.'

'Exactly.'

It rained heavily, torrentially, that night – so forcefully that the sound of it woke Horatio in the early hours. He went to the window and switched on the terrace lights, then watched hailstones, like ice-cubes, as if a thousand bartenders were emptying ice buckets from a thousand feet high, bounce off his teak table and chairs and rattle across the paving stones before melting rapidly with the day's accumulated ground heat. Hail, in his experience, was usually like mothballs; but these were falling as cubes with sharp corners.

He knew that there would be floods in the morning, not only in the valleys and gullies but also in the hillside roads that previous administrations had never thought to provide drainage for. Unable to get back to sleep he went into his study and called police headquarters for a situation report.

They had bad news for him. The floods had washed away the outer half of the road in front of the Porto Hotel where there was now a hundred-foot drop into the harbour. A civil protection unit was there, and the contractor, mayor Morano's cousin Pisani, had been called and had set up concrete blocks to stop traffic going up what was left of the road. Horatio told the duty officer that he was awake and wanted to be kept informed.

There was worse news about three hours later. The *tenente* called him to say that a second flood stream had poured down the hill, hit the concrete barriers and, having nowhere else to go, had swept off the remainder of the road outside the hotel. The hotel portico now hung over a cliff edge. Access was available at the back of the hotel, but the entire structure would need supporting at the front. Furthermore, he said, there were now about a dozen cars or trucks bobbing about in the harbour.

'Nobody inside any of them?'

'No, they had been parked on the pier overnight. Mainly fishermen and maybe some foot passengers using the ferry. One driver had unwisely got out of his car on the jetty and been swept into the sea, but he managed to swim back; he is okay.' The downpour had damaged several other roads, flooded many and washed away patches of what Horatio described as 'water-soluble tarmac', and lifted the surface off a few more, but none was as seriously and dangerously damaged as the one leading to the hotel.

Horatio said he would meet the chief of police in their operations room, then called Aldo at home, briefed him with what he knew and told him to get down to the harbour with a couple of reporters and a photographer.

Cesare turned out to be an expert in organisation and logistics; he said he'd been trained to do it while at staff college in Modena, but it was the first time he'd needed to use the knowledge. He called in the corps' own mobile unit and engineers from Sicily for immediate assistance and deployed his own team and the local police on dealing with traffic and diversions. He also alerted the Italian army's engineers for back-up. Horatio sent his directors of transport and of engineering to the harbour, telling them to take contractors Portelli and Pisani with them and report back to him with an assessment of what needed doing. Ex-mayor Morano phoned and offered help, and Horatio asked him to base himself at the hotel and do whatever was needed there to calm tourists and staff, while assessing the damage from the inside.

They all reported back to the council chamber at 9am, with Horatio chairing the meeting. Army and *carabinieri* engineers were already on their way by air and sea, said Cesare. The director of engineering had told the two contractors to shore up the cliff face. The police mobile unit was rescuing the vehicles from the harbour. There was no panic among the guests at the Porto Hotel – most of them were excitedly taking photographs to show their friends back home. They were mainly north Europeans; they'd seen heavy rain before.

The two contractors, working together, produced a list of equipment that they had available, and another list of what was additionally needed immediately to carry out repairs. Manuel said he would organise that; there was a relief fund available for such contingencies.

Horatio thanked them all; he was impressed by the way they had responded. Then he suggested that they should go down to the harbour and examine the site.

All the island's roads were awash with silt, mainly rich brown topsoil washed off the fields. The mountain, usually matt black or a dirty brown when covered by the Saharan sand that blew in with the Scirocco, now gleamed shiny bright like a guardsman's toecaps, reflecting the golden morning sunshine and the fields around it glowed emerald green, refreshed by the storm. Gullies and valleys, normally parched from the start of spring, had become fast flowing rivers carrying a swirling scum of vegetation and litter down towards the sea. Most of the bamboo crop that was cultivated in different grades, from sturdy poles to flexible weaving material, had been flattened. A number of farm walls had collapsed into the roads and the floodwater had lifted several manhole covers along the sewerage system, but he was pleased to see that the council workmen – his workmen – had already made a start on clearing and cleaning.

He stood in the mud at sea-level in the harbour, staring up at what had once been the cliff face beneath the Porto Hotel. It was a sheer wall of dark brown earth, not a rock in it.

'No wonder it collapsed,' he said to the two contractors. 'It's just soil. There's nothing to support the road. It must have been only a footpath once, maybe a cart track along the coast since the time of the Romans, or even earlier. It wasn't designed for the weight of modern traffic. Who did the road?'

Pisani hung his head. 'It's been re-laid several times. Last time, we did it.'

'But there are no foundations. It was just tarmac, on top of soil.'

'There was nothing to build on. When we repaired the road we only covered the existing surface. That's what we were contracted to do.'

'No rocks, no foundations… and no drainage. Well, let's get it right when we re-do it. It needs a complete rebuild, from sea level. Masses of huge rocks, then infilling, then what we call in English hogging, then a new surface. And bloody drains, too, eh? We need to get into the habit on this island of building drains for roads.'

'It rains so rarely, here,' said Portelli. 'It must be six years since it rained like it did last night…'

'But when it rains… *Madonna!* It really rains. The police say there was the equivalent of two months rain in as many hours, last night. Who knows when it will happen next? It's just happened twice – two separate flash floods – in one night!'

He told the two contractors that it was vital that they forget business rivalry and work together, quickly but efficiently, under the direction of the council's own engineer. They assured him that it wouldn't be a problem.

Still shocked by the effects of the downpour on the badly built road, he told them: 'You two should merge your companies. Then you could also combine your names and go into business as Pis-Por Road Construction.' Only Cesare with his fluent English appeared to get the point of that message.

Morano, driving him back to the *municipio*, alternately swishing through the floods and crunching over rubble, said: 'That's real bad luck, in your first week. A baptism of fire, eh?'

'A real baptism – with water.'

# *Eight*

Dealing with the flood and the collapsed roads took the best part of a day out of the schedule Horatio had planned for himself, so he asked his clerk and his secretary to come in to work on the Saturday. Since the deluge they had enjoyed stifling tropical heat with high humidity so that stepping out to the street from an air-conditioned office was like having a hot damp velvet blanket dropped over your head. He'd told them to dress casually; he and Manuel wore polo shirts and light cotton trousers; Sophia opted for a cotton shirt, tied under her breasts so it exposed her midriff, and a mini skirt. He had also suggested that they work through lunch in an effort to finish as early as possible, and around noon laid out plates of *antipasti* he'd brought in from the delicatessen – cold meats and spicy local sausage, fresh and sun-dried tomatoes, artichoke hearts, stuffed olives and cheese, a dozen quail eggs, plus a couple of bottles of chilled white wine – on the conference table in his office.

While they ate, they chatted. Manuel asked whether Horatio had given any thought to appointing a deputy mayor, somebody who could relieve some of the burden of at least the routine work.

'Who would you suggest? Is there anybody on the council who's reliable, who would be capable of doing the job?'

Manuel said that, without wishing to appear disrespectful, there weren't many on the council who were up to it.

'Suppose you were me; who would you want?'

The clerk said that he, personally, would offer the job to Marco Bonnici, a Labour councillor – 'but one who puts his people before his party' – a retired headmaster. In fact he had been Manuel's headmaster, years ago, at the *liceo*.

'And mine,' said Sophia. 'Not quite so long ago.'

Aldo, who regularly reported the council meetings, had also told him that councillor Bonnici was probably the pick of the bunch.

'Give him a call. See whether I can see him on Monday.' He had decided that the assistant magistrates (something of a misnomer because, unlike Horatio, they were all qualified lawyers) should start working through the backlog of minor cases on Monday; he would start dealing with the more important ones on Tuesday and continue through the week.

When Manuel returned to his own office and Sophia started to collect the plates, he told her: 'I'm also going to need another secretary. This is no reflection on you but I can see that, if I'm going to do the job properly, there's going to be twice as much work. Give it a thought, will you? See whether there's anybody among all the secretaries that we employ who could make both our lives easier.'

Sophia said she could recommend somebody immediately. She had a good friend, Francesca, who was an excellent secretary and worked in the judiciary department.

'I could call and ask her to come and meet you this afternoon. She's not doing anything. If I hadn't been working we were only going to the beach. Would you like to see a photograph of her…?'

She returned to her desk, took a paper wallet of postcard-sized photographs from a drawer and handed the contents to Horatio. The first four were photographs of Sophia herself, black-rimmed sunglasses on top of her blonde hair, sunbathing topless, wearing only the bottom part of a lime-green bikini, little more than a thong. She had a fine pair of breasts that he hadn't really noticed before her appearance that day. He thought he shouldn't spend too long looking at them, but also that it would be impolite to ignore photographs that his new secretary was showing him.

'They're in Sardinia. We went on holiday together last year.'

The other photos showed her friend, equally only half-dressed, slimmer and smaller breasted with elfin short hair and a mischievous smile. He felt that he should say something.

'Very pretty girl.'

54

'She has an inverted nipple, can you see? But it comes out if you suck it. I'll get her to come over, if you like.' He didn't ask how she knew about stimulating the nipple.

He was standing beside Sophia's desk, planning the following week's diary, when her friend walked – sashayed – in through the glass doors wearing short – very short, shorter than her shoulder bag was deep – blue shorts and a white T-shirt with *Porto Cervo, Sardinia*, printed across it. Fairly clearly, no bra. As they were introduced she appeared to pose, slightly provocatively, Horatio thought, as she pushed out her rib cage towards him.

'He's already seen your *tette*,' Sophia told her sharply. 'I showed him our holiday snaps. The mayor wants to talk to you, not look at you.' Horatio thought he'd like to do both.

'I want to talk to you about a job. Come in.'

She followed him into his office and closed the door behind her.

As Sophia had suggested, Francesca seemed to be exactly the sort of secretary who would be useful to him. She said she had good typing and shorthand skills (he didn't test them); but she was also bright, intelligent and even amusing. She knew in detail how the judicial department worked, and how the individual magistrates operated; she even said that if she knew who was in the dock and who was on the bench she could accurately predict what the outcome – the verdict and the sentencing – would be. She had regular contact with her opposite numbers on 'the mainland' (Sicily) in both the legal directorate and the prisons department.

She confirmed Horatio's impression that it was extremely rare for anybody – 'apart from foreign drug dealers or illegal immigrants' – to receive a term of imprisonment.

He decided to offer her the job, but she continued to appear to pose for him and he thought it would be wisest to keep her at arm's length, and place her in an office at the courthouse. His own responsibilities were basically twofold, the council and the courts; Sophia could look after the municipal side of things, while Francesca could handle the judicial area, working in an office of her own in the magistrates' department.

The new role would include a pay rise, he said, and she told him she'd be 'thrilled and honoured' to accept it and delighted to work for him directly. So he called Manuel and asked him to arrange for her to be transferred to the mayor's direct payroll on Monday.

He walked her to the door. As she started to open it she offered her cheek to him – by no means an uncommon act on parting – but as he bent to kiss it, she tilted her head to take his mouth on hers. They kissed quickly and he stepped back.

'She really showed you the holiday pictures?'

'She really did, yes.'

'Better in real life,' she said, touching the front of her T-shirt.

'So I know you have a piercing in your navel.'

Francesca grinned, and lifted up the front of her shirt – far higher than necessary, he thought, exposing the lower curves of her petite breasts. 'No. It was glued in. Just for sunbathing.'

'Behave yourself,' he told her. 'You're working for the mayor now, and for the chairman of magistrates.'

He didn't know how he resisted patting her tight round backside as she glided out of the door and winked at him.

The two secretaries left the town hall together, arm in arm, and he stepped into the clerk's office.

'Has Sophia ever shown you her holiday pictures?'

'Topless in Sardinia? Yes. I think she also sometimes appeared topless in your own office, when it belonged to mayor Morano...'

'It can't be the right thing, can it?'

'Oh, I don't know. Consenting adults, and all that. It isn't sexual harassment – not, at least, unless you feel harassed by it.'

After his marriage had broken up, Horatio had enjoyed relationships with a couple of secretaries in his own or other newspaper offices around Fleet Street. He knew editors who had had affairs with secretaries and some who'd even married them. So office relationships were by no means unusual. He thought he might be in danger of a holier-than-thou or a hypocritical attitude. But he wasn't sure.

Manuel appeared to intercept his thought process. 'I think it's ok to shag your secretary, if that's what you're wondering. So long as it doesn't interfere with business.'

Horatio called in at the newspaper building on Monday morning to check that everything was running smoothly without him, then dodged the traffic to cross Anton Vella street to the *municipio* and handle yet more bureaucracy.

He telephoned Vincenzo in the court office to tell him about Francesca's new appointment, then asked him to present the court lists to the magistrates who were sitting that morning and tell them to transfer all cases, however trivial, that involved any personal or business relationships – 'you know how I define those' – for another magistrate to hear.

Retired headmaster Bonnici came to see him, mid-morning, and Horatio explained what he needed from a deputy mayor. Basically, he said, what he thought he required would effectively be a chief of staff, somebody to act as a buffer between the mayor and the roughly 40 departmental directors. Anybody who could organise a school curriculum and keep 500 rowdy children, and their teachers, in order should be more than qualified for that task, he suggested. Except in emergencies – and the previous week's flooding was an excellent example – the first point of contact with the *assessori* should be via the deputy's office.

Bonnici said that he was of course flattered to be offered the job, but he needed to speak to his party's executive, which might think that there were longer-serving or more experienced councillors who should be given priority for the position of deputy mayor.

'There may be,' Horatio told him. 'But they are not being offered the job. Your party should be happy that one of its members is about to be appointed deputy to an independent mayor. Anyway, I'll give you a week to think about it. A decision earlier than that would obviously suit me better.'

Portelli, the contractor, telephoned at lunchtime, to say: 'I understand that you are hearing the child-rape case tomorrow.'

'That's true. But I obviously can't discuss a case with you – or with anybody – that is coming up in court.'

'Forgive me. I fully understand that you can't do that. Only the two accused both work for me. One is my brother-in-law. They know that I know you so they asked me to speak to you. That's it. As far as they, and I, am concerned, I have now spoken to you. End of discussion.'

'One of them is your brother-in-law? I wasn't aware of that. Is he your wife's brother or your sister's husband?'

'Sister's husband.'

'And... although, as you understand, we are not discussing the case in any way, what does his wife think of it?'

'Oh, she's left him; thrown him out of the house.'

'And you, my friend... you have daughters...'

'I have three.'

'What's your view of the whole thing – I mean, without discussing the actual case?'

'If it were one of my daughters I would cut off their cocks and balls slowly, with a blunt knife.'

'Then feel free to assure them both that you have spoken to me and whatever penalty they receive in court tomorrow will be less severe from me, than it would be from you...'

Before the end of the day's business he had an appointment to meet Alessandra Debattista, a young lawyer who he'd heard was now representing Giuseppe Benedetto, Montebello's first and only bank-robber. She had insisted that she wanted to discuss 'a matter of court procedure' – not the case itself – so he invited Vincenzo the court clerk to sit in on the meeting.

She was stunning to look at, but her enquiry seemed straightforward enough. Her client had been in jail for almost a year, awaiting trial by jury, as so serious an offence demanded. But it hadn't come to court for the simple reason that it had proved impossible to find a jury of twelve people on the island who didn't know him.

'Without discussing the actual case,' said Vincenzo, 'if an accused person pleads guilty, he obviously doesn't require a jury to determine a verdict.'

'You and I know that,' she said. 'But his previous lawyer thought he might get away with a not guilty verdict, bearing in mind all the circumstances. He's dumped that guy and instructed me, and I've convinced him to change his plea. So… without, as you say, discussing an actual case, if an accused person pleads guilty he could just appear before the magistrates for quick sentencing.'

'Sounds sensible to me,' Horatio said, as Vincenzo nodded in agreement. 'And, in some purely hypothetical case, how long do you say an accused person might already have spent in jail?'

'Eleven months.'

He turned to the clerk. 'And if we had such a hypothetical case on the list, how quickly could we get it on the calendar?'

'With a bit of rearranging, you could probably hear it a week from today. Without, as you say, discussing any individuals, you might think that such a case might have been going on for long enough.'

'Thank you. Fix it, then,' said Horatio. That business concluded, he offered the lawyer and the clerk a drink. Vincenzo said he ought to go back to the court house, but Alessandro said she would happily join him for a glass of wine.

She was wearing a tailored trouser suit of pearl grey over a pink and white striped fitted shirt. As she crossed the room to sit on the sofa he said, 'By the way, nice suit,'

She inclined her head, acknowledging the compliment. 'Nice ass, you mean.'

What was it, he wondered, about the young women of Montebello that made them so obsessed with their bodies?

'No; I meant it's a smart and stylish suit. I mean, yes… a nice ass too. But in fact I was commenting on your clothes.'

She shook her head, waving her long dark curly hair. 'But I think you were actually looking at my *culo*.'

'I think that's a little unfair. If I complimented you on your choice of shirt – which, incidentally, I also think is very smart – would you interpret that as being a comment on your *seni*?

'It's English, from Jermyn Street. But... yes; I have good tits, too. Great tits, actually. So if you said it, you'd be right.'

To change the subject he asked whether she had any other trials pending before the court and she told him she hadn't because she normally did property, contracts and international work. She'd taken on this case only after a chance meeting in a café with Benedetto's girlfriend who was visiting him in prison, and who was also paying her costs.

'So,' she concluded, 'when this court hearing is over there would be no conflict of interest if you invited me for dinner.'

# Nine

Taking his seat on the raised platform for the first time as chief magistrate, Horatio suddenly experienced an instant flashback across the decades. He was a young reporter, maybe 20 or 21, attending Leeds press ball and wearing a midnight blue dinner suit with metallic gold lining that he'd had specially tailored for the occasion. His partner, Jessica, still in sixth form at a prestigious public school, wore a full length evening gown. As they danced he told her that the town hall, where the ball was being held, also housed the law courts where, in those days, the assizes and quarter sessions sat.

She asked him to show her round the building and they walked hand in hand along the half-lighted corridors until they reached court number one. He had been surprised, trying the handle, to find it unlocked and they'd gone inside. He pointed out the dock, where the prisoners stood, and mentioned a couple of important trials that he had covered, then the press benches where he had already passed many hours filling pages of his shorthand notebook, then the elevated dais where the judges sat and passed sentence.

'Can we go up there?'

They could, and they did and Jessica, sitting in the judge's high-backed leather seat, said: 'Wouldn't this be just the most exciting and original place to have sex?'

It would be and it was. She unbuttoned his flies with one hand, raised her skirt with the other and leaned back along the judge's table. He could recall the scene vividly; illuminated only by the lamps in the street outside, his mind's eye could clearly see his girlfriend, top down, skirt up around her waist, small breasts with stiff nipples pointing at the ceiling, black stockings and suspender belt, her legs waving wildly beneath the royal coat of arms with a lion and a unicorn proclaiming 'God and my right' and 'Evil to him who evil thinks'. And Jessica shouting 'Do me… do me!'

And he remembered that he'd been thinking… if a cleaner heard her and came in and found them, could they be arraigned before a judge in that same room the following morning on a charge of contempt of court?

Apart from having much longer hair and a square cut fringe, Jessica had looked very much like his new court secretary, Francesca, he thought.

They say you never forget your first one, and in any case Jessica had been back in his consciousness that week after reading about him in *The Times* and sending an email saying how distinguished he now looked with his 'new' (to her – he'd had it 20 or more years) goatee beard which she cheekily suggested might compensate for the declining amount of hair on top of his head, and adding, as if as an afterthought, that she had never been to Montebello. A request for an invitation, perhaps.

He filled a glass from the water jug in front of him, took a sip and ordered a start to the day's business.


Two construction workers – Portelli's employees – stood in the dock wearing checked shirts, ties and tight-fitting suits: probably the first time either of them had worn a suit since their weddings.

The prosecuting attorney, who also had the title of magistrate – prosecutors were called 'standing magistrates' while those who sat in judgment were known as 'sitting magistrates' – outlined the charges. The men were accused of defilement of a thirteen-year-old virgin, of aiding and abetting rape, indecent assault and making an obscene video.

The evidence was that, in anticipation of the girl's 14th birthday, they had invited her into one of their homes, plied her with vodka and persuaded her to undress. Then they had taken turns to rape her, while each of them filmed the other with a video camera. They had also forced her – and it was clear from the video that she had not been a willing participant – to do what the prosecution coyly described as 'perform a sexual act' on both men.

Each of the accused was represented by a lawyer and they both said more or less the same thing – that the girl was mentally backward and had led them on, and that she had consented to having sex. The filming had not been done for profit, but merely in order to entertain themselves, and the camera itself was their birthday gift to the girl.

Horatio interrupted: 'But presumably not the film?'

'That had certainly not been the intention.'

The lawyers asked the court to deal with the accused men leniently. The girl had been one day short of her birthday at which point she would have reached the age of consent under Italian law; they were pleading guilty in order to save the court time and also to avoid the embarrassment to the victim of being called to give evidence. Neither of them had previously committed any crime, both had families and were fully employed, and witnesses – their employer and their village priest – would testify to their good character.

'I am tempted to suspect,' Horatio interrupted, 'that the reason the men are pleading guilty has less to do with the court's time or the girl's embarrassment, and is more closely connected to the fact that the police had a video recording of the offences taking place…'

Before deciding on a sentence, he said, he wanted to hear from the girl's mother who he had been told was sitting in the public gallery.

She took the oath and told him that although her daughter was well developed physically she had been a slow learner at school; nevertheless it was disgraceful of them to describe her as being mentally retarded. However, she said, following the offence she had cut off contact from her friends, done even worse at school, and nowadays rarely left the house. Her daughter, returning from a neighbour's house 'and clearly in a disturbed state', had shown her the camera, describing it as a birthday present. But when the mother switched it on, reading the instructions to see how it worked, it had somehow retained some of the filming and she had immediately taken it to the police. She said the effect on the entire family – there were four other children – had been so profound that there had been times when she wished she'd taken up the village priest's offer to accept a big sum of money as compensation in return for asking for the charges to be dropped.

Horatio leaned forward. 'Tell me about the priest's offer.'

Vincenzo, sitting at the clerk's table in front of and below the magistrate's bench, stood up and whispered to him: 'You realise this is going to be hearsay…?'

Horatio nodded. 'Just tell me how much.'

'Thirty million lire, if the case was dropped. My husband wanted to accept it, but I didn't. Not at the time.'

He turned to the defence lawyers. 'This would be the priest who is present in court as a potential character witness? Let's hear from him.'

The priest, short and stout in a shiny black suit and a greasy white dog-collar, began with his prepared script. Both men, he said, were of previously good character, regular church-goers and supporters of his parish. Both were family men and totally contrite and ashamed about the way they had behaved, on this one single occasion in their lives. They wished to apologise to the court, to the girl and her family, and to the community. They had offered financial compensation or reparation to the family.

'You made this financial offer on their behalf, I understand.'

'I did, yes.'

'But not as compensation, was it? It was conditional on the charges being dropped by the family.'

'My hope was that the offer would avoid embarrassment to all parties.'

'It was effectively a bribe, wasn't it?'

'No, no,' said the priest. 'Nobody could undo what had already been done. On the other hand, no advantage could be gained by the unhappy incident resulting in the publicity of a court case and the potential effect and possibly even the break up of more families.'

'You mean except for the advantage of the guilty participants receiving their just deserts with a court sentence.'

'As I said, I couldn't see what advantage…'

'You don't think that there would be an advantage in seeing justice done? What was your incentive,' Horatio asked him, 'to act as go-between in this case? What motivated you to decide to attempt to interfere with the due process of justice?'

'My only motivation was to attempt to assist members of the parish. Of my flock.'

'The girl and her family were also members of what you call your flock, weren't they?'

'Of course.'

'What I am asking, father, is how much the two accused men offered you in return for your intervention on their behalf.'

The priest shifted about in the witness box, shuffling his feet. 'Oh, nothing.'

'Nothing directly or indirectly?'

'Both men supported the church and the parish financially and in other practical ways, for example with building work and repairs.'

'And if you didn't help them in this venture, that support and assistance might have ceased, did you think?'

'I don't think so.'

'But it might have? Whereas if the scheme worked their support might have increased?'

'I don't think it would have stopped.'

Horatio told the priest that he would discuss with the prosecution service whether he should be charged with attempting to interfere with the process of justice. Then he called Portelli the contractor whose only contribution as evidence was that both the accused were good workers, good timekeepers, and that they both had secure jobs.

'You're a character witness. You've heard the evidence, which is undisputed by the accused. What would you now say, in the circumstances, about the personal character of these two employees of yours?'

'I'd rather not comment,' said Portelli.

Before adjourning to consider the sentences, Horatio asked for final submissions from the defence lawyers. Again, they each said the same things. They asked for non-custodial sentences to avoid families being split up.

'They are each still currently living with their families?'

The man representing Portelli's brother-in-law said that his client was working hard to save his marriage.

They asked for a ruling of anonymity for the two accused – 'to protect the identity of the victim who lives in the same street'.

'Is there anybody in the village who is not aware of the identities of both the accused and of the victim?' Horatio asked.

Probably not in the village, but elsewhere on the island, the lawyers said. And the victim could be identified by the fact that she was described in the evidence as being a neighbour.

Horatio said he thought that anonymity might serve the accused men better than the victim, but said he would give an instruction that the proximity of the households should not be referred to by the press. 'I can assure you that such an instruction will be complied with,' he said.

And he left the courtroom, lighting and drawing heavily on a cigarette as the clerk closed the door behind them.

He asked: 'Maximum sentence?'

'Ten years, for defilement,' said Vincenzo. 'But you should take into account that the girl was only one day short of the age of consent. Six years, suspended, would be normal.'

'You don't have a daughter.' – 'No.'

He tamped out the half-smoked cigarette and put another in his mouth. 'I do.'

The two men in the dock looked fairly relaxed, he thought, as if enjoying a joke, when he resumed his seat on the bench. He was about to wipe the smiles from their faces.

'For making a pornographic video of an illegal and obscene act,' he said, 'two years.'

One of the defence lawyers was immediately on his feet, to interrupt. 'Suspended…' he said.

Horatio ignored him. 'For defilement, and for indecent assault, and for aiding and abetting the assaults, four years…' The lawyer rose again. 'I haven't finished. Please sit down… these terms to be custodial sentences, and to run consecutively: six years. In addition there will be a fine of 15million lire to be paid to the victim's family by each of the accused. If that sum is paid into court within seven days the sentences will become concurrent, so they will serve only four years each in total.'

The defence lawyers started whispering frantically to each other. Horatio waited.

'We will of course appeal against the sentence.'

'Any appeal will obviously need to be heard in Sicily. I will therefore transfer both men to prison in Sicily to make life easier for all concerned. Whatever you decide, though, I'd commend your clients to consider making the reparation payment before the due date.'

He looked around the court. 'Could the priest return to the well of the court?' The cleric waddled towards him.

'This court takes a dim view of your attempted intervention in this matter. In my view you exceeded your duty of care in one aspect, and totally neglected it in another. But your pastoral duty is not my concern. What is my concern is that you attempted to interfere with the due process of justice and you should consider yourself fortunate that you have not been charged with that serious offence, and are not about to share a prison cell with child rapists. I shall ask the clerk to write to the bishop informing him that such behaviour by priests will not be tolerated in future…'

He snapped shut the book in which he had been making notes. 'Take them down.' He knew the terminology. 'We'll adjourn for lunch.'

He was to hear a case of assault on a policeman in the afternoon; then he intended to return to the newspaper office and do some journalism.

Francesca, intercepting him in the corridor, grabbed his elbow. 'Congratulations, boss,' she said. 'Jail sentences for child rape – that's a first. Well done.'

She had a request. The director of tourism wanted him to hear a case urgently because the island's most popular night club and disco had been shut down by the police for operating in contravention of its licence. The urgency was that the tourist season had started and the club was a major attraction and revenue earner. He could fit it in, she suggested, after the police assault.

He told her to ask Vincenzo to add it to the afternoon list, and watched her walk to the clerk's office in a smart grey pin-striped jacket and knee-length skirt tight around her small round backside, mid-height heels emphasising the shape of her slim legs.

He decided he would send an email to his childhood sweetheart, Jessica.

# Ten

Standing at the sub-editors' table in *La Gazzetta*, Horatio told Dino, the chief sub, that the warning to priests – that they shouldn't interfere with the law and could go to jail if they did – and the letter to the bishop, should be on the front page, cross-reffed to coverage of the child-rape case which should be an inside page lead, but not too prominently displayed, perhaps on four or six.

'That's how they'd do it in...?'

'In Fleet Street? It would have been page two in the *Guardian*; you know, they once reported a sex case and a witness was asked whether fellatio had taken place and she said no, it had never entered her head. Only the *Guardian* thought its readers would understand that one... The *Daily Telegraph* would use it on page three; the *Mail* on four, the *Mirror* on five. In the old days the *News of the World* might have splashed it on the front, but we're not competing with the *Screws*. Another thing... we don't want the paper to be filled with court reports just because they've suddenly started to become interesting, or because you think it's what I would want. Cover the results, but keep them brief unless they're good stories. We are not competing with *Police Gazette*, either.'

Nevertheless he suggested that the assault on a policeman – two men who had objected to being stopped after driving through a red traffic light and attacked the officer – should be given reasonable prominence. The driver and passenger had actually come out of the altercation worse (one of them suffered a broken nose), but several witnesses said that they had started the fight. Horatio had given them both a 28-day sentence.

'What about the licence for the Caverna?'

'Well... cover it, so people know that it's open again.'

'But it's a funny, isn't it?'

The night club owner had been accused of playing music after two in the morning, at which time the noise was legally supposed to cease. Horatio had asked to see the licence and it was handed up to him.

Was this the current and only licensing document? – It was.

'It has expired,' said Horatio, reading. 'It is three months out of date. So the club was not operating in contravention of its licence. It has been operating without any licence at all. But that isn't the charge. So the case for operating in contravention of its licence is dismissed. On condition that the owners renew the licence, backdated to when it expired, before leaving the court building, they can re-open for business tonight. And, in future, perhaps the standing magistrates should read what they presume to be evidence before producing it in court.'

Horatio told Dino he didn't think it was funny; he thought it was ridiculous. But if the chief sub thought it would amuse readers, so be it.

He decided he quite liked being a magistrate. It had nothing to do with sitting in judgment over his fellow men – indeed, he hadn't actually sat in judgment yet, because he'd dealt only with guilty pleas – but he felt he had a fair and proper sense of what was just, and of justice. Nor was he over-impressed by the surroundings and the trappings of courts; he'd watched brilliant advocates and duff lawyers, QCs who mumbled because they were inept or inadequate performers and solicitors who fumbled because it was part of their act. He had witnessed bewigged and red-gowned judges who could cut a straight line to the facts and others who seemed to lose track of what was going on before them. He wasn't overawed by judges, either – certainly not since, after an over-indulgent Old Bailey dinner, he'd finished up in bed with one (although their extravagant consumption of fine wines and port had meant that neither he nor she had actually been able to consummate the otherwise platonic relationship that had long existed between wig and pen).

It wasn't a power trip either. *Madonna!* He was mayor, magistrate and editor of the local paper. Who was there on the island with more power than he had suddenly achieved?

But he thought that, even in an island where most people seemed to have two jobs – the government workers reappeared after lunch as plumbers, electricians, fishermen, farmers, car mechanics, plasterers, painters and decorators and air-conditioning contractors – three jobs was at least one too many.

He spoke to Hannibal, his publisher and effectively his partner, about taking leave of absence from editing *La Gazzetta* for the duration of his role as mayor. He recommended that Dino, the chief sub-editor, was amply able to take over as acting editor.

Hannibal had been against that plan. The circulation had increased during Horatio's editorship and had soared during the election, and it would increase again when people realised that the court reports were suddenly worth reading. The print run was being enlarged virtually ever week. He said that Horatio could become editor-in-chief, and oversee the newspaper when it went to press, two nights a week.

'In any case,' he'd said, 'you are now the major source of news on this island. You can control what goes into the newspaper by deciding what you do as mayor and magistrate. You don't need to be in the office in order to do that.'

Hannibal also told him that he'd been summoned to the bishop's palace to be admonished over the paper's front page story about priests who exceeded their duty in the eyes of the court.

'I'm sorry that happened. But should I be surprised?'

'He even made the point that he had supported you in the election.'

'Obviously I have no idea how he voted, or whether he even voted at all. I was aware that he spoke against Labour and the Communists. Perhaps that's what he meant. But he can hardly expect that his vote for a mayor in an election is going to alter the way a magistrate makes decisions or the way the newspaper editor reports those decisions. That may have happened in the old days, but not under this administration.'

'That's more or less what I told him. But you can separate your three roles, can you? Mayor and magistrate and editor?'

'I have to try.'

'Don't try too hard to make this a perfect island, my friend,' said Hannibal. 'The population isn't used to it. They won't like it.'

He was also visited, as arranged, by former headmaster Bonnici. Horatio asked him: 'Before we discuss the deputy mayor's job, would you be interested in becoming director of education? That's an alternative paid position and, like the other one, good for five years.'

Bonello said that he wouldn't. He already had a pension and wasn't interested in restricting himself to one department. Also, if he became a director he would have to give up his seat on the council. – 'But if you have problems with education I suppose it would be part of my new responsibility to find a replacement for the current incumbent. I could make suggestions.'

'So you're accepting the job as *vicesindaco*? Excellent.' He held out his hand.

'But…' he didn't take the offered handshake '… the party asked me to demand certain conditions before accepting.' He produced a folded sheet of paper from his jacket pocket. Horatio didn't take it from him.

'Didn't you make it clear to them that the vacancy was being offered to you, personally, and not to the party?'

'I did. But their point was that if the deputy mayor was a Labour councillor, that fact should be reflected in the administration's policies.'

'And if I refuse to accept their demands…?'

'Oh… I'd be honoured to take the job in any case. I'd like to think that I could make a contribution.'

'In that case, the job is yours.' The two men shook hands. 'Now let me see their piece of paper.'

Horatio read it. Most of the items on the list, he said, were policies that he would be happy to consider, and even to introduce. The exception was the 'extended guarantee' of already permanent employment for government workers.

'Some of these people work a three-hour day, a maximum 15-hour week, but some of them additionally find the need to claim for what they call overtime. I want to cut some of those jobs. In fairness, I want to create new employment so that nobody should be out of work – and I'll reduce the government workforce fairly gently, by non-replacement when people retire, things like that. But what I want to do is reduce the official payroll where previous administrations have simply created non-jobs for their friends.'

He said he also wanted his new deputy to use his personal experience and somehow improve the standard of teaching. 'Clear out the dead wood. Move teachers around so they are doing what they are good at and if they are good for nothing, clear them out totally.'

'It sounds like a good theory, but people here don't care much for government, only for government jobs; in practice it will be very unpopular.'

'Not among the parents, it won't. Nor among the pupils who suddenly start finding that they have the qualifications to find decent jobs when they leave school. In any case, I'm not here on a popularity kick. I don't plan to seek re-election after I've done my term. I am not in this job hoping for votes, next time round.'

Not surprisingly, considering that it had proved impossible to find a jury of a dozen citizens who didn't know him – plus the fact that most people had seen bank robberies on TV but never before had one on their doorstep – the public seats were packed for the hearing of Giuseppe Benedetto.

The standing magistrate outlined the prosecution case: how the fisherman, wearing a stocking mask, had driven to the bank in Salinas, threatened the guard with a shotgun, demanded money from the cashier and driven away 'at speed' to his home, where he was immediately arrested by police officers who had been alerted to the crime and were awaiting his return.

His lawyer, the attractive Alessandra Debattista, wearing a dark pin-striped trouser suit over another crisp white fitted shirt, said, firstly, that her client had changed his plea from not guilty to guilty, then outlined what she described as mitigating and extenuating circumstances. She told how her client's girlfriend had trusted him to the extent that she left large sums of money in his home, and how he had misguidedly misappropriated it to use as stakes for card games with friends who visited his home… how he had suddenly realised the overwhelming amount of indebtedness he had accrued, and how – being by nature a very simple man – had thought that robbing a bank was his only solution.

Although there was no doubt, she said, that his crime had been premeditated, it was important for the court to note what had not been said in the prosecution evidence – namely that the shotgun had not been loaded, and the officers who arrested him had found no cartridges on his person or in his car.

Horatio interrupted her: 'Of course, there is no way that either the guard or the cashier could have known that.'

'No… except that the cashier, having recognised my client (in spite of his attempted disguise) clearly considered him to be no real threat because he initially refused to hand over any money.'

'But the guard obviously took a different view. And the gun was being pointed at him, rather than at the cashier.'

'My point is that the cashier obviously didn't think the guard's life was in any real danger, either. Otherwise he wouldn't have been so bold.'

She wasn't only beautiful, he thought; she was also bright. For somebody who didn't normally do court work she was doing well. Every few seconds she had to keep brushing back her long hair which kept falling over her left eye, but it didn't distract her from her task, and Horatio found it more attractive than irritating to watch. She mentioned that her client's English girlfriend, who she described as a secondary 'victim' in the case, had forgiven him, had visited him regularly in prison and was standing by him, and was in court to hear the sentence. Then she pointed out that he had already spent eleven months in jail, awaiting trial, then awaiting sentencing.

Horatio dragged his eyes away from the advocate and studied the man in the dock: a rough broad-shouldered son of the Sicilian sea and soil, standing uncomfortably in a jacket and tie. Then the girlfriend, a teacher from England, small and slight, quite pretty, in a knitted dress that emphasised her slim waist and heavy breasts. He could see what attracted him to her, but… presumably it was proof of the saying that opposites attract.

He couldn't see any advantage in keeping the man in jail. He had no previous convictions – not so much, apparently, as a parking ticket.

'I am going to sentence you to twelve months in prison,' he said. 'With one month reduction for good behaviour, that means you can now walk freely from this court. But in doing so, I hope that you have learnt the error of your ways.'

'I sure have, sir, magistrate, your honour,' Giuseppe replied. 'I shouldn't have worn the Liverpool shirt…'

Horatio beckoned the police chief to the bench and spoke quietly, asking whether the baker, the taxi driver and the electrician who had led the fisherman astray with their game of poker were in the court. They were, so he asked Cesare to bring them to his office.

'Between you,' he told them, 'you relieved your friend of some 800,000 lire. I appreciate that by the nature of gambling you probably didn't win equal shares of that amount, but somehow I expect you to repay half of the total, each in proportion to the money you took from Mr Benedetto. I don't intend to impose this as a fine; it is merely a recommendation that I expect to see fulfilled within one month. There will be no formal penalty if you fail to do it, but you might each bear in mind that, at some time in the future, you will be coming to the court or the council seeking permissions, or renewal of licences or even building permits or contracts… who knows? You might like to consider how difficult things can be for people who don't co-operate with the administrative services.'

The three men said they understood the message and left for La Spada to celebrate Giuseppe's release.

Outside the court the freed bank-robber and his girlfriend posed happily for the photographer from *La Gazzetta*. He positioned the girl so that she was facing Giuseppe and half turning towards the camera, showing her breasts in profile. 'Bank robber's girlfriend with big boobs,' the snapper thought. 'Page one picture. That's how they'd do it in Fleet Street.'

# Part Two

# *Eleven*

They were obsessed with cars on Montebello. Delivery charges from mainland Europe and Sicily, heavy import duties and taxes, and expensive registration meant that the purchase of a vehicle was likely to be a once-in-a-lifetime commitment. So they hosed off the dust every morning, burnished the brightwork once a week, and gradually learnt how to do their own routine maintenance, especially those repairs made necessary by the use of low-grade over-leaded fuel and exhaust-crunching pot-holed roads that appeared to have been surfaced by a designer of patchwork quilts.

Previous generations had devoted the same sort of loving care to grooming their donkeys and horses and painting their flat-top carts in bright colours. They may never have learnt properly how to drive their cars – the driving test involved passing between two oil drums, in forward and reverse gears, but if this proved difficult the examiner would widen the gap. The test did not include any reference to parking, to the use of mirrors, indicators or lights, to hill-starts, overtaking or emergency stops, traffic lights or roundabouts, to turning left or even to which side of the road motorists were expected to use. There was a 98 per cent pass rate, possibly because it was widely held that if you bunged the transport department's examiner a few thousand lire you didn't even need to show up for the test. It made experienced drivers wonder about the two per cent who failed.

But they cherished their cars, which seemingly lasted for ever. They hung lace curtains inside their garage windows and pictures of saints among the tools racked on the walls. A film producer wanting to make a movie depicting the 1960s need look no further for a collection of period vehicles: the local Alfas, Buggatis, Fiats and Lancias were matched in number by British Ford Zodiacs, Consuls, Cortinas, Capris and Anglias, Triumph Heralds and Dolomites, Morris Minors and Oxfords, Austin A40s and 1100s and mark-one Land Rovers. The single-deck buses, most of them dedicated to Jesus or the Madonna and with names like *Indominatable*, were the sort from which you might expect to see Humphrey Bogart step down.

So the arrival of a shiny new Maserati, disembarking from a rust-caked ferry in the frantic harbour at the island's only commercial port, was unlikely to escape notice. Charcoal grey and chauffeur driven with a priest – a monsignor, no less – and another man on the back seat, it was clocked first by the taxi-drivers polishing their white veteran Mercedes on the sun-baked quayside, then by fishermen eating *pastizzi* in Gianni's café, and of course by the duty policeman who routinely (and pointlessly) logged the number of all arriving vehicles.

Except in the glossy pages of imported car magazines, nobody on Montebello had ever seen a Maserati. A few motorists with nothing better to do followed its route past the boat-builder's shed and La Spada pub, round the corner of the island's only main road where a couple of boy racers with smoke-spewing exhausts competing in decibels against their car radios roared past solely for the pleasure of being able to boast later that they had overtaken a Maserati. Everybody else stayed in line along the roller-coaster ride towards the town. When the longest journey takes about twenty minutes, who needs to hurry? It passed the orphanage, the filling stations, the football ground, two banks, the opera house, the police headquarters and the Bishop's palace, through the main square of the *Souk* and into Assumption Square where it turned off into ancient narrow winding streets leading towards the isolated village of San Pietro.

Either the driver knew his way around or the priest was a local and giving directions. The followers didn't pursue the car any further. They wouldn't want to appear nosey.

Late that night it drew up outside the door of Giosetta's restaurant, where Horatio was enjoying dinner with the lawyer Alessandra Debattista. The short spring had evolved into a steaming summer and he had decided to leave what he considered to be a decent gap between the court case and her invitation to take her out to dine.

The restaurateur had produced a new bottle of olive oil for his approval. They had each sipped it from sherry glasses, identified scents of grass and mustard leaves, and declared it to be 'smooth, round and rich but soft, with a perfect level of pepper on the finish'. When Giosetta challenged the diners to name the olives, Horatio said he thought they were *frantoio*, and *moraiolo*; Alessandra guessed at *leccino*. They checked the label and discovered it was a fusion of all three.

This girl wasn't only beautiful; she shared his passion for olive oils.

Sitting opposite her, he tried hard to concentrate as she told him about her life. But while his ears were attending to what she was saying, his eyes flicked uncontrollably from her deep eyes, high cheekbones and long nose straight down to the hint – something more than a mere hint – of cleavage. She had been right: she certainly had good tits, even great tits.

She was telling him that her parents had lived only long enough to enjoy the pleasure of seeing her graduate in international law at Bologna. Driving home their car had been crushed by an out-of-control articulated lorry in one of the hundred tunnels on the *autostrada*. She remarked that, apart from him, she was probably the only person in Montebello who didn't have any family members on the island.

But with each movement of her arms or shoulders, and as she frequently raised her left hand to move the long flowing hair from her face, her silk blouse shifted slightly and exposed the upper crescents of her magnificent breasts.

And – Horatio thought – she knew that she was teasing him in this way.

He was brought back to reality when Giosetta reappeared at their table to announce that she had a special delicacy on offer that evening – *fungo di carrubo*, the mushroom growth that occasionally appeared on a carob tree, which she knew was a particularly favourite dish of Horatio's. Alessandra had never heard of it, so he thought he'd impress her by explaining that it was a rare but popular dish in the Ragusa region of Sicily; a woody parasite, it was often shaved off and thrown away or used as fertilizer. But the *cognoscenti* harvested it and presented it in a tomato sauce with pasta or risotto, or cut it in strips like steak and cherished it as a delicious *secondo*. It tasted, he told her, a bit like pork loin.

But, he asked, wasn't it still a bit early in the year for such a fungus to appear? Giosetta said that the unusual change in the weather, the storms followed by intense heat, had probably brought the seasons closer. They both said they had to have it. And because it was such a rare opportunity, they opted for both the risotto version and the *secondo*, in steak form with small potatoes.

He'd decided to offer her a job as director of legal services, overseeing everything from courts to traffic, registry, contracts, licensing, and international trade. She had a good degree – he'd looked her up – and a good brain. With no relations on the island she was unlikely to be expected to provide personal favours. And she had great tits. His dilemma was that he didn't want to appear to be trying to bribe her into his bed with the offer of a job; nor did he want to bed her and then appear to reward her with a job.

'You never thought of becoming a magistrate?'

She waved a hand dismissively.

'Magistrate jobs go to the people who can't hack a living as a lawyer. You've only to look at them; not one had a decent practice. A good advocate can easily earn twice as much as a magistrate's stipend. Haven't you asked yourself who's got the jobs? They are all lousy lawyers who voted for mayor Morano or his father. And the women magistrates – there are three – happen to be the wives, or in one case the daughter, of guys who voted for him. Some coincidence, eh?'

She was impressive, no doubt. He was still wrestling with tactics when the Maserati drew up outside and its occupants walked in to the restaurant. They were guided to a table in an alcove, already ordering Sicilian wine as they crossed the room.

A few minutes later, as she topped up Horatio's glass, Giosetta told him: 'The bastards have all gone for the *fungo*. That means that there'll be none left for Patrizio in the kitchen. He has to cook it, but doesn't get to eat any of it. He's really pissed off.'

Horatio said he thought he vaguely recognised one of the men; he had a feeling that he had met him, or seen his photograph, years ago, but couldn't place him.

'The monsignor is Sicilian, but he works here, teaching at the seminary. The other two are also Sicilian,' Giosetta said. 'Rough Sicilian, peasants; going by their accents they are from the north west. It needs a whole lot of effort from me to understand what they are saying.'

'They may be peasants but they have a Maserati.'

'That's how it is, in the north west. Nobody asks where their money comes from, because everybody knows.'

When they finished their meal Horatio sent compliments to Patrizio, along with condolences that he hadn't been able to enjoy any of it himself. Horatio asked whether she'd like to go on somewhere for a coffee; he was going to ask 'your place or mine?' But she said she'd prefer a glass of rough red wine, to further complement the *fungo*, and suggested going to La Spada, which she said would still be open.

They drove their cars in convoy down to the harbour, found two stools at the bar beneath the fishing nets that were draped across the ceiling, and directly under a balsa-wood replica Swordfish aircraft with a 24-inch wingspan. This was *la spada* – the bar was named in honour of the aircraft that had 'liberated' Montebello and not, as most visitors assumed, in recognition of a popular species of fish. They ordered a bottle of local red; it bore the Morano label. While they chatted a man came in and stood beside them. He asked the barman whether *dottore* Ferra had been in and was told he'd just missed him.

'He'll be in again tomorrow, I expect,' the barman said.

'Will you give him this?' He handed what looked like a birthday card envelope across the bar. 'And can I pay you for a bottle of *prosecco*, that you can also give him tomorrow, from me, Bruno Peppone? It's his birthday.'

When he'd paid and left, Alessandra said: 'You see what happened there? Ferra, in case you don't know, is one of your magistrates. How much do you want to bet that this chap has a court case coming up in front of him?'

Horatio was more determined than ever to offer her the job.

They walked to their cars. 'I'm not inviting you home,' she said. 'Not tonight.' But she held him tightly and kissed him with her mouth open. 'Thanks for dinner. Let's do it again, soon. My treat, next time.'

Driving the short distance to his home Horatio thought there were a couple of reasons why she might have said 'not tonight'. One of them was that some women had a rule about first dates. However, she'd invited him to see her again... soon. And that kiss, *profondo*... He'd make sure the second date happened soon.

# Twelve

There was a message on his answer-phone when he got home asking him to call the police chief. He had the number on speed dial so he found him at the touch of a button.

'Bad news, boss,' Cesare told him. 'We have lost our virginity. The first-ever car theft in the history of this island.'

'You're calling me at home because somebody has stolen a car?'

'Well, because somebody stole a car and has already been arrested and is in custody. I plan to keep him in custody, pending a trial, so you might want him in court in the morning.'

'A trial? He is denying stealing the car?'

'It's his mother's. He says he had permission. But in addition there were two stolen shotguns on the back seat, he was driving without a licence and without insurance, and driving while drunk. Did I mention that he is only 15...? And that he was already on probation for a previous offence of driving without a licence?'

'If he's pleading not guilty I'll need two more magistrates. Okay, let's try to arrange to have him in court tomorrow afternoon...'

The first car theft... and it was to be his first trial.

Next morning the Maserati drew into Assumption Square and the two passengers, and then the driver, alighted and sat in the sunshine facing the baroque fountain outside the Del Monte snack bar to order café *espresso*. Priests, even monsignors, were two-a-penny on Montebello – there was a saying that if priests were trees, the rest of Montebello would be as beautiful as its mountain – but Maserati-owners were something else. Local residents visiting the offices of the transport department, next door to the Del Monte, or sipping *cappuccino* in the Rosa Nero café opposite, gazed at the man with some kind of awe, although they tried hard not to make their interest apparent. Montebellans didn't interfere in other people's business.

What they saw was a short, squat man with a thick shock of hair, prematurely greying at the sides, that appeared to have been cropped in a kitchen, rather that at a barber's. Those within earshot noticed that the visitor was very softly spoken. He was polite to all around him, nodding in friendly acknowledgement of other coffee drinkers who caught his eye, or who rearranged the pavement furniture around him. He didn't read while at the snack bar, and the priest – who they all recognised as a member of the seminary – appeared to be telling him what local and foreign news was in the pile of morning papers on the round metal table, and occasionally taking notes, writing down the man's comments on a pad.

Alessandra telephoned to thank Horatio for dinner and he asked whether he could see her later.

'I have a client in the early evening, so…'

'I meant late afternoon. At the *municipio*.' He had already accepted an invitation to dine with Cesare.

'Oh.' Did he detect a note of disappointment that he wasn't offering a follow-up date?

'It's business,' he told her.

When Horatio arrived at the court house Vincenzo said he'd had difficulty finding two magistrates to sit with him who didn't know the accused.

'He's a 15-year-old boy, isn't he? How many magistrates does he know?'

'Not him; his father. He's a Camilleri.'

'So are lots of people. It's a common enough name.'

'But this end of the family… Anyway, I've found you two: Brusco and Ferra, both old-timers.'

The boy's lawyer told the court that his client had answers to all the charges and would be pleading not guilty but, since the arrest had occurred only the previous day, he needed more time to prepare a defence. He asked for the case to be delayed for a week, and for the boy to be allowed out on bail in order to assist the defence.

'You'll be ready to proceed in one week?' asked Horatio.

'We will.'

'In that case he will be remanded in custody to the police cells, where his legal advisers can have full and instant access to him at any reasonable time.'

Magistrate Ferra leaned over to Horatio and whispered: 'He's only 15. We could allow bail.'

'But he was already on probation,' he whispered back. 'He has broken his probation order.' Brusco nodded his agreement and the case was adjourned for a week. The defence lawyer did not look happy. Nor did magistrate Ferra when Horatio wished him *buon compleanno* and then enquired whether he had a case coming up involving a defendant called Peppone.


Experiencing difficulty, after going to bed the previous night, in getting Alessandra – and her breasts, and her kiss – out of his mind, he had reached a conclusion about what to do. He wanted her to have the job because he thought she'd be good at it, not because he thought she'd be flattered and grateful and might reward him with sex. If she had told him at the start that there was no chance in hell of their going to bed together, he would still want her to become his director of legal services. So it wouldn't be a bribe. If she was going to be offered the job in any case, and if they got into bed afterwards, it wouldn't be a reward but simply an unconnected relationship between two working colleagues. The point was really that he shouldn't offer her the position in a restaurant while staring down her front; it should be done formally and in the office – business, as distinct from possibly being confused with pleasure.

Nevertheless, when she entered his office, having no suspicion about why she'd been invited, she appeared surprised when he offered his hand instead of kissing her on the cheek. She was wearing a high-necked cotton sweater; the shape was still visible but there was no cleavage on view.

When he offered her the job she prevaricated. She protested that she was too young, too inexperienced, and lacked the authority for such a role. But Horatio was determined and persuasive. He told her she would have his authority as both mayor and senior magistrate. He said he needed somebody who was not bogged down by previous systems nor was involved in old, possibly corrupt, practices and unlikely to be open to lobbying or impressed by who people were or what they did. He needed a director who understood how things worked, but who also knew how they should work. He needed somebody who understood law, who had sussed out the magistrates, and had a good – he called it a 'forensic' – eye for detail.

'If I took it on, to whom would I report?'

'For routine matters – staffing, administration, bureaucracy – to councillor Bonnici.'

'Marco? The ex-headmaster? He was my headmaster at the *liceo*.'

'He was everybody's headmaster, it seems. What did you think of him?'

'Oh, he was good. And when he ran things the school got much higher grades.'

'I've appointed him deputy mayor and chief of staff.' He made a note on his pad to call Dino and suggest a belated profile of the new deputy in *La Gazzetta*, announcing his appointment and getting quotes from former pupils about why he would be good in the job. '… but in all legal matters affecting the court or the council, you'd have instant access to me, day or night.'

She smiled at that. 'Night might be more fun,' she said. She finally agreed to take the job as soon as she could clear her current list of clients, probably by allocating them to other lawyers.

'You live alone?' he asked her. A leading question? – Yes, she did.

'And you cook at home, for yourself, and sometimes for guests?' Angling for an invitation? – Yes, she did.

He walked to a cupboard. 'Here's a small gift to celebrate your new appointment.' He handed her a bottle of olive oil. She studied the label, then held it up to the light.

'Slightly hazy. That's how it should be. You can't buy it in the shops; the grower is mainly a wine man and he sells this only to people who buy his wine direct, from the vineyard. He let me have half a dozen bottles. The olives – I'll save you guessing – are *Biancolilla, Cerasuola* and *Nocellara del Belice*.'

'A perfect team.'

'Like you and me, I hope…'

They shook hands. 'You're going to call me?'

'You call me, when you're ready to start work.'

No mixing business with pleasure. But she had great tits, and a nice ass.

Cesare told Horatio that he thought the chief magistrate and mayor should have a driver.

'A driver? Why? It's impossible to drive more than ten miles on this island.'

'For security.'

'Security…? Against what?'

'Against attack, against assault. I'm talking about a bodyguard. I will provide you with a car and a driver who will take care of your security. Nothing flash – an unmarked Alfa Romeo, a driver in plain clothes.'

'You are joking – aren't you?'

But the police chief wasn't smiling. 'Look, a traffic warden was shot and killed a couple of years ago. If they'll kill somebody for issuing a ticket, what do you think might happen to somebody who sends them, or their children, to jail? I am already assuming that that's what you have in mind for the Camilleri kid.'

'Assuming he's found guilty, yes.'

'There's no doubt that he will be. There's no other possibility. But you know, don't you, that his father is… connected.'

Horatio forced a laugh. 'Connected? To what? Mains electricity?'

Cesare replied in English: 'Don't be so fucking naïve, Horatio. You know exactly what I mean when I say connected.'

'To the mafia, you mean? But he can't be, can he? There is no mafia here. Your corps is based here solely to make sure they don't have a presence here, and of course I have absolute confidence that you are doing your job properly and efficiently.'

'The mafia – what you mean is the Sicilian mafia – isn't here, but that doesn't mean that people here can't be connected to it. That's what I mean. You know what they say in Sicily? – That Montebello is where the *cosa nostra* comes to learn.'

Horatio shook his head. 'I obviously know that we have corruption here, albeit on a small scale. We have cheating and double-dealing. We have nepotism on a grand scale. We have bribery, sometimes fairly blatant and unashamed. But if the mafia really comes here to learn they must all be total cretins.'

'Why so?'

'Because everybody and his mother has heard of the mafia. And nobody in the world has ever heard of Montebello. The whole point of the *cosa nostra* – isn't it? – is that it's a secret society. So how come that everybody knows about it? On that basis alone I'd accept that our version, whatever it is and however it works, is better.'

'Okay. So it's a different sort of mafia. But it is connected. And what I want is you to have a bodyguard. I am responsible for your security.'

Horatio asked: 'Did mayor Morano have a bodyguard?'

'He didn't need one. He didn't do anything. He didn't create any waves. And he never sent anybody to jail. Whereas you…'

'You think Camilleri is a threat?'

'Not necessarily. I don't know who is a threat, or whether anybody is a threat. If I knew about threats, well… they'd be less of a threat. What I am saying is that it could be anybody. Or it could be nobody. I am not saying there is a threat at all. What I'm saying is that if there is one, I want it covered. Your safety is my responsibility, and whatever you think about it, I am not prepared to take the risk. So I am not only talking about protecting your back, but also protecting mine.'

'Let me think about it, eh?'

'Sure. Think about it, and I'll send a driver round in the morning.'

# *Thirteen*

Next day the monsignor and the Sicilians were at the Del Monte snack bar again and this time the other customers nodded in greeting. They tried harder to get a measure of the man who sat with his back to the wall, with his driver beside him. He didn't look like the sort who would own a Maserati, a car they associated with big business or even with nobility. He was, compared to most Montebellans, well dressed, but otherwise he could have passed for a local farmer or businessman. Like most of the regulars he was thick-set, with broad shoulders. His fingers were thick and stubby. He wore no jewellery. And yet he owned, or at least had the use of, a Maserati and he was treating the monsignor like a personal secretary. He was clearly a man of some esteem, and they eventually concluded that he must be doing a deal, buying or selling land, with the Church.

There was a saying, 'never do business with a priest or a monk', but the Montebellans didn't believe it; the church was rich in land, as well as in cash, and despite the government sequestration of most of its agricultural and non-clerical properties before the war, appeared to have retained a lot of both, courtesy of intermediaries that the bureaucrats had not managed to trace through the labyrinthine curia documents. There were still plenty of deals to be done, by people who had the contacts. And this particular monsignor was the man who could arrange those contacts and contracts.

To anybody who knew him, the monsignor introduced the stranger as 'Don Salvatore', a businessman on holiday, no more than that, from a small town a few miles outside Palermo, the capital of Sicily. If the priest had mentioned that the town happened to be next to Corleone, his friends would have been more interested for they had all been to the cinema to see Marlon Brando as 'Don Corleone' in *The Godfather*. Don Salvatore himself appeared friendly enough, courteous and even generous, offering coffee and drinks for the all-male company to whom he was introduced. But his Italian was thick with Sicilian regional dialect, and wasn't easy for them to understand.

This morning the coffee drinkers were joined by a Montebellan, a man they all knew, who pulled up in a battered old car, parked wherever he felt like it, shook hands with the visitors, dragged up a metal chair beside the Don and ordered cheap local red wine, the sort that came in a carton. This was Portelli the developer's father, a big landowner and plant-hire contractor, a man who, at least in public, famously had no time for the church – his own elderly parents had been threatened with excommunication following a former bishop's edict warning against supporting the Labour Party. But that was personal. What was being discussed was obviously business. And on Montebello business always superseded all other considerations. So did secrecy: when people enquiringly mentioned the visitor's presence to the landowner, he put his forefinger and thumb together and drew them along his pursed lips, as if closing them with a zipper.

There was a Sicilian proverb: *Cu' ammuccia zoccu fa, è signu chi mali fa*: a secretive person is up to some mischief.

But there was another saying: *Flies can't get into a closed mouth.*


Two of Cesare's officers, a man and a woman, both sergeants, had appeared at Horatio's door early that morning. They made a point of showing him their credentials and introduced themselves. 'I said I didn't want a bodyguard, so he's sent me two?' Nevertheless, he invited them in and made coffee.

'You have the two of us because you work long hours and you have three offices as well as this house,' said Giovanni – 'Johnny'. 'Between us, Teresa and me, we'll be on duty or on call 24 hours.'

Pouring the coffee, Horatio asked: 'But most of the time I am sitting behind a desk. What do you do all day?'

'When you are in an office, one of us will normally be outside it. When you're in court, we'll be in the courtroom. When you're at home, we'll see you safely inside it and go home or wait outside. But we'll give you a bleeper. If and when you want us, you just press it and we come.'

'What if I go out for dinner?' – 'We'll sit outside, if it's a restaurant. If it's somebody's home, again, we'll see you safely inside, then disappear until you want to go home. Like calling a taxi.'

Now, said Johnny, he'd like to look around and check the security of the house. 'Is there anything you want to put away, that you don't want me to see?'

'Nothing at all. But you don't want to check my computer, do you?'

'Not at this stage. But we might talk about it later.'

Horatio didn't even know why he had asked. There was nothing on the computer apart from email correspondence with old colleagues, a childhood sweetheart, an ex-wife and his daughters; nothing that was confidential relating to court or council matters or to newspaper stories. And then there was that novel that he'd always intended to finish, but now realised was a fairly vain hope.

Johnny asked whether there were spare keys for the house, and whether he'd object to the officers having copies. He wouldn't. They asked about the days his cleaning woman came, and whether he was expecting visitors or tradesmen to call.

'There's a chance that some of Portelli's workers might come round. They are going to clear the field at the back so I can plant olive trees.' He noticed the officers exchange a glance, but Teresa only asked: 'But they don't need access inside the house or any buildings?' And he confirmed that they didn't.

Fine, said Johnny. So if everything was otherwise okay, Teresa could drive Horatio to work while he had a look around the house and made a report about recommendations for improving security.

'You know, don't you, that I think all this is crazy, unnecessary, a waste of time and money and resources?'

'Most people think that,' said Johnny. 'But then, sometimes…' He left the sentence unfinished with a shrug.

Outside the house Teresa held the back door of the car open for him. 'The safest place is behind the driver. This may be a bit of a problem for you with Johnny because you both have long legs, but the best thing will be for you to sit behind him at an angle, so your feet are in the well on the other side. There's nothing unusual about somebody with a driver sitting on the back seat and reading papers, or whatever you want to do. If we are out in the evenings, and you want to look a bit less conspicuous, you can sit up front beside me, like a couple, out for the night. But always remember that behind the driver is safest.'

'It must be a boring bloody job for you, isn't it, body-guarding people who don't need bodyguards, sitting outside offices all day. What do you do while you're sitting there?'

'Yes. We drink a lot of coffee. But I am studying for my promotion exams, so when I have nothing to do there's a lot I can be reading.'

A thought suddenly occurred to him. 'Hey, are you armed?' She nodded. Of course she was; all *carabinieri* officers were armed.

'What are you – I think the expression is – carrying?'

'A small Beretta 8000, the Cougar, the one with the rotating barrel' – as if to suggest that the additional information would identify it for him – 'on my person and an M12 Beretta in the glove compartment, although it might sometimes go in the door. Johnny has a bigger Beretta sometimes, if he wants people to know he's carrying.'

'Where… I mean… where on your person, is your gun?'

'Right now it's in my handbag. Sometimes it's on my belt. Sometimes, when I'm in the car, on my ankle because it's the easiest place to reach quickly when you're seated. Johnny's is usually in a shoulder holster, if he's wearing a jacket. Or on his ankle.'

'Have you done this sort of work before, or am I your first subject?'

They were drawing up at the *municipio*. 'We say principal,' she told him. 'You're not my first.'

Horatio introduced her to his secretary Sophia and asked her to organise the maintenance department to bring an extra desk and chair for her. 'I'm afraid you'll have to share your office,' he said. 'When Teresa's not here, you'll have a handsome young sergeant for company. But do not... do not... show him your holiday pictures.' If everybody was taking this thing seriously, the last thing he wanted was a distracted bodyguard. It also occurred to him that if Sophia and Teresa became friends it might not be long before he was shown semi-naked pictures of his bodyguard. He looked at her for the first time as a woman; shoulder-length hair brushed back from a widow's peak, square shoulders, athletic build, perhaps a tennis player. She looked like a girl that worked out in a gym; she probably did, *carabinieri* officers didn't carry much surplus weight.

He closed the inner door and sat at his desk. He had a pile of mail every morning, even after Manuel had sifted through it. Most of it was about European Union rules, policies and subsidies and would find its way to the directorates.

A young man in his twenties sauntered through the open door of the secretary's office, holding a ten-by-eight card-backed envelope. He said: 'Good morning, lovely lady,' to Sophia. He raised a quizzical eyebrow at Teresa, who he hadn't seen before and asked: 'Is he in? Can I go in?' then found Teresa standing between him and the door.

'Beppe. He works for the mayor... a reporter at the newspaper,' Sophia told the policewoman.

Teresa knocked on the door and opened it. 'Beppe, from the newspaper. Can he come in?'

Horatio waved a hand to signal that he could.

'New secretary, boss?'

'New bodyguard.'

Beppe laughed, then realised that Horatio wasn't joking. 'Shit... You serious? Shit...'

He got straight to the point, opening the unsealed envelope and placing three photographs on the desk. 'I stopped for a coffee at the Rosa Nero and saw these guys sitting across the square at the Del

Monte. They arrived in a Maserati… One of them… well, the one on the end is that poser, Mons Cremona. The one on the left I don't know, but the guy in the middle, I am pretty sure, is Don Salvatore…'

The name meant nothing to Horatio. 'He's a capo from Lercara Friddi. He's on the most wanted list. And he's here… On Montebello. In Assumption Square. That camera I got for my birthday –' He lifted a miniature camera from the pocket of his shirt – 'you said it'd come in useful one day… I took these snaps, got the film developed and enlarged at the office, showed them to Dino and he said I should bring them to you because you'd want to tell the cops.'

'You're sure this is who you think it is?' – 'Pretty positive.'

'Let's see.' He buzzed Sophia and asked her to tell Teresa to come in. 'These faces mean anything to you?'

She didn't hesitate. 'Barracato; they call him Don Salvatore. That's his driver and bodyguard. The other one looks like a priest…'

'We know him. Local monsignor at the seminary. I guess I'd better call your boss.'

When Cesare arrived Horatio asked him: 'How is it that my boys are more observant than yours? Here's Beppe, stopping for coffee when he should have been at work…'

'I was on my way to court, with plenty of time…'

'And he sees these guys sitting under the noses of your officers.'

Cesare studied the photographs, turned to Teresa and asked: 'Barracato, right?' She nodded.

'And… Bruno somebody?'

'Used to be a hitman. Now his bodyguard and driver. They are both on the list.'

Cesare told Teresa to take the photographs, and Beppe, to the *antimafia* team. As they left, Horatio said: 'We have no mafia here, but you have an *antimafia* team? What does it do all day?'

'It ensures that we have no mafia here.'

'It's fucked up, then, hasn't it? And, now that we have found we do have mafia men here, I suddenly don't need a bodyguard. You've sent her away. How does that work out?'

'She'll be back. Right now you have me, my friend. But the truth is that you are as safe as houses if Don Salvatore is here. If anybody was planning a hit, he would be miles away.'

Cesare, operating mainly from Horatio's office, kept the mayor in the picture as events moved forward. First, every off-duty officer was quietly tracked down and called in to headquarters. Arms and ammunition were issued and checked. Vehicles were fuelled up. Rations were sourced and issued, then the troops – the *carabinieri* were soldiers as much as they were policemen – settled down for the night. Meanwhile the *antimafia* team somehow established where the Don and his minder were staying. It was a fairly remote farmhouse belonging to the monsignor's family.

'I don't want to storm the house and I certainly don't want a scene in Assumption Square,' said Cesare. 'So, on the basis that they'll leave the house in the morning again for coffee, we'll stop their car along the road, and that will be all that's necessary. Then we'll get them away to Sicily before anybody knows what's happening. No problem, no danger, no difficulties.'

Nevertheless, he asked Horatio whether he had a spare room at home and whether Johnny, the bodyguard, could stay in it overnight – 'just in case anything happens.'

And in the morning Cesare called at Horatio's home to brief him. Everything had gone according to plan. The car had driven away from the farmhouse towards town and been confronted by a road block and surrounded by armed *carabinieri*. The occupants – the two Sicilians and the monsignor – had offered no resistance and had all been handcuffed. Seconds later a helicopter had set down in a field beside the road and the three men put inside it with armed guards before flying off to the Ucciardone prison yard in Sicily.

'You know what?' said Cesare. 'They had been looking for him for 30 murders for 30 years. And it was your boy Beppe who found him. We should buy him a drink. You've got page one for your next edition and I've got the Godfather behind bars. Let's take the rest of the day off.'

'Why not?' replied Horatio. 'That's what we would have done in Fleet Street.'

# Fourteen

The linage pool at the paper cleaned up in Fleet Street – probably the only place outside Hollywood where the mafia enjoyed a romantic, rather than a brutal and criminal, image – and elsewhere with stories about GODFATHER ARRESTED AFTER 30 YEARS ON THE RUN. Some sub-editors in London with time on their hands sent to the library for cuttings to find out where Montebello actually was. They discovered that the island had an English mayor, which added to the colour, and two of them assumed he must have led what they described as a dawn raid.

A reporter Horatio had never heard of on the *Daily Mirror* took the initiative of making a phone call: 'Hi, Raich… well, it's all happening down your way, eh? So… what can you tell us?'

Horatio told his reporters on *La Gazzetta* that, apart from the fact that he was nowhere near when the arrests were made, and that it was an ambush or simple road block, rather than a raid, the reports were about as accurate as he would have expected. Fleet Street, he added, didn't start operating until the streets were aired, so any time before noon could be described by them as dawn. And, well… that was how they did things in Fleet Street… these days.

He and Cesare, having written the day off, took a car down to the harbour and walked along the waterfront, impressed by the speed with which they noted the road in front of the Porto Hotel had been rebuilt. It had sewer pipes, flood drains, channels to hide electricity and telephone cables and even – the first on any road in Montebello – a camber. 'Your first problem, and your first success. I have never seen any construction work on this island move so quickly.'

'Good teamwork. Your people, my people… everybody mucked in.'

The bodyguards trailed behind at a discreet distance.

'Teresa told me I'm not her first ...er, I gather I'm called a principal. So who did she guard before me?'

'She won't tell you about it. It would probably be a good idea for her to talk about it, but they never do. She was part of a team guarding a politician in Catania, and somebody shot and killed him. One officer stayed with the principal and Teresa set off in pursuit of the gunmen – there were two of them. She chased them down a busy street, crowded with people, and realised she wasn't going to catch up with them, so she stopped, drew her gun and shot them both.'

'On a crowded street, while they were running?'

'Shooting between the people. She got one in the back of the head and the other through the throat. Both dead.'

'What is she – lucky, brilliant, or stupid?'

'A brilliant marksman. You should get her to take you to the firing range, and see her in action. At 50 metres, which is officially more than the limit of that little gun she carries, she can place three rounds within five centimetres; within two centimetres at 25 metres. Which is what she did that night. Anyway, that's why she was in the job. They had to move her out of Sicily after that and she was transferred here. So you can believe me when I tell you that you've got the best.'

'I like her,' said Horatio. 'She seems bright, intelligent, pleasant company.'

'She's all that. And by the way, if you're going to some function and want to take her ostensibly as your date, she'll hold her own in small talk. And she'll look good. In fact she's entitled to a dress allowance, so you'd be doing her a favour if you invited her along with you. Then she can buy something nice to wear. She'll do anything you ask... except have sex with you.'

'Boyfriend?'

'No. She's married to the job. For the time being she's married to you, except, as I say...'

'It must be a boring job, though, being a bodyguard.'

'Not really. They observe. They see everything. Right now they're aware of everything that's a hundred yards ahead of us and everything a hundred yards behind. And they look up. Most people never notice any architecture that's much above eye level. But a bodyguard does. They look at rooftops and balconies and upstairs windows and they know who is where, and what they are doing. They're often a prime source of intelligence. Trained observers.'

'Yet none of them noticed Don Salvatore sitting outside the Del Monte snack bar.'

'No… I'll give you that. I owe you one for that.'

Horatio enjoyed Cesare's company. His English was fluent – he said he'd learnt it from reading Agatha Christie and Conan Doyle detective stories as a teenager – and the two of them could switch languages, even mid-sentence. As they walked towards the Café Jubilee for coffee they presented an impressive sight: the two tallest men on the island, *il gigante delicato* and *il sindaco inglese*, the gentle giant and the English mayor. A pair of good-looking, single – Cesare was a widower – middle-aged and influential men. Women of all ages smiled and waved at them; men stopped them as they walked to shake the hands of one or both of them; shopkeepers came to their doors to wish them *buon giorno*.

As they sipped *macchiato* Horatio checked that nobody was within earshot, then asked: 'And you… have you ever shot anybody?' Although he would probably describe himself as a pacifist, he had spent his share of time in battle zones and was fascinated by people – soldiers and policemen – who lived on the front line of danger, and who had killed people.

'I told you… we don't talk about that sort of thing.'

'Just a yes or a no would suffice.'

'Okay. Yes… two shot, neither of them fatal. Both in prison… How are things going with the traffic wardens?'

Horatio told him that he'd insisted that the clerks work a full day. They didn't like the idea. The director had announced that he'd resigned on principle over the new working regime and was being seen as a sort of local hero among his staff. So now they were looking for a replacement. The deputy wasn't a suitable substitute because he was too close to his boss and lacked authority.

'Could be a job for a recently retired police officer?'

Horatio laughed. 'You planning to retire?'

'Not me, but I have somebody who could probably fit in well. Somebody who has run departments, including traffic, who can organise things, who would have the necessary authority, and command respect.'

'Sounds good to me. Get him to talk to Marco Bonnici; he's the guy who will make recommendations. But if you think he'd be a good candidate, I guess he's halfway there. In fact there are a lot of vacancies; most of the *assessori*, the executives, were appointed by mayor Morano as favours for friends, not on the basis of experience or competence.'

'Like the magistrates…'

'Been talking to my new girl Alessandra, have you?'

'The one we call The Body? Now, my friend, that was another interesting appointment. I guess you gave her the job just so you could look at her. Or are you…?'

'I've hardly seen her since she got the job. But we're having dinner tonight, so… But, just a minute… what do I do about the bodyguard? I can't have an intimate conversation in the car with Johnny or Teresa sitting in the front.'

'Use your own car, if you like, and they'll follow you in theirs. It's no big deal as long as they know who you're with and where you're going, and when.'

It didn't make much difference, in the end. He drove out to pick up his date, then back to the restaurant, with Johnny in the Alfa bringing up the rear. Over dinner they chatted a little about wine and a lot about olive oil, then they discussed Alessandra's plans for her new role as director of legal services, and the magistrates, and the relative competence of some of the local lawyers. It was as if neither of them wanted the evening to end.

She sat across the table from him, once again displaying the depth of cleavage that he normally associated with an Italian TV newsreader, most of the time staring straight into his eyes. She reached over and put her hand on his, inscribing circles or figures of eight with her middle finger on the back of his hand. Shortly after midnight she moved back the cuff of his shirt to look at his watch and said: 'Time for bed, I think. Would you like to take me home?'

Johnny stopped his official car a discreet distance away from, but in full view of, her house. Alessandra put her hand on his shoulder and thanked him for an enjoyable evening, then kissed him, her tongue delving deep inside his mouth. But when, with their tongues still jousting frantically, he lowered a hand onto one of her breasts she removed it gently, turned her head away and said: 'I'm not inviting you in. Not tonight.' She kissed him again, this time chastely, and disappeared indoors.

'Not tonight...' Again. What was going on? Were there women who held back until the third date, or maybe the fourth?

He passed a restless night, thinking about the four relatively new women in his life. Three worked for him directly and one, Teresa, indirectly, but Manuel had said that office relationships were okay so long as they didn't involve harassment or sexual favours. Three of them were flirtatiously touchy-feely, never missing the opportunity to hold his arm or brush their fingers across his hand. And the fourth hadn't actually touched him at all, although she was personally and professionally committed to him – lock, stock and revolving barrel. All four were single, and attractive in their different ways. And he was a single man and – in his bedroom at least – a relatively lonely one. He fleetingly wondered what it would be like to have all four of them in his bed at the same time – who would be doing what, and to whom? Who would be sucking on the inverted nipple?

By the time he was being driven to work the following morning he was sitting behind Johnny thinking that his childhood sweetheart might be his surest and safest bet.

# *Fifteen*

The Camilleri family lawyers asked for a further adjournment of a week, with the boy being allowed out on bail meanwhile. They said he would be entering a not-guilty plea on all counts and that there was overwhelming evidence from all parties concerned that would surely result in an acquittal.

Horatio, sitting on the bench with a lawyer on either side, said he would adjourn the hearing for an hour. The magistrates would discuss the request for bail, first, then he wanted to see the core participants – defence, prosecution, police – in the conference room.

Closing the door behind him he shoved a cigarette into his mouth and said he couldn't see how bail could be an option when the boy was in breach of a probation order.

'He's in breach of it only if he is found guilty,' said magistrate Ferra. 'You are pre-judging this trial. I appreciate that you are not a lawyer, and that is why we are here to assist and advise you, but –'

'What's to pre-judge?' interrupted Horatio. 'He was on probation for driving without a licence and insurance, and he is accused of yet again driving without a licence and insurance. What's the penalty for breaching a probation order? More probation?'

'He's still legally a child,' said Ferra.

'A bloody dangerous one. No licence or insurance, shotguns on the back seat, driving while drunk… oh, and stealing his mother's car.'

'That's if he is guilty.'

'Yes; if he's guilty.' He turned to Vincenzo: 'Wheel them in, will you? And ask Francesca to come in and take a note.'

When they were all seated Horatio said he was not starting the trial behind closed doors, nor was he starting to prejudge the evidence; this was a preliminary and informal meeting and

Francesca would take notes that would be available to all parties so that there could be no confusion about what was being discussed.

'But I am concerned about wasting the court's time,' he said. 'We have a defendant on probation who is accused of committing the same offence for which the original order was made. He was the only occupant in the car when it was stopped, so whatever the defence for that might be, it would need to be a bloody good one.

'There were two shotguns on the back seat and they had been reported by their owner as having been stolen two days earlier. I suppose it's remotely possible that the owner had made a mistake, or made a false declaration, but I trust that he has received independent legal advice because either way it would amount to a firearms offence and that would potentially carry a custodial sentence and a ban on any future ownership or use of firearms…

'Driving while drunk – and uninsured – is a serious offence and, while as I say I am not prejudging anything, the evidence from the police will be that he was drunk when arrested, and carrying liquor and, as I say, he was the sole occupant of the car.

'And then we come to the question of whether or not the car was stolen. He either had his mother's permission to use the car or he did not. If he took it without her prior knowledge, then it was stolen. If she gave her permission for him to drive it, obviously aware that he was neither licensed nor insured, nor even old enough to be licensed or insured, she was aiding and abetting a crime and also the breaching of his probation order.' He turned, questioning, to the court clerk.

'Accessory before the fact,' confirmed Vincenzo.

'Again,' Horatio continued, 'has she been advised of her legal predicament, here? That crime could carry a custodial sentence. I suppose it might be reduced to a suspended sentence, or even probation, in her case. Either way, the mother would have a criminal record, if that were the way the trial went.

'So here, as I see them, are the options: a guilty plea and twelve months in jail that could be served here, or a not-guilty plea and the possibility of a guilty verdict followed by a minimum of two years, which will be spent in prison on Sicily. Now, gentlemen... any questions?'

There were none. But when the defence team had left magistrate Ferra said he wanted it on record that he didn't think that the meeting had followed correct legal procedure. Horatio told his secretary to make a note. Then magistrate Brusca said he thought everything had been 'legal and above board'; Francesca made a note of that comment, too.

Then they all trooped back into court to hear the defence announce a change of plea. Sentence was passed and the court adjourned for another day.


Horatio's routine slowly started to evolve into a regular but variable pattern. The mornings and some evenings – for as mayor he needed to attend committee meetings – were usually spent on council work; afternoons and some full days were mainly reserved for court hearings and two nights each week he would approve and oversee the production of *La Gazzetta*. He was also, by the nature of his official work, in fairly constant touch with the editorial team at the paper.

Marco, his deputy at the *municipio*, proved to have been a good choice as chief of staff, producing new nominees for the executive positions, and encouraging new attitudes among those who were staying on. The clerks, Manuel and Vincenzo, were hugely supportive and hard working, appreciating that their particular areas were now being properly run, at last. The two secretaries, Sophia and Francesca, continued to flirt with their boss while working with great efficiency. The traffic department's new shift patterns caused a lot of dissatisfied rumblings, but so far no action had been taken. The new road outside the Porto Hotel was completed, with the mayor cutting a ribbon to declare it officially open, his first such engagement.

Horatio even found that, with a bit of juggling, he could find some space in his timetable and one afternoon took up Cesare's invitation to visit the police shooting range and watch Teresa in action.

Driving there she asked whether he had any experience with guns and he told her he'd fired a Tommy gun on the FBI indoor range in the Hoover Building in Washington, and a sniper rifle and a tripod-mounted machine gun during an army exercise in Germany. He'd also used a shotgun for shooting wildfowl and rabbits when he lived in the north of England.

She gave him protective glasses and ear defenders, then set up a paper target with the outline of a human torso 25 yards behind the line and fired three rapid rounds, followed by another three. Then she wound the target in and Horatio could see six holes – all connected – in the centre of the head.

'Do you want a go? I think your hands are too big for this one, but try the 93R. The R stands for *Raffica* – burst-fire – because it can fire a single shot or three rounds at once.' She took the second gun out of her holdall and showed him how to hold it, and to use the forward grip for greater stability.

It was on single-shot. Horatio aimed carefully at a new paper target and missed it completely. She moved up behind him, wrapping her arms tightly round his body so that he could feel her firm breasts pressing into the small of his back. She held his arms and he fired again, this time hitting the paper, but not the torso. 'You should practice,' she told him. 'If we were in an incident and anything happened to me, then you could at least defend yourself. As things are, you wouldn't hit anybody, but you might scare them to death.'

'I'm much better with a shotgun.'

'What do you shoot?'

'Nothing, these days. Used to shoot pheasant, wood pigeon, rabbits, that sort of thing. And I rarely missed. In fact I became quite proficient. The trick with rabbits is to get the shot all in the head, so people who eat the meat aren't chewing on lead pellets. So you need to work out how the shot spreads at different ranges. With pigeons, their wings are like armour plating, and the thing there is to shoot so that when the shot reaches the bird its wing is up, and not protecting the body. It takes practice, that's all. But it takes a lot, because a shotgun is hardly a precision weapon.'

'We have one here. Would you like to try it?'

'No thanks. I might have lost the knack, then I'd just embarrass myself in front of you again. Anyway, why do cops need shotguns?'

'All sorts of reasons. It would be handy to shoot at a car that looked like it wasn't going to stop at a roadblock – just firing into the radiator... or to blow the hinges off a locked door... or even to shoot into a crowd of armed rioters. I've never used one myself, so you can show me.'

She went to the armoury and returned with a 12-bore and a box of cartridges and handed both to Horatio. It was another Beretta – the *carabinieri* obviously believed in supporting local industry. He felt the weight of it, then fed in two cartridges, aimed at one of the paper targets they'd already used, fired one round, and told her: 'Now you can see how the pellets spread, at this range. So with the next shot, you just adjust your sighting and fire higher.'

He fired the second cartridge. This time, the pellets went into only the top left quadrant of the target. 'That would be the head of the rabbit,' he said.

Teresa took the weapon from him and tried for herself. 'Your first shot had been at the centre of the paper, right? So if I raise the barrel a bit, and move it slightly to the left...'

All her shot went into the same place as Horatio's second attempt.

'You're a natural. You should take up hunting.'

'I don't think I could do that, shooting animals. All I've ever shot is people.'

'What is that like?'

'We don't talk about it.'

She would, and could, talk about virtually any other subject that he raised, and he was impressed by her range of knowledge. On evenings when he fancied a restaurant meal but had no dinner dates pre-planned he would invite her to join him, rather than leave her sitting outside alone in the car. She appeared to be something of an expert on Italian wines, especially Chianti, her favourite, but she never drank alcohol in his company – she was always working when she was with him; they didn't date because it would have been against the rules. Horatio introduced her to the mysteries of olive oil and she gradually came to share his enthusiasm for it. Like him, she had been on Nato exercises, but unlike him had also worked with Interpol and even with Britain's Special Boat Service; like him, she enjoyed the telling of a good story. She was fascinated to learn more about England, a country she hadn't visited, and Horatio mused about the fun he would have in taking her there, and showing her ancient Roman cities like York, Chester and Bath, if only the circumstances had been different. She confessed to being 'fiercely ambitious' and told him, without embarrassment, that her job as his bodyguard was basically a stop-gap in her career until a suitable vacancy for promotion appeared.

He greatly enjoyed her companionship. In a different situation he would have invited her out. There was more to male-female bonding than sex, or the prospect of it; Horatio preferred women he could talk to. But then… if he were able to invite her on a date, who knew where the relationship might progress…? For the time being they were simply good friends, good mates, and selfishly he hoped that her promotion didn't arise too soon.


Just as his scheduling appeared to be dropping into some sort of shape, it was interrupted by a call to attend a meeting in Sicily, to discuss the effects of the European Union on *communes* and municipalities. It was to be a seminar in separate sections – for mayors (who handled policy), clerks (who did the paperwork) and directors or *assessori* (who got down to the detail).

De Giorgio, responsible for Montebello's tourism portfolio, had suggested sharing transport with Horatio but Cesare vetoed that idea. Horatio and Teresa travelled to Palermo in a police helicopter then were driven to the Hotel des Palmes on via Roma, where – Horatio delighted in telling her – Wagner had composed part of *Parsifal* in 1882 (a bit of useless information that he'd picked up somewhere); the rest of the Montebello delegation, whose meetings were being held elsewhere, made the crossing by car and ferry.

Horatio didn't learn much that interested him at the set-piece lectures and discussions, but he was intrigued by what he learnt from his fellow mayors over coffee and at mealtimes. He mentioned how impressed he'd been by the rapid reaction of the EU relief agencies when a major road collapsed, saying that his biggest problem was how to return all the equipment that had been sent – earthmovers, bulldozers, cement mixers, cranes and concrete pumps – now that they were no longer needed.

The delegate nearest to him was aghast. 'What…? *Madonna!* You don't return that stuff. Why do you think they would want it back? It's all yours now. It belongs to the *commune*.'

'No: we didn't pay anything for it, and it must be worth a fortune.'

'You don't understand, do you, how the EU works. Providing heavy construction equipment for member countries means work – industry, jobs, money – for the factories in the other member countries that make it. In this case they will be mainly in England and Germany, two countries that are always complaining that they put millions, or billions, into Europe and never get anything back. So they're delighted to get the contracts, and the EU is also delighted because it keeps those two countries quiet for a while. So they certainly don't want any of it back. The manufacturers don't want it back.'

'But what am I supposed to do with it?'

'Keep it. Hire it out to your local contractors. Or sell it to them. Only, don't suggest that you could send it back.'

The Sicilian mayor went on to relate how contractors in a *commune* near Naples had planted dynamite on a cliff edge, exploded it, and reported an earthquake, asking for immediate relief aid. 'There's an earthquake or at least a tremor somewhere in the Mediterranean every four days, so it was no big deal. They got so much equipment – even though the earthquake was officially downgraded to a landslide because it hadn't registered a reading anywhere outside the region – that they repaired the chasm they'd created, then bought the stuff at half price from the council and had enough new vehicles and machinery to replace all their existing gear for years to come...'

When another of the delegates noticed him studying the label on a bottle of olive oil, they started a conversation during which Horatio mentioned that he was planning his own olive grove.

'Planted, or in pots?' Planted, said Horatio. How on earth could you plant olives in pots?

'Big pots. You need a fork-lift to move them.'

And what would be the advantage of doing that?

The man smiled. 'You get a grant if you have more than a dozen olive trees. They don't trust Sicilians so they send a man from Brussels or anywhere outside Italy to count them. But they can't just turn up and expect the farmer to be on site, so they make an appointment. The grower shows the inspector his trees – there is nothing in the rules about them being in the ground – and they are counted. Then he gets the fork-lift and a low loader and moves them across to his friend's land, where they are counted again, usually the next day.'

'But...' Horatio thought he could see a flaw in the plot.

'You can't mark olive trees, not it any way.'

'But they could mark the pots.'

'They haven't thought of that yet.'

Another mayor asked him how dairy and beef farmers were benefiting from the EU on Montebello. Horatio said he wasn't sure, but he remembered a story in his own newspaper about a call to reduce the size of herds because of the so-called 'beef mountain' and the 'milk lake', so he said he assumed they were not benefiting very well at all.

'They need to wise up. As proof that you have killed a beast you are required to submit an ear from it. It obviously hasn't occurred to the brainboxes in Brussels that cattle have two ears...'

'*Madonna!*' said Horatio. 'But they will eventually realise, and start asking for two ears.'

'Yes, of course they will… eventually. But cows produce milk and bulls produce beef whether they have ears or not.'

The man continued: 'Tomatoes. You produce great tomatoes on Montebello…'

'They're expensive, though.'

'That's because the best ones are exported. But the question is, where do they go? Instead of being shipped to Sicily they should go to Malta – at least until they join the EU.' He smiled: 'If they let them in, with all the corruption there is on that island. Anyway, that's an international export because it's still outside the European community, so there's a grant for it. Malta converts it into tomato sauce or paste for pizza and *bruschetta*, then ships it back. Your people can put it into tins and export it again; you get a grant to open a canning factory to do that. That creates employment. And it also means another export grant when it is shipped. Malta puts a label on it and re-exports it to Europe – another grant. Everybody's happy, especially the EU which only sees itself assisting growers and canners with exports to countries outside the community.'

There were grants, it became clear, for just about everything: roads and parks, communal buildings and office blocks, repairs to walls, communications systems including the internet, fishing and farming, manufacturing and exporting, education and hobbies and playgrounds, sports facilities including playing fields, welfare, any new employment opportunities, ecological improvements, solar heating, beaches, tourism… Horatio wondered where was the need for his *commune* to spend any of its own money. Certainly, he reckoned, with a bit of judicious research and planning he could save untold millions and replace the financing with EU grants.

# Sixteen

As the delegates poured out of the conference hall and into the heavy night air Horatio heard a short crisp crack, a sound he instantly recognised as one that he'd heard before, somewhere, and in the same split second that he heard it there was a thud, a dull blow, on the side of his head. But before his memory cells could identify the noise he was thrown to the ground and was flat on his back on the pavement.

Teresa, who had downed him by kicking his legs from under him with an instinctive judo move, was sitting across him, the fork of her trousers covering his chin, holding her gun and shouting: 'The roof... he's on the roof!'

He knew what it was now; he'd heard it often enough when covering the so-called Troubles on the streets of Belfast: a sniper rifle. Teresa, trained to scan the skyline as well as all around her, had seen the muzzle flash and was directing the rest of the police squad. But what about the blow to his head?

She was holding him down firmly but lightly. He wriggled his hand up slowly under her bottom and towards his face. In different circumstances, in a different place... She told him to keep still, but was allowing him room to breath. Her holdall – the one in which she carried her armoury – had appeared as if from nowhere and now was at the top of his head as protection from the line of fire. Without averting her eyes from the roof she dropped her small handgun into the bag and retrieved the heavier, ten-inch, burst-fire model, the one he had used with the forward grip.

Horatio felt sticky blood on the side of his face and thought: 'Christ! A head shot.' Then he remembered – because he'd seen it in the movies – that it was important for him to retain consciousness;

he recalled that in Hollywood shootings people always said 'Stay with me... Stay awake.' Then he passed out.

He recovered on a bed inside a speeding ambulance, a uniformed *carabiniere* and a paramedic sitting opposite him and Teresa perched on the bunk beside him, holding and stroking his hand. Her holdall was at her feet and her handbag, its flap unfastened, on her lap.

She looked concerned, ashen. She was shaking. She didn't want to lose another principal.

'How are you feeling?'

He checked the extremities. He had feeling in his legs and could wiggle his toes. He could move his fingers. He thought he must be okay. He tried to swing his legs off the bed to sit up, but they were strapped down.

'Okay, but... Head wound...'

'No... Flesh wound, I think. It is your cheek.'

'That's the face. Part of the head.'

'Only a flesh wound,' she said.

As the ambulance pulled up to the hospital doors and the paramedic prepared to wheel the stretcher bed out, Horatio said: 'I'm all right. I think I can walk.'

'Lie still,' said Teresa. 'Head wound.'

The trolley crashed through rubber doors, through the emergency room and through more doors to a side ward where doctors were waiting for him. There were policemen everywhere.

The initial examination took no more than a couple of minutes. 'Shrapnel,' said one of the doctors. 'Here it is.' He placed a sliver of stone in Horatio's hand. 'A souvenir for you. Looks like the bullet hit the wall behind you and it chipped out a piece of stone and that hit you in the fleshy part of the cheek. No harm done.'

Nevertheless the doctors kept saying 'head wound' and insisted on a skull x-ray before releasing him to the police cars that drove him and Teresa in convoy back to the Palmes hotel.

She followed him into his bedroom, dropped her holdall on the bed and placed her handbag, open and with the small Beretta back inside it, on the bedside cabinet. When he sat on the bed she checked him out again, expertly, almost exactly as the doctors had done it at the hospital. 'Shock?'

'I guess so. I need a Scotch. There's a bottle in my wheelie bag.'

'Probably not a good idea.'

'I wasn't given any medication. Anyway, whisky is supposedly a good antidote for shock.' She looked more tired than he felt. He told her: 'You could probably do with something yourself.'

She thought about it. 'I'll join you, if you take a coffee with it. There's a coffee-maker over there. It'll be only instant, but...'

'Instant is how I'd like it: instantly.'

They sat side by side on the bed, sipping whisky from glasses she brought from the bathroom. Horatio put his arm around her and hugged her. 'Thank you for all that,' he said. He kissed her forehead and she pressed her cheek against his, the uninjured one, then turned and kissed him on the mouth, opening hers slowly. They held the kiss for several minutes. Then she moved slightly away and told him: 'I'll stay with you tonight, if you like. It might make us both feel better. But what I'm saying is, I'll share your bed, but we don't have sex. That's the rules. We'll just curl up in each other's arms and feel secure and go to sleep, okay?'

'Just a cuddle?' It sounded okay to Horatio.

She picked up her handbag, with the little gun inside it, and went through the connecting door to her own room, checking that it was locked from the inside, then double-checked the chain and the bolt on the inside of Horatio's corridor door.

'Another whisky?' she asked.

'And another coffee,' he said. He didn't like the instant stuff but he felt he wanted to stay awake for as long as possible, to enjoy the promised cuddle. She refilled the small electric kettle from the bathroom tap and made another two cups. Then she started to undress him, as if he were an invalid, incapable of doing it for himself. When she removed his boxers she looked and said: 'You are well built. A tall man, everything in proportion, as it should be.'

114

Horatio removed the counterpane, pulled back the sheet and swung naked into bed, watching her remove her own clothes. She stripped totally and for the first time he saw her breasts, relieved of the pressure of a sports bra, round and firm, with a slight upward curve and with prominent nipples, standing like pink pearls on small circular rose petals. As she moved across the bedroom he noticed – he was looking for it – her small triangle of dark curly hair.

She picked up his shirt from the back of an armchair and put it on, fastening alternate buttons, then stood hesitantly and demurely at the side of the bed. He thought she looked even more sexy wearing his shirt than she did when fully naked. He extended a hand, sideways, through two of the lower buttons and caressed her thigh, then moved it upwards so that his thumb could stroke in circles in the soft hair at the top.

'Don't do that,' she told him, moving slightly backwards and just out of reach. As she joined him in the bed the shirt rode up above her waist. He put his hands there and pulled her towards him, and they were kissing again. Horatio's hands continued under the shirt and up her body, and began encircling and cupping her breasts.

'It wasn't much use, was it, your shirt?'

'For what?'

'As protection.'

'You need protection, from me?'

'I suppose not.'

He easily forced a leg between hers and moved it until he could feel the soft moist fur at the apex. She could obviously also feel him. He took her hand and steered it down his chest and across his stomach. 'I know the rules are that we don't have sex, but could you do something about this?'

'Of course,' she said. 'This part of a man's body has rules of its own.' She kissed his throat then applied pecking kisses all the way down until her lips were encircling his unruly member.

Later, she aroused it again. 'I want you inside me,' she whispered.

'What about the rules?'

'The rules of engagement can always be changed, according to the circumstances. I need you inside me.'

What was a fellow to do? 'Okay,' he said. 'You're in charge.'

When he woke she was lying with her head comfortably in the crook of his arm, her dark hair splayed across the pillow. He had been sleeping only lightly and had been woken by the telephone on the locker beside him making a clicking sound as it was connected, prior to ringing. He kissed her gently and moved his arm away to answer it. He paused and listened.

Looking pointedly at Teresa he said, loudly: 'Ah, Cesare, old friend. How are you?'

Teresa was out of the bed and through the connecting door, Horatio's shirt flowing, now totally unbuttoned, behind her.

'…I'm fine, thanks… you heard what happened… just a flesh wound, in the cheek. No harm done…'

Cesare asked for Teresa. 'I guess she'll be in her own room, next door… well… she was probably in the shower. In fact, I think I can hear her moving about now.'

The police chief asked him for an account of events the previous night and Horatio told him as much as he knew, up to the time when they had started on whisky, coffee and sex.

'Did they get the shooter...? Great. So, has anybody asked him why, with more than a hundred mayors present, I was the target for assassination? Not, surely, because I've sent a handful of people to jail.'

'You weren't the target.' Cesare told him. 'She was.'

'Shit!' said Horatio. 'But she put herself between me and the gunman as soon as the shot was fired.'

'That's her job. And she wouldn't have known what was happening at the time. She will have worked out fairly quickly, though, that, as you say, with all those mayors present at the conference, more than half of them representing different mafia factions and the rest being staunchly anti-mafia, the member from Montebello would have been the least likely target of all. They got the guy and he's admitted that he was after Teresa. Luckily for you

116

both he is a *picciotto*, a young punk, and a bad shot. They are picking up the man who sent him – he's the brother of one of the assassins she shot that I told you about – right now. In the meantime, stay together; the hotel is safe but do not order room service. You'll be picked up in an hour or so by people that she will know.'

He rang off and Horatio heard the phone ringing in the next room as Cesare called Teresa.

He was still in bed when she returned to his room, steaming and damp from the shower, a short towel knotted just above her breasts. She sat beside him and tenderly stroked his wounded cheek. As the towel slid down her body she told him: 'One more time… We have an hour to occupy. Then we'll get you home to safety.'

# PART THREE

# Seventeen

John Richmond knelt painfully on the sole of the cockpit of his 29-foot Bermudian sloop, his knees raw from constant contact with the hard teak. He was sanding down the cabin hatch in preparation for its twelfth coat of marine varnish.

Experience had taught him that in the rock-cracking heat of the Mediterranean a dozen coats – each application thinned down slightly less than the previous one – was the minimum number of applications, for the salt spray boiled on the varnish and blistered the gloss finish, leaving it pock-marked and ugly. 'Hot salt water,' he would propound to the fishermen at the bar of La Spada: '...That's the best way to remove varnish.' And they would generally stare at him blankly, because they didn't varnish their fishing boats. But he took immense pride in the appearance of the yacht he and his wife had sailed from Burnham-on-Crouch, across the Bay of Biscay and round Gibraltar into the Med. They had intended to spend their retirement island-hopping, John finding odd jobs in marinas to eke out their pensions; but after the long crossing from Mallorca to Montebello they had decided to go no further. Richmond found occasional winter maintenance work in Porto Vecchio, and in what they called the shoulder months – when there was sufficient wind to drive the sails, but it wasn't yet too hot to stay on deck all day in the sunshine – he and his wife were content to cruise around the island with a picnic lunch and a chilled bottle of wine.

It was only light sanding, removing miniscule bubbles and the occasional wayward paintbrush hair from the previous coat, but the friction and the monotony, with the morning sun beating down on the back of his neck and his shoulders, made it hot work. He took a rag from his pocket and mopped the torrent of sweat pouring from his hairline into his ginger stubble. He noticed two young men, Africans, barefooted in jeans and T-shirts, standing on the pontoon watching his progress.

'Can I help you, gentlemen?' All boat owners in the marina kept an eye on strangers; it wasn't unknown for odd bits of equipment – ropes and boathooks and sometimes even bits of diving equipment left causally on deck – to disappear, even on a crime-free island.

They appeared hesitant, looking about them. 'We want to go to Sicily.'

He nodded towards the terminal. 'No problem. There's a ferry.' But he recognised their predicament. Illegal immigrants, having somehow reached Montebello, needed to get to the European mainland. In theory part of the EU (which was chiefly how the locals saw their status: more theory than practice), there was – in the same theory – no frontier, no passport control, within the community. Nevertheless, because of its closer proximity to Libya and Tunisia, there were sometimes spot-checks on papers when the Montebello ferry docked in Sicily. Once in Sicily, however, you were in Europe: you could travel as far as England or Ireland without being stopped and asked for ID.

He asked: 'Do you have money?'

'We have a hundred dollars.'

'Okay, I'll take you. Come back here at midnight.'

They appeared doubtful. 'We go in this boat?'

'No. Meet me here. I have another boat, a faster one.'


Next morning, Jim Hipwell, another English ex-pat, parked in the marina and, with a copy of *La Gazzetta* under his arm and a flask of fresh water in his shoulder bag, stepped down from the concrete pier to the floating pontoon. He didn't take his boat out often, rarely more than once a week; but most mornings he sat on board reading the paper – sometimes one of the English newspapers that arrived two days late and cost a fortune – drinking coffee from his

12-volt percolator while thinking of odd jobs that needed doing to the boat, and occasionally attending to some of them, or asking JR to do the work. He realised immediately that his gleaming white cruiser was missing. Refusing to believe what he was seeing – or not seeing – he walked along to his mooring. No boat, and the mooring lines were in neat circles on the pontoon.

He walked back along the waterfront to the harbour police station and announced that his vessel had been stolen.

'Not stolen,' said the desk sergeant. 'Nobody has ever stolen a boat on Montebello. Perhaps you didn't tie it up properly and it has just drifted away.'

'No, it has gone. The mooring lines are coiled up on the pontoon. It's been stolen.'

'Then perhaps,' suggested the sergeant, 'it has just sunk.'

'It's a bloody 36-foot Fairline. 'There isn't sufficient depth of water for it to sink.'

'I'll come and help you look.'

But, standing on the pontoon as it bobbed gently with the waves, and staring incredulously at the space where a motor cruiser should have been, the sergeant had to concede that the boat had been slipped from its mooring lines and driven away. The policeman and the boat owner strode back together towards the police station in order to file a report. As they walked, the sergeant pointed towards the tiny island called Calvo at the entrance to the harbour and said: 'Just a minute. Isn't that your boat, over there?'

Jim Hipwell said that it certainly looked like it. They took out the police inflatable and motored the short distance to Calvo. There, stranded on the rocks, was the missing boat. Also there, totally bewildered on the island, were two illegal immigrants. The sergeant waded ashore and enquired what they were doing.

'Is this Sicily?' asked one of the Africans.

The immigrants, correctly believing that it was no crime to attempt to cross the sea from Montebello to Sicily, told their story. Asked to describe the boatman, one of the Africans used the word *hamri*, which means reddish in Arabic.

'*Barbarossa*,' announced the sergeant. All Sicilians believed, for some reason, that Judas was red-headed and John Richmond happened to be the only man on the island with ginger hair and beard. The sergeant had always thought there was something dodgy about the Englishman.

Hipwell and the officer returned to the marina and stood at the stern of Richmond's yacht. 'My flippers… and one of my life-jackets,' said Hipwell, pointing into the cockpit of the sloop. He shouted: 'John… Come out here!' And the head of a bleary-eyed Richmond, red hair awry, poked out of the hatch.

'We need to talk to you,' the sergeant said. 'Get dressed and come to the station.'

Richmond's story was that, as a law-abiding citizen, he was not – of course – willing to assist two obviously illegal immigrants to get to Sicily. But nor was he going to miss the opportunity to make an easy hundred bucks. He had simply borrowed his friend's boat, driven out of sight of land, then made a wide gentle turn back towards Montebello; his passengers were not astral navigators, and had no idea of the direction in which they were travelling. As they approached the harbour he had pointed out the lights and told them it was Sicily. That wasn't exactly a lie, for it was a Sicilian island. He had put them ashore on Calvo and told them to wait until sunrise when they would be able to get their bearings and travel inland. But after disembarking his passengers he had driven away too quickly and hit the rocks. So he anchored it and took a lifejacket and flippers and swam back to his own boat where he dried himself and went to sleep. He fully intended to report everything to his friend Hipwell, he said, and retrieve the cruiser as soon as he woke in the morning.

'But you didn't have your friend's permission to take his boat?' asked the sergeant.

'I didn't need it. I look after his engines. Whenever I do a job it's perfectly normal for me to take it for a run to test the motors.'

'But – on this specific occasion – you didn't have his permission to take it out? And in the middle of the night?'

'As I said, I didn't need it. If I am performing an engine test I can do it any time I like, day or night. I had replaced a gasket for him. I wanted to see how it ran after that.'

'So,' said Cesare as he recounted the story to Horatio: 'What do you suggest we do about all that? I have two illegal immigrants in the police cells, and two Englishmen, one with the bottom ripped out of his expensive boat and another who admits to damaging it, but says he didn't steal it. Any ideas?'

Horatio took a long draught on a cigarette and pondered. 'The Africans are easy,' he said. 'They want to go to Sicily; they can go there. We'll arraign them in court here and I'll send them to Sicily for sentencing. Let the Sicilian authorities deal with them. They'll either jail them as illegal immigrants, or send them home, or both. As for Mr Richmond, he must be made to pay for the immediate repairs to Hipwell's boat, in the boatyard, to a standard acceptable to the owner, so he doesn't have to claim on his insurance. I think he should also return the Africans' money, since he didn't do what they paid him to do. Otherwise he will be charged with stealing the boat and with reckless behaviour at sea, and probably go to jail.'

'I'm sure he'll find the cash, somehow, if I tell him the alternative is a prison sentence,' said Cesare. He paused. 'And perhaps when the Africans are convicted you might wish to commend the sergeant on his powers of observation in spotting them on Calvo...?'

'Absolutely.'

'Splendid. Then we have had no boat stolen on the island and we keep the troops happy. And there is still no crime on Montebello.'

# Eighteen

Horatio's local popularity had soared after the headline ISLAND'S MAYOR SHOT BY MAFIA GUNMAN had appeared on the front of *La Gazzetta*. And the linage pool for the journalists' drinking fund at the Ireland pub had increased considerably when ENGLISH MAYOR SHOT IN SICILY BY MAFIA HITMAN had been retailed to Fleet Street where some sub-editors dramatically upgraded 'shot' to 'gunned down', and others called for cuttings, found the story about a mafia godfather's arrest on Montebello, and put two and two together with the not unusual result of making five. On the express instructions of the *carabinieri* there had been no mention of the mayor's bodyguard.

Immediately following their return to the island, Teresa had been relieved of her duties. As Cesare explained it: 'We can't have a bodyguard who may herself be a target – we'd never know who was shooting at whom.' She was sent to the comparative security of staff college in Modena with the promise of fast-track promotion, followed by a probable transfer to the *antimafia* commission, and with the likelihood of an eventual posting back to Montebello, which – because it was properly policed – was considered to be free of organised crime and gunmen.

Horatio's ratings rose even further when the traffic wardens and clerks announced a strike for the late summer months. Motorists were unanimously in support of anybody who could remove the scourge of the irritants they generally described as 'blackshirts'.

He waited until the strike actually took effect – no wardens on the streets and no clerks in the traffic department offices – on the day after pay-day, then called a meeting in the council chamber, having asked his deputy and the clerk to invite the appropriate participants.

On one side were the general secretary of the government employees' union, the leader of the traffic section of the union, and the leader of the labour party. On the other side with Horatio were his deputy Marco Bonnici (a labour councillor) and the new director of the traffic department, a former policeman. Also in attendance were Cesare, as head of *carabinieri*, Manuel the council clerk, and Alessandra, his head of legal services. His secretary Sophia was taking notes.

While they were being served with coffee and biscuits Horatio thanked them for coming. When everybody was settled he gestured towards them with his hand, palm upwards, and asked: 'So, gentlemen… where do you think we go from here? I mean, what is going to happen to your members?'

'We have a list of demands,' said the general secretary, producing a few sheets of paper. Horatio nodded to Manuel who got up from his chair and crossed the room to take a copy from him. 'First, we wish to put on record that we totally reject…'

Horatio raised his hand, palm outward, now, to silence the speaker and then turned the list of demands face downwards on his desk. 'I apologise if you were given the impression that you were invited here today to negotiate. That is not the case. It is not the way that this administration operates. Negotiation – whenever negotiation is necessary – takes place before labour is withdrawn, not afterwards.'

He took a sip of coffee while the delegation looked at each other in confusion.

'When I asked what was going to happen to your members, I meant where were they going to find new jobs. The point is that we don't really want to add to the queue of unemployed. Jobs, even at the best of times, are difficult to find, even for skilled workers. In the case of your workers…' Horatio shrugged, as if in doubt about the amount of skill involved, and left the sentence unfinished.

'They are government employees,' said the labour leader; 'Their jobs are guaranteed.'

'Past tense,' said Horatio. 'Yesterday, they were government employees. Today they are among the ranks of the unemployed. And some of them, from what I have seen, among the ranks of the unemployable.'

The section leader was clearly offended by that obvious slur on his members and colleagues, but Horatio showed him the palm of his hand, again, as the man started to object.

'Let me tell you something,' he said. 'I, too, am a trade unionist. Still a paid-up member. I used to work in the newspaper industry in England. I'd be the first to admit that I use the terms "work" and "industry" somewhat loosely in that context, and it was a pretty ineffectual union. But in the workplace we knew how to behave and more importantly we knew how the employers behaved, and were likely to react, whatever we planned to do. For example, if you want to bugger up the system, you don't withdraw your labour: you work to rule. That means you do everything strictly according to the rules, and it generally means that nothing works properly at all.'

He paused to allow that to sink in.

'So if you are a traffic warden and you want to attract somebody's attention to the importance of your work and the state of your grievances, and you work to rule, you'll ticket every official car that's badly parked, every police car stopped on a yellow line, any ambulance that stops near a pedestrian crossing, any van selling fish or bread in the street, every doctor on call outside a house, everybody who pops out of the car for 30 seconds to use a cash machine. And you cause so much fuss that people decide they need to talk to you. And, more important, to listen to you. Workers who work to rule always screw everything up. But what they do is legal, because they are following the rules.'

'But,' blustered the general secretary, 'if our members worked to rule they would have to work their contracted hours…'

'Ah,' said Horatio, shaking his head, as if with sadness. 'There we have it. They'd be required to do what they signed up for when they started the job.' He nodded to Manuel who distributed a single sheet of paper to each person present. 'This is a letter posted today to your individual members at their home addresses, informing them that they have broken their contract and their employment has been terminated. That, of course, includes all pension rights. This weekend's edition of *La Gazzetta* will advertise vacancies in the traffic department. The number of recruits will be fewer than was previously employed, but I promise that every applicant will be interviewed. The main stipulation – for those who are considered suitable for the job – will be that they are prepared to work according to their contract, including their contracted hours.'

He put his pen in his jacket pocket, a signal that the meeting was over.

'Now, if you'll excuse me, I have a luncheon engagement.' As he walked towards the door the general secretary stood up. Horatio patted the man on the shoulder. 'You fucked up,' he told him.

As they walked back to his office he told Cesare that he didn't want the absence of wardens to lead to 'parking anarchy' on the streets. 'I'd like the police to be helpful to motorists, courteous as I know they usually are. Help them find places to park – and no automatic ticketing of tourists' hire cars, just because they're easy.'

Alessandra, pearl grey trouser suit, white blouse with one button too many unfastened, followed him into the room. 'You have a lunch date…?'

'At the newspaper office.'

'Fancy a dinner date?'

He had been avoiding her company, keeping himself busy with evening engagements of which there were many. And keeping her busy, too. She was handling the chamber of advocates and the professional magistrates, rearranging cases – with Francesca's help – in the court office to avoid any obvious conflicts of interest. He also fed her all the contract work and the ever-increasing pile of EU regulations that always needed somebody to translate into language that even the most devoted bureaucrats could understand. She had been doing an excellent job. 'Legal services' was all-embracing, even including unofficial strike action.

126

But when he looked at her, and at the half-open buttons, he wondered whether it could be a case of third time lucky. He pretended to be thinking about the offer.

'Dinner at my place,' she offered. 'I'll cook for you.'

It was, he decided, an offer he couldn't refuse.

In the afternoon Manuel told him that by tradition the mayor's office formally requested permission from the curia to hold the big annual fireworks display to celebrate the feast of Santa Maria – the island's patron saint – in *piazza duomo*, the square in front of the cathedral. The paved central area was church property and the fireworks were a civic, rather than a church, affair. It was, the clerk repeated, a mere formality: permission was requested and permission was automatically granted. But the request normally went from the mayor to the bishop.

'Isn't this something, then, that can be handled quickly and simply between the mayor's clerk and the bishop's chaplain?'

'Probably. But it's a case of *noblesse oblige*. It is, after all, Santa Maria. The most important day – well, apart from Easter, and possibly Christmas – in the Christian calendar. That's why it is done by the two top men.'

'Can it be done on the phone?'

'I don't see why not.'

'Get him on the line, then.'

It was, as the clerk had said, a mere formality, although the bishop made the point that, 'in the old days', the mayor had presented himself at the palace, the two community leaders shared a bottle of wine while discussing matters of mutual interest, and permission was granted just as the final glasses were poured.

'We are both extremely busy men,' said Horatio.

'Changing times,' said the bishop. 'A pity that old courtesies can't be maintained. But yes, of course, the council has our permission to hold its display on our *piazza*. I shall greatly look forward to watching it.'

'I am assured it is going to be the biggest and best *festa* ever,' said Horatio.

'Then I'll enjoy the spectacle even more.'

Towards the end of the afternoon Marco Bonnici came in with what he described as 'a problem'.

The street cleaner who regularly maintained the road and pavements around *piazza duomo* had complained to the director of sanitation and cleansing that the women volunteers who swept the central area of the square simply brushed the dust and rubbish into the street, usually after he had cleaned it. The council cleaner had spoken to the women and told them that if they would kindly put the rubbish into bags, he would take it away for them, but they'd shrugged and said it was the way they had always done it. The director didn't want to approach the church authorities personally; his view was that matters between the curia and the council should be handled only at top level. So he had taken the problem to Bonnici.

'The street-cleaner's solution seems highly sensible to me,' said Horatio. 'The cathedral obviously wants its *piazza* to be clean and tidy. All that the women appear to be doing is redistributing the rubbish. Call the bishop's chaplain, give him the mayor's compliments, and tell him that if they'll gather it up, we'll take it away. But we don't want the mess to be brushed on to our streets. Church and state… we should co-operate however and whenever we can.'

She had prepared him baby tuna – so-called because nobody, fishermen, fishmongers, chefs or restaurateurs could agree on the proper name for the peculiar species. A perfect replica of the yellow-fin tuna, when fully grown it was not much bigger than a trout. She simmered onions, thinly-sliced new potatoes, herbs and garlic with olive oil in a pot then placed the fish on that base, leaving it covered only long enough to cook through.

'It's delicious,' he said. 'I love fresh tuna.'

'Couldn't be fresher; today's catch, compliments of our friend Giuseppe, the bank robber. He doesn't let me pay. But if I don't visit his stall he sends fish to my office; I'd rather go to the *Souk* and choose it.'

'Shouldn't you be wary, then, about a conflict of interest between a merchant and a government employee?' Horatio smiled, to suggest that the question was only half serious.

'There could be no conflict unless Giuseppe was ever likely to appear in court again. I think the odds are against that. In any case, it is payment in kind. I didn't charge any fees in the end, partly because it was an easy case with little or no work beyond clearing up a couple of points with you; and also because it was through representing him that I met you, and I got this job.'

'He caught this fish himself?'

'Somewhere behind Calvo.'

'It's gorgeous, and beautifully prepared. My compliments to you both, defendant and advocate, fisherman and cook.'

He refilled their glasses with a light Sicilian red and they talked as they ate about work and work colleagues, then took a second bottle to a coffee table and sat together on the sofa. She curled her long legs beneath her, forcing the short skirt to ride halfway up her thighs. Trying to concentrate on small-talk, he asked how she normally spent her evenings.

'I bring a lot of work home. Have you any idea of the size of my workload? I read the Italian newspapers and the London *Times*, I try to catch the news on TV, then I go to bed and usually masturbate until I fall asleep.'

'You…?'

'Masturbate. Doesn't everybody? I have a great body – you know that – and I enjoy touching it. And I have very sensitive hands.' She took the glass from him and put her hands on both of his. 'You're picturing it in your mind, now, aren't you? Me lying naked on the bed, writhing, as my hands move over my body, stroking, nipping, exploring, penetrating. Sometimes I pretend that they are your hands – yours are lovely and soft.'

'Never done a day's work in their lives,' said Horatio, desperately trying to sound normal, although his mouth was dry.

She stroked his palms and along the lengths of his slim fingers: pianist's fingers, some people had said, although one former lover had described them as penis fingers. Then she brought his hand to her mouth, nibbling his fingertips and stabbing gently with her tongue.

'Do you know what they say in the *Souk* about the difference between you and mayor Morano? They say he had no balls, but you are a man who has real balls. I think about that, a lot, too.' Still holding his hand, she stood up. 'Let's go. Perhaps you could lend me a hand.' And she led him to the staircase.

Johnny put down the novel he'd been reading in Alessandra's driveway and sprang out of the car to open the rear door for Horatio. He was grinning. 'You had a good time, boss.' It wasn't a question. As they drove away he said: 'It's a good thing that villa is isolated. She's a real loud one. I had to put on the radio to drown her noise.'

# Nineteen

Horatio was in the buoyant mood the following morning. He'd finally bedded – third time lucky was right, after all – a girl who could have graced a Page Three in Fleet Street or the gatefold of *Playboy* magazine. He now slightly regretted having invited his childhood sweetheart out for a holiday, but that would be only a week, and hopefully wouldn't interfere too much with what he planned, or hoped, to be a longer relationship with Alessandra.

He was still contemplating his good fortune when Cesare popped in for mid-morning coffee, grinning and claiming that he had an interesting story to tell.

'We've had a reported rape,' he said. But the look on his face somehow suggested that he was not, in fact, referring to a serious crime.

'A *reported* rape?'

The police chief hesitated, briefly. 'Yes; reported, but not yet confirmed. A certain lady in Santa Lucia… you won't know her but by reputation she is – how do you say it? – no better than she ought to be, reported that she had been raped. Or her husband reported it. She said she couldn't identify the man because he was wearing a ski mask.'

'A ski mask? In Montebello? So you sent your men round the sports shops to find out who on this island has bought a ski mask. They have ski-ing on Etna in winter, but…'

'Good thinking, Monsieur Poirot! Except that they are not so uncommon as you might suspect, because the fishermen often wear them when putting out to sea in the bad weather. Lots of fishermen own one. In fact my local man believes that it wasn't a rape at all; that she was in bed with her boyfriend when the husband came home unexpectedly early. The guy leaped out of the window, just as the husband came into the room, so what else could she say, except that she had been raped by an unknown intruder?'

'But there's no actual evidence that she knew the man?'

'No; but my guy thought he knew who it was likely to have been, and he had no alibi, so we offered a *confronto*, an identity parade.'

'Even though her evidence was that she hadn't seen the man's face?'

'Exactly,' said Cesare. 'But she did say she could identify the man's body. However, pulling ten guys in off the street and asking them to stand, as you would say, bollock-naked in a line-up is no easy prospect. So I sent to the bakery for some large brown paper bags, got ten policemen to strip off and stand in line with the bags over their heads, and invited the suspect to stand anywhere he wanted. Then I called the woman in.'

The *commandante* paused, for effect, anticipating what was coming next.

'And she identified the suspect?' asked Horatio.

'No... but she identified three of my officers.'

Horatio laughed. 'I think we might open a bottle, on that one.'

As he walked back from the fridge the phone rang. Manuel told him the bishop was on the line.

'I offered him a solution to keeping the *piazza duomo* clean and tidy,' said Horatio, happily.

The bishop was not on the line, but the chaplain said he'd connect the mayor with his excellency.

'How dare you insult my holy ladies?' the bishop shouted. 'How dare you suggest they behave like slatterns when performing church work?'

'I – I don't think that anybody could ever have suggested any such thing,' said Horatio.

'Your deputy, that labour man, told my chaplain that they did not sweep up properly, and that they only redistributed the dust and the litter.'

'He was merely making a very helpful suggestion – that if they gathered the litter as they swept it, the council people would take it away and keep the whole of the *piazza* – your *piazza* – clean and tidy at all times.'

'Well,' said the bishop, 'they, and I, are insulted. Only yesterday I gave permission for the fireworks display to be held on the square. Now, that permission is withdrawn.'

'But the fireworks are the highlight, the culmination, of the *festa*. And they are always held in the *piazza*. I fear that you are over-reacting, your excellency. In any case, where else could we hold the fireworks display?'

'I never over-react, as you so rudely put it. You'll need to find another square, I suppose. This is just another symptom of your attitude as – and I regret to say this – as a protestant, towards the holy Mother Church that has been on-going since you were elected. You abuse and threaten my holy fathers in court when they are performing pastoral duty, and you refuse the traditional church blessing for your office. You don't even call at the palace when you are seeking a favour from the church. You have no respect. No respect whatsoever. Good day.' He hung up.

When Horatio had given him the gist of the other side of the conversation, Cesare told him that there was no other square. In any case, he said, it was the feast of Santa Maria; the square was Santa Maria's; it was in front of the cathedral of Santa Maria... nowhere else would be appropriate.

Horatio buzzed Manuel. 'Ask the office to find Aldo and tell him to come round here,' he said. 'I have a story for him.'

He poured a drink for the two of them.

'Oh dear,' he said. 'And I'd thought the day was going so well.'


Rumours had started and, he told Aldo, would soon be all over the island, that this year's Santa Maria *festa* was to be cancelled.

Aldo sat across the desk sucking the end of his pencil and not believing a word that he was hearing.

Horatio nodded at his spiral-spined pad to signal to Aldo that he should be taking a note in it.

The bishop had banned fireworks from the *piazza duomo* and the conclusion was being drawn that the council would say, no fireworks… no *festa*.

The situation had arisen from confusion, he said. The council had generously offered to maintain the *piazza* in a clean and orderly state and the bishop had over-reacted – and Aldo should be sure to use that expression – and mistakenly taken it as a slur against the ladies who normally swept the square.

'Now,' said Horatio, 'I'd like you to go down to the Ireland bar and then maybe to La Spada and ask ordinary people what they think about the rumour. Have a couple of pints while you're there; no doubt it will help you write more fluidly. It would be helpful if somebody, even somebody you don't name, says something like "What's he going to do next, cancel Christmas?" Or words to that effect. Then type up the story, take it and show it to the bishop's chaplain, and ask him for a quote from his boss.'

Aldo could quote the mayor as saying that in his view there had been a simple misunderstanding and he was sure the matter would be quickly resolved.

'But,' asked Aldo, still disbelieving, 'are there actually rumours flying around that Santa Maria is being cancelled?'

'There will be... when you start asking questions. They're already flying around this office. And you know how fast rumours travel on this island.'

'That's how they do things in Fleet Street?'

Horatio nodded.


Before he left the office that afternoon there was a call from the bishop's chaplain. 'His excellency presents his compliments and –'

'Did he actually say that?'

'Perhaps not in so many words, but he invariably acknowledges certain proper courtesies… And he wishes me to tell you that he has changed his mind.'

'Changed his mind again, you mean?'

'He means that he will of course accede to tradition and permit the fireworks display to be held in *piazza duomo*.'

'Has he said this to anybody else?'

'He said it to the reporter, along with his express and personal wish that no story about any misunderstanding will appear in the newspaper.'

'I'm sure he can count on that,' Horatio told the chaplain.

It had not, after all, been such a bad day.

# *Twenty*

Portelli, the contractor, called with an invitation to dinner. Horatio said that was kind, but he was trying to implement new rules under which council members and employees did not accept hospitality from people with whom they did business. Portelli laughed and told him that it was the way business was usually conducted everywhere in the world, but that if it was a problem the two of them could dine at Giosetta's and split the bill, so that nobody felt compromised. That sounded fair enough to Horatio so they arranged to meet that night.

Portelli wanted to talk about olives. Horatio would get his first harvest this autumn – only a small one because it was the trees' first year on his land, but sufficient fruit to make a few bottles because the stock his men had planted was already mature.

'It takes five kilos of olives to make only one litre of oil,' said Horatio. 'I looked it up.'

'Yes, and you'll get more fruit every year. When the trees are settled and five or six years old they will be fully established, and you'll be swimming in oil.'

As they chatted they went through the tasting ritual with a new label that Giosetta had sourced in Italy: a piece of bread to cleanse the palate, the gentle pouring into a small glass, warming it in the hands while swirling to release the aroma, holding it to the light to examine and admire the colour, inhaling deeply over the rim of the glass… and only then putting a few drops onto the front of the tongue, moving the soft liquid slowly around the mouth for twenty seconds, and pronouncing on its degree of excellence.

Giosetta stood patiently beside their table, awaiting their approval, and then went about the rest of her work, attending to other, less pernickety, patrons.

As they ate their meals – quail for Horatio; Giosetta's husband Patrizio reared his own birds – he said: 'I have been meaning to ask you this for some time… how does your father know the mafia *capo* from Lucky Luciano's home town?'

'Don Salvatore? I don't know. How does anybody know anybody? I suppose they did business some time in the past. Dad is big in plant hire, as of course you know. He sometimes even supplies to Sicily.'

'He can supply all Italy now, he has so much machinery.' Portelli senior had bought the entire consignment of EU 'relief' equipment supplied to Montebello when the road outside the Porto Hotel had collapsed.

'But when the don came to Montebello, your father was his point of contact, eh? Or one of them.'

'Yes, but how many people on this island can a man from Lercara Friddi know?'

'So what was he doing here?'

'I think he was planning to buy some land and buildings, as an investment. From the church, of course. Interesting, isn't it, that the curia distances itself from labour voters who are devoted churchgoers, but will get into bed with the mafia to do business? Anyway, he was arrested before he'd done the deal. A pity, really, because if the mafia wants to invest its money legally we should have it here. They have to spend it somewhere, so why not here? And then when he was arrested the government could have confiscated it and sold it again. That way the church makes a profit, the government makes a profit, and everybody's happy.'

'Except Don Salvatore, who is now rotting in Ucciardone.'

'Not rotting so much, I think. They wear designer clothes, Gucci and Armani, in there. And they keep their flashy jewellery. It isn't like England; Italian prisoners can't be forced to wear uniforms.'

When they ordered coffee, Portelli came to the point of the meeting. He wanted to buy a parcel of land from the council. More particularly, he proposed buying it as a joint venture with Horatio, and planting trees on it; he said it was a potential source of oil. The land was called *Zarafa*, from the Arabic: *zara* meant beautiful and *afa* meant distant or afar; the land was not itself very attractive, he said, but it had stunning sea and cliff views. His soil expert had recommended it as a likely place for producing oil, he said.

'It is scrub land, virtually barren. But planting trees would be good for the ecology of the island. Ecology is the flavour of the month. There'll probably even be an EU grant available, to pay for it. You and I could go 50-50, as partners.'

Horatio said that, as mayor, he could hardly buy council land – it would be like selling it to himself.

Portelli appeared shocked at this response. 'What I am suggesting is a transaction that would be totally transparent and legal and above board,' he said. 'You get the council's own valuer to set a price for it, and between us we will pay whatever is the fair market rate. No favours, no special deals. But, if your conscience or your new set of rules won't allow you to buy from the council, I will buy it all and sell half of it to you at the same rate. That way you are not buying from the council, but from me. Presumably there's no rule to prevent you buying land privately, from a friend.'

Horatio said he wasn't sure he wanted more olive trees. Growing olives beside his own house was an interesting hobby. But he wasn't in the olive oil business, nor intending to be.

Portelli sighed. 'What I am proposing is an investment. We are talking about a piece of land that the *commune* owns, but nobody wants. Everything has a price, a value, even rubbish land. But then we plant trees on it and it increases in value. I'll make you an even better deal: you pay half, but if at any time in the next five years you change your mind about it, or you need the money for something else, I will repay in full what you paid for it. Now… what can be wrong with that?'

Horatio said he would think about it, then called Giosetta to the table and paid the bill for both of them.

Cesare came to the mayor's office, his familiar friendly smiling face grey, even ashen, and announced that there had been a murder.

'It's not so unusual, is it?' asked Horatio, who had been contemplating olive trees. 'You told me some time ago that sometimes – in the Sicilian way, was how you put it – it was necessary for somebody to be killed. I appreciate that murder is always a serious matter, but what's special about this one?'

It wasn't just a killing, said the police chief, taking a deep draught on his cigarette; not an unfaithful spouse or a family feud, or somebody who felt cheated in a deal between friends. It was a professional hit: a gunman on a motorbike, in broad daylight, two shots to the head, almost point-blank, what they called a 'double tap'.

He said: '*Avvocato* Piscopo. You know him?'

Horatio nodded. 'I have met him. But I suppose a good lawyer – and, even worse, a bad one – makes a lot of enemies. Who was he representing, do we know?'

That was the problem. The police needed a search warrant in order to go through his files; Cesare wanted the chief magistrate to approve and sign it for him. Horatio didn't want to delay the investigation but he was concerned about professional confidentiality; he had a vague idea that confidentiality ended with the death of the client, but didn't think it necessarily applied on the death of the lawyer. He asked Vincenzo and Alessandra to drop whatever they were doing and come over to advise him.

Alessandra's view was that there would be no difficulty in asking the lawyer's secretary for a client list, as a start. Vincenzo thought long and hard, then eventually suggested that if the legal practice were to be sold, as it surely would be, the lawyer who purchased it would inherit the confidentiality. So the answer was another lawyer. He said that the police probably could not have automatic access to the files, but another lawyer could. The solution would be for a prosecuting magistrate to take possession of the files, although they shouldn't leave the office and even then it was highly doubtful whether they could be used in evidence, without the consent of each individual client.

'What they could do, though, is provide you with some clues and possibly even with a motive and maybe some leads,' he said.

In the first instance it was the list of clients that raised Cesare's bushy eyebrows. Among the names of people represented by *avvocato* Piscopo were Don Salvatore Barracato, and his friend the monsignor from the local seminary who had been arrested in the company of the Sicilian *mafiosi*, but then released after questioning in Palermo.

'You going to arrest a monsignor, for a second time?' asked Horatio when Cesare told him the news. 'That will surely make the bishop's day.'

'Not arrest him, but certainly bring him in for questioning. My guess is that it will be about property or money laundering. I am going to turn over the inquiry to the *antimafia* commission. Meanwhile we have the matter that there is a professional hitman on this island. We need to find him.'

Page One of *La Gazzetta* would be busy for the next couple of weeks, thought Horatio – first the killing of a prominent citizen, then a monsignor brought in for questioning, the Don Salvatore mafia connection re-run, and the hunt for a hitman on the island.

# Twenty-one

An old friend rang from Basingstoke and asked whether Horatio could spare a couple of minutes for a chat. Tony Peagam was a former journalist, a motoring correspondent who had left Fleet Street to handle public relations for the Automobile Association but regularly returned to his old haunts for lunch or drinks with his newspaper colleagues. Horatio therefore said he could have as many minutes as he wished.

'I have this chum,' he said, 'who is planning to build replica models of classic British cars, like the E-type Jaguar and maybe the Triumph Stag, in resin fibre. So he's looking for somewhere he can set up a factory with cheap – or cheapish – labour, and maybe get a grant for introducing new industry, and perhaps even some sort of tax break.'

'Rules out Blighty, then,' said Horatio.

'Precisely. He looked at Malta; they have some interesting incentives but they also have this mad rule where you are forced to take on a local partner who then shares the profit in return for no investment and no work. Then he thought of Montebello. And he was mighty impressed when I told him I know the guy who runs the island, so he asked me to call you.'

Friends of friends, thought Horatio. The whole world was becoming Sicilian.

He assured Tony that there were tax breaks and grants available for new employment prospects on the island, plus ready-built but empty factories on the industrial estate that could be rent-free for five years. There was also no shortage of labour, some of it skilled because the locals built glass-reinforced plastic fishing boats. They talked briefly about former colleagues with whom they each kept in touch and the conversation ended with Horatio inviting Tony and his friend to come out to the island and have a look around.

It had given him an idea. He asked Sophia to bring him the file on the department of development: the pages that showed how many were employed, how much it cost to run, and how much investment it had brought in.

When he'd read the notes he called Marco and told him to tell the director of development that his department appeared not to be cost-effective; unless there was an immediate increase in new industries being attracted to the island the mayor was thinking of closing the entire *assessorato* and saving money.

'It wouldn't actually save much money,' his deputy told him. 'They are government workers so if you close the department the staff would need to be redeployed.'

'Tell them there are vacancies for traffic wardens,' he said.

Then he phoned Franco di Giorgio at Campenello public relations and offered him a government contract.

'We already handle your advertising for tourism,' Franco reminded him.

'We need a big campaign to attract new industry and investment for employment,' Horatio said. 'I've just had one potential investor on the phone – the first since god-knows-when. You could start with some of your international clients. Persuade them to open up factories and offices here on the island. Easy, eh?'

'Put like that, it sounds easy,' Franco said. 'Nothing is ever that easy. But I'll draft something and come round to talk to you.'

He rang Portelli and said he'd decided he was interested in the Zarafa project and would pursue the matter with the official valuer.

Yes, the valuer said when Horatio called him. He knew the piece of land called Zarafa. In fact he'd had an enquiry about it a few months ago. He said he couldn't remember who was asking, but maybe he had a note somewhere. He hadn't actually made a valuation, but it wouldn't be much; it was waste land and outside the scheduled development zone, so there was no possibility of any

142

owner getting permission to build on it. It was therefore virtually worthless.

Jessica the childhood sweetheart was talking to him from half-way down his bed. 'When I accepted your invitation to come out for a holiday, I didn't envisage that we'd be doing this.'

Horatio grunted. He didn't believe a word of it but, after all, she was a married woman; perhaps she was trying to convince herself.

He'd recognised her walk from a hundred yards distance as she strode across the tarmac from the aircraft steps. Her head held high, looking straight ahead, one hand carrying a light bag (he'd told her she'd not need many clothes for a visit to the middle of the Mediterranean in mid-August); the other upper arm close against her body and the lower arm out at an angle, as if she was about to instruct staff. Three decades after public school lessons in deportment had changed none of that.

She'd been impressed to discover that he had a driver; less impressed that Johnny didn't offer to take her bag. 'He's a bodyguard, not a servant,' Horatio told her quietly. 'He doesn't carry luggage. He needs to keep his hands free.'

On the way home he told her there was nothing to worry about, but that there had recently been some 'minor mafia activity' on the island and the bodyguard was merely a routine precaution, insisted on by the local chief of police. When she reminded him that she had read in the English papers about the shooting in Sicily, he told her that, typically, the newspapers had got everything out of proportion and that there was definitely no known threat against him.

He had carried her bag upstairs and taken it to his second bedroom. 'This is the guest room. And… this is my room. Of course you can choose where you want to sleep.'

She looked in at his king-size bed. 'I think this one looks like it may be more fun.' She had walked into his bedroom and started to undress.

All government offices and most businesses closed for the week of *Santa Maria*. Some residents left the island to escape the crowds, the intense heat and the blinding sunshine; some simply stayed put and went to the busy beaches; hundreds of ex-pat Montebellans returned from their new homes in Sicily and New York and even in Melbourne to celebrate their traditional annual *festa*. Horatio also had little to do except catch up on some reading, so the week was virtually free for him to show his childhood sweetheart around his island.

He took her – more precisely, Johnny drove them both – to see the remains of a Roman villa, the mouth of the extinct volcano, and the ancient salt pans. He showed her the rock 'window' cut into the cliffs by constant sea and salt erosion, the fossils that had been left on the rocks by the withdrawing tide following a great flood – said by some to be Noah's flood – before which the Mediterranean had been a low-lying land area, protected from the Atlantic until the rocks eroded close to Gibraltar. And he showed her the parcel of land called Zarafa, where he planned to create a new olive grove.

There was a man in the middle of the field doing something with an agricultural auger, pulling soil samples from below the surface.

'Who's that? What's he doing on your property?'

Horatio had no idea at all, but he guessed: 'He'll be the soil analyst. He's checking the quality of the earth. Olives are very hardy trees but you need to ensure the best type of soil for the optimum yield of fruit.'

'If you don't know him, you should ask him what he's doing,' she said.

They walked together across the recently ploughed land – Portelli's men had already cleared it of scrub.

'Excuse me, but this is my land. What are you doing here?'

'Checking the soil quality and content.'

'And what are you finding?'

The man left his auger in the earth and picked up a clipboard from on top of the canvas pack near his feet.

'The hydrocarbon content. I am taking samples, then I'll be measuring it.'

'Good for oil, would you say?

The expert appeared surprised by the question but wasn't giving anything away, even to somebody who said he was the owner. 'Could be good for all sorts of things, I'd say.'

'There; I told you,' said Horatio with renewed confidence. I'm going to become an oil mogul.'


On the eve of *Santa Maria* he took her to dinner at Giosetta's, where he and the restaurateur enlightened (and possibly bored) her with depictions of various local wines and olive oils. Jessica said she used only Italian oil when cooking at home, even though it was considerably more expensive than oil from other countries. Giosetta told her to be wary about what she bought from the supermarket; even if the label was green, white and red, even if it said 'bottled on our estate in Tuscany', that was no proof that the oil was actually Italian.

'Italy doesn't produce sufficient good oil even for its domestic market,' she said. 'So it imports cheap-quality oil from Spain by the tanker load, or from Greece or even from Tunisia, where there are something like 85million olive trees. Then the Italians bottle it – possibly sometimes even on their own estate, so they can say that on the label – and export it. Most Americans insist on Italian olive oil, but what they get may be bottled here, but not produced here. You need to look at the label and see whether it actually says that it was grown in Italy, rather than just shipped in and poured into a bottle with an Italian label and re-exported.'

'It's just another EU scam,' said Horatio. 'I can tell you all about EU scams…'

'She's a pretty girl,' said Jessica when Giosetta had returned to her other customers. 'Are you…'

'Certainly not. She's a close friend but she's happily married to the chef here. In fact I don't actually approve of extra-marital relationships – although, in your case, I'm obviously more than happy to make an exception.'

While eating – he'd suggested she tried fresh barracuda, which she'd never tasted before – he looked round to check the intimacy provided by his usual restaurant alcove, and said: 'Tell me, when did you get into oral sex?'

She also looked about her, then told him: 'When I went up to Durham, I guess. It was the big thing there, even more popular than screwing.'

'But we never did it.'

'We never had time. We always just went straight at it. We were constantly in a hurry to have it, anywhere we could find. And when you took me home there was always the possibility that my parents might wake up.'

'I just wondered whether it was a generational thing, whether people didn't do oral in those days, because I never heard of people doing it, either.'

'No,' she told him. 'The convent girls did it all the time. They were told by the priests that they could do it – apparently they even recommended it – to avoid contraception and losing their virginity, while at the same time relieving their boyfriends of their otherwise uncontrollable animal lust. And the Jewish girls did it, so they didn't lose either their virginity or their boyfriends.'

He reminded her that the last time he'd seen her had actually been at her wedding. 'Good god, I really fancied you that day, dressed all in white like the virgin you weren't.'

'You should have told me,' she said. 'You might have been in with a chance. We didn't even have sex that night and we haven't had it very often since that day, all those years ago. We don't even live in the same house these days.'

'But you were a very – how can I put this politely? – active woman. How do you manage?'

'I have a friend,' she said. 'Actually he's our family GP. We get together once a week – more often, if Roger's away on business.'

146

They finished eating early and skipped coffee because Horatio said he wanted to show her something. They walked together through the gathering crowds to the court house where he told the *portiere* he could go out for an hour to watch the fireworks, because Johnny the bodyguard would be stationed at the door.

'Here's what I want to show you,' he said, opening a door. 'This is the courtroom – my courtroom. Now… does this bring back any memories?'

She gazed about her, thoughtfully. 'Just a minute. Do you have to dress up?'

He took her hand and led her through an inner door to the magistrates' chamber where he opened a wardrobe. 'A *tricolore* sash, a black gown, fancy tassels and white linen bands around the neck.'

'Put them on. Let me see…'

They returned to the courtroom and she spread herself along the judicial bench, raising her skirt. 'Wow,' she said. 'You certainly know how to treat a girl.'

An hour later the crowd in the street parted to let them through to the front of the fireworks display, a few people shaking his hand and congratulating him on the occasion, and some even thanking him for having ensured that it was taking place, for the rumour about its possible cancellation had predictably spread from the bar rooms.

The people, he told her – not the church and not the council – paid for the fireworks by playing bingo twice a week and holding lotteries and other fund-raising activities. Every time she heard a simple bang, a *petardo*, it was costing the equivalent of about fifty pounds: 'a genuine example of burning money, or of money going up in smoke, but they like to make a noise'.

He pointed to a figure in the centre of festivities. 'See that little fat guy, all decked up? That's our bishop. He had thought about banning the fireworks this year. Now they're happening after all, and he needs to be the centre of attention.'

'Catholics call that the sin of pride,' she told him.

In the car on the way home she said she'd noticed that some people in the restaurant and some on the street had addressed him as *Don Orazio*. 'Does this mean you're now, like… you know… Don Corleone?'

'*Don* is just a sign of respect,' he told her. 'Although a few people, perhaps the ones who have seen *The Godfather*, actually call me Don *Coglioni*. It's their little joke. *Coglioni* are testicles. They say the previous mayor had no balls, and I am the one with real balls.'

'They've certainly got that right,' she said, nestling her head on his chest and resting her hand on his crotch, in the back seat.

# Twenty-two

Cesare came round to the *municipio* for mid-morning coffee. It was becoming part of the daily routine. He always phoned first, to check that Horatio wasn't engaged on any mayoral or court business, and then announced that he was about to pop round for a chat.

Ostensibly, he was providing an update on the *carabinieri* murder inquiry, although there was rarely anything to report.

For one thing, the eye-witnesses – and there had been several – could not agree on what they had seen. The assassin's motorcycle was variously described as having been black, blue, grey, and even silver. He had worn a full-face crash helmet (on that, they were all agreed), and blue denims, but there was disparity about whether he was wearing trousers, shorts or rip-off jeans, and no agreement whatsoever about his footwear. It was generally agreed that he was 'on the short side' – most Sicilians were. One witness even described him as being 'dark', admittedly without having seen either his face or his hair, but it was the impression he'd had. He was either 'young' or 'in his twenties', or 'in his thirties'. Nobody had taken note of a vehicle number, even if there had been one.

What especially concerned the chief of police was the knowledge that there was, or apparently had been, a professional mafia hit-man on his island.

The mafia, he had explained to Horatio, hardly ever employed contract killers: gunmen who were not part of 'the family' could not be trusted, and on the rare occasions when they were employed they were usually killed themselves, shortly afterwards, to ensure secrecy. If advocate Piscopo's killer had been an outsider, Cesare reckoned, his own body would have turned up somewhere by now; his men had been searching valleys, ditches, gulleys and wells.

So, he said, there were two likelihoods: either the shooter was an experienced killer – what he referred to as 'a career assassin' – or he was a new member undergoing the final stage of the traditional *cosa nostra* initiation procedure that demanded a murder to ensure perpetual secrecy and loyalty to 'the family'.

'According to what we know,' said Horatio, 'it surely seems unlikely to have been anybody's first hit, does it? By all accounts the gunman was calm... and, more importantly, deadly accurate.'

That was also the police theory. But the bullets had been removed from the lawyer's skull for examination in their forensic laboratories and there was nothing to connect them with any previous shooting, anywhere on Sicily or mainland Italy.

'So we're left looking for a young, or youngish, man, not tall, pprobably dark, with access to a motorbike which, at the end of the day may even have been borrowed or temporarily stolen without the owner's knowledge. In other words, it could be almost anybody.'

Cesare was in despair. In the past year or so he'd seen the island's first bank robbery and its first car theft (although he thought that taking your mother's car without asking didn't amount to much of a theft); there'd been the first-ever theft of a boat (although it wasn't on record as having been stolen); he'd had one of his own officers targeted by the mafia (albeit in Sicily) and shot at, and a principal's life endangered; and now a prominent citizen – a lawyer, no less – had been gunned down in the street in broad daylight, in front of witnesses.

Horatio tried to placate his friend.

'Nevertheless, in a period a little over a year, it doesn't really damage our claim to be more or less a crime-free island... relatively, I mean.'

'Relatively? No; it isn't unusual for Sicily to have more than 700 murders in a year. That's mafia-related murders, not including domestics, or friends who fall out – nor even people who object to getting parking tickets and kill the traffic warden. No: they can get two or more a day, over there. What I'm saying is that it doesn't happen here. Or it didn't. Now it does.'

And the prime role of the *carabinieri* on the island – Cesare said it couldn't be repeated too often – was to prevent crime, to ensure it didn't happen in the first place. Unlike police forces elsewhere, which were generally judged on their record of crime detection, the *arma dei carabinieri* was rated according to the lack of crime in its area.

Sophia, having realised that the meeting was running longer than usual, knocked and brought in fresh cups of coffee. The two men sat staring at the cups, waiting for the grounds to settle – Sicilians didn't stir their coffee, which they believed could taint it with metallic spoons – and lighting cigarettes.

When it was cool enough for drinking, Cesare raised his cup, then replaced it on the desk without having tasted it.

'You are doing deals with the Portelli family.' It wasn't a question.

'Deals? We're growing olive trees,' Horatio told him. 'As you know, olive oil is something of a fetish of mine.'

'You are doing secret deals, though.'

Horatio frowned, wondering of what interest his olive trees could be to anybody, least of all to the chief of police. 'A personal deal, maybe,' he conceded. 'Even a private deal – insofar as it is nobody else's business. Certainly nothing is secret.'

He explained how Portelli, sharing his interest in olive oil culture, had told him about the possibility of obtaining free vines under some EU initiative to encourage oil production, and the contractor's workers had planted a few trees on spare land attached to his villa.

'A few? Five hundred is a few?'

'About that number, yes. But it was a big paddock, something close to four acres, and I had no other use for it. I don't keep horses or cattle.'

'And his labourers worked for you, clearing the land and planting the olives, free of charge.'

'In their down-time. When Portelli had no construction work to keep them occupied. But it isn't free of charge – we agreed that I would pay him in oil produced from the vines. Tell me, Cesare, where is this going? What are you getting at?'

'But this happened, this deal was struck, only after you became mayor.'

Horatio laughed. 'You think there's something corrupt here? You think I've turned Montebellan?'

Cesare didn't join in the laughter. 'Here's what I think, and what I see.' He touched his left thumb with his right forefinger. 'First, he helps you with the election...'

How did anybody know about that? Horatio smiled: 'Yes; he said his family would be good for something like 18 votes...'

'More like 50, I think. And maybe far more than that, if you count his workers who will do what he tells them, even vote the way he tells them. There were seven hundred guests at his wedding, all family or personal friends. How many were there at yours?'

'One hundred. But big weddings are the Montebellan way. I was one of his seven hundred guests, but he didn't influence the way I voted.'

'*Al contrario*, I think that's exactly what happened, don't you...? Then...' he touched his left forefinger, counting. '...he offers you free olive trees. Then...' his middle finger '...you are elected mayor. Then...' his ring finger... 'he immediately gets a share of the contract, on your personal insistence, for work on the collapsed road outside the Porto Hotel... Then...' the little finger of his left hand... 'his men start work clearing your land and planting olive trees, everything without payment...'

Horatio was still unable to take his friend – the man who he thought of as his friend – seriously. 'What are you suggesting, Cesare? That there is something corrupt about this deal? *Madonna!* If it were corruption, which it isn't, it would still be pretty small beer in the Mediterranean, wouldn't it?'

The police chief said he wasn't suggesting anything, merely listing facts.

But there was more to it, he said.

The council had acquired a mass of construction equipment to repair the road, and it had sold the entire fleet to Portelli's father.

'Now, there's a man I don't like. He's a friend of Don Salvatore; they met together here, on this island. And there is a saying, you know it, *pesci fet d'a testa*: fish stinks from the head down. It also applies to families.'

'You want to quote me Sicilian proverbs, Cesare? I'll give you one: *I palori nimici fannu ridiri, chiddi di l'amici fanni chianciri* – the words of my enemies make me laugh; those of my friends make me cry. We fixed a price for the entire stock of machinery as one lot; we didn't want to sell it piece-meal. It was advertised for sale in *La Gazzetta*, and Portelli senior offered the asking price, which nobody else even came near. So tell me… Are you really investigating me for corruption?'

'As I said, I am reporting facts. Reporting to you. We are, of course friends, good friends. But I am warning you to take care. You are claiming to be Mr Clean on Montebello, forcing people in authority to declare their interests, and I honestly think that you are doing a good job. But you should beware, because there is more to it than what I have said already.'

He lobbed another cigarette into his mouth.

'When they were going through the files of lawyer Piscopo, your name came up.'


Cesare hadn't touched his coffee, so Horatio buzzed Sophia and called for fresh cups. He reached into the bottom drawer of his desk and produced a slim yellow folder. It contained a copy of the deeds for the plot of land called Zarafa, and a single sheet of paper, Piscopo's headed notepaper, an early draft to witness the transaction with Portelli and the agreement to buy back the land at any time within five years of the deal.

He handed the agreement to Cesare. He explained how, being loath to make a personal acquisition of property owned by the *commune*, he had gone along with the developer's suggestion of buying it, then selling half to him 'as a purely private arrangement, between friends'.

He said: 'I wasn't his client, Portelli was.'

'It was a secret deal,' said the police chief.

'It was nobody else's business, just a joint private venture to plant olive trees for the betterment of the ecology of the island.'

'So tell me – under your own guidelines – is Portelli a friend, or is he a developer to whom the *commune* from time to time awards competitive contracts?'

Framed like that, Horatio wasn't sure of the answer.

'...Because you didn't declare it. You didn't declare the work on your property in return, as you say, for only a few bottles of oil. And you didn't declare the roundabout and intentionally complicated deal to buy council land in partnership with Portelli. It was you, not Portelli, who asked the valuer to price the land, and you who ended up owning half of it.'

He sipped his coffee, now.

'Then you have been investigating me.'

'...So what we have is a dead lawyer who, among his clients, numbers the head of a mafia family in Sicily, a monsignor doing business with the mafia on behalf of the church, a major developer who does deals with the council, a plant hire magnate who rents machinery to the *commune* and associates with a mafia godfather, and his honour the mayor of Montebello. Interesting bedfellows, wouldn't you think?'

'Put like that, perhaps. But –'

'What I am telling you, as a friend, a good friend, is that the *antimafia* commission finds it interesting.'

# Twenty-three

Portelli had been right about one thing: sitting beneath, or among, your own olive trees in your own olive grove was an excellent place for thinking. He had taken a deckchair and a book out into the sunshine to read, or to re-read, for he'd devoured it many times in the past. It was *Publish And Be Damned!*, the history of the first 50 years of the *Daily Mirror*, written by the newspaper's former editorial supremo, Hugh Cudlipp. Horatio thought that, despite its age, the book contained plenty of lessons for modern journalists. He had opened the book on his knee, but instead of reading any of it, had simply sat, deep among his thoughts.

It was Saturday, a day off work, and also his birthday. He enjoyed parties, but didn't celebrate his own birthday. The date invoked only bad memories. First, his mother had died on the day before his birthday; the following year his father had died, on the day after it. If that wasn't sufficiently glum, his birthday had also been the day on which his wife told him she was leaving him. The memory of that was still fresh.

'We need to talk,' she had said.

'Sure… About what?'

'About us.'

'Go ahead.'

She bit her lip. She'd thought about what she was going to tell him, but now wasn't sure how it would sound when the words came out.

'I have been seeing somebody.'

'Are you going to tell me who?'

'Eric.'

'When you say seeing, you mean shagging?'

She nodded. 'Yes.'

'And this has been going on… how long?'

'Three or four months.'

Eric was one of Horatio's drinking mates at their local in the village. The two couples played bridge together; the two families had gone together on outings, and on picnics; they had looked after each other's children. Horatio had been helping Eric's elder daughter with research as part of her course at university. The two men had nothing in common professionally – Eric was a double-glazing salesman who had never read a book, nor even a newspaper, apart from the sports pages – but socially they shared a similar sense of humour, and both of them liked a drink. Horatio felt doubly betrayed.

'Did you pack your bags, before deciding to tell me about this?'

'No.'

'Then you'd better go and fucking pack them now.'

He offered to drive her to wherever she wanted to go, to get the bitch out of his home, but while she was packing in the bedroom she rang Eric who said he would send his sister to collect her.

She returned to the drawing room with one wheelie bag in tow.

'I'll phone you about coming round for the rest of my things,' she said.

'What have you told the girls?'

'I thought you would want to decide what they were told. You can tell them the story in your own way. But don't worry; when I talk to the twins I'll tell them it was all my fault.'

'Have you thought who's going to look after them while I'm at work?'

'I've asked your mother to come and stay. I didn't tell her why. She'll be here in the morning.'

'And what about Eric and Rosie's girls?'

'He told them this afternoon.'

'So he told his family before you told me. And he also told his daughters, and you're leaving that to me.'

'I was worried because I didn't know how you would react…'

Women, he thought: fucking women. And birthdays: fucking birthdays.

And now, as if there was some magnetism for bad news on that particular day of the year, and the days either side of it, there was the matter that he was already thinking of as The Mafia Connection. It had been only yesterday that Cesare had warned him of the *antimafia* commission's 'interest' in his innocent olive ventures.

He hadn't done anything criminal; he was content about that, in his own mind. But nevertheless he had probably been careless, or possibly over-confident. The biggest problem he thought he could face would be guilt by association – being on the same list as people who, maybe only remotely themselves, might be considered to be 'connected'. He remembered an English MP who had been named in court – only named, not accused of any crime – because he had received a small gift from an architect who turned out to have been corrupting other politicians. But that slur had stuck.

He wracked his brain for what he could remember about the definition of corruption in English law; the Italian law would, surely, be basically similar. It was something along the lines of offering or receiving a gift, reward or inducement in connection with your principal's business. In his case, the principal would be the *commune*. He remembered the QC leading the prosecution in the architect's trial explaining the meaning of the civil service *Establishment Code*: if your aunt sent you a pair of cufflinks for Christmas, that was okay, but if she had, or was tendering for, a government contract, you were expected to return them with a polite note (always polite, the English civil service), and you should report the fact of the gift to your superiors.

Had he done that? In his own case his superior would be the council of the *commune*.

He closed the book, unread, went into his study and telephoned Manuel, apologising for disturbing him at home on his day off.

'Did I ever mention to you that I was having olive trees planted at the house?'

'Yes,' said the clerk. 'Several times. Portelli's men were planting them, and you would be paying for them in bottles of olive oil. Why are you asking?'

'When would you think was the first time I mentioned it to you?'

'I have no idea. But it was right at the beginning. Certainly when you got the bodyguards, anyway, because you had to tell them that Portelli's men would be appearing on your property from time to time. What's the problem?'

'Did I ever mention to you that I was buying a piece of land, called Zarafa, from the council?'

'I don't know whether you did. But you told me you were interested in it, because you wanted the council valuer to tell you what it was worth. Why?'

'Just a minute… did you make a note, in your diary or anywhere, about any of this?'

'No. Why would I have done that? It was personal business, surely.'

'But perhaps nothing is personal, when you're the mayor. Can you please check your diary on Monday morning, and double-check whether you ever made a note?'

'Sure,' said the clerk. 'And if I didn't, I'll make one.'

Horatio apologised again for the interruption. He already felt better. He had told the police; he had told his clerk. He had done nothing secretly or untoward. He was about to return, light of heart, or at least lighter, to his trees and his book when he heard the wrought iron gate swing squeakily on its hinges and the clack-clack of wooden sandals crossing the paving stones outside.

His two secretaries, Sophia and Francesca, stood at the open doorway in T-shirts and brief shorts. Each of them held a bottle of *frizzante*.

'Happy birthday, boss,' they said in unison.

# Twenty-four

'We checked your diaries, and we checked with the cops,' Francesca told him. 'And you have nothing on for today, and it's your birthday, so we thought...'

'Johnny's sitting outside on the drive, is he?'

'He's okay, said Sophia. 'We brought him a copy of *Penthouse*, the English edition. He'll be studying it all day.'

'Even longer, if he ever gets round to trying to read the words.'

'But I do have an appointment, this evening,' Horatio told them.

'That's tonight. The rest of the day you can enjoy yourself, with your favourite secretaries. Now, where do you keep the glasses? And which way is the pool? We're both sweating like horses.'

He collected a wine cooler and three glasses from the kitchen and padded barefoot out to place them beneath a parasol on his big poolside table, just as the secretaries were starting to strip. T-shirts off, no bikini tops; no surprise there. Shorts off, the tiniest of thongs underneath. Wooden-soled sandals kicked away, and the girls jumped into the water. He threw big beach towels across a couple of sun-loungers, thinking that when they emerged the towels would protect something of what other young women might refer to as their modesty. Fat chance, he thought.

Once refreshed, they clambered out over the side of the pool and walked towards him, salt water droplets running into narrow rivulets between their breasts, forking around the navel and then converging at the soaking thongs and dripping down the insides of their legs as they stood beside him.

'There are towels...' he said.

'No need. We'll be dry in seconds.'

He was, he thought, a healthy single man, not much past his prime, and he knew what he wanted and intended to do with the two nymphs who were flaunting themselves beside him. But he had another pressing matter, more immediately important than the pressing matter he could feel inside his shorts. And, as always, it was business before pleasure.

He cast aside sinful thoughts and asked Sophia whether she remembered when he had first mentioned his plans for an olive grove beside his house.

'That was ages ago,' she told him, surprised at the question. 'Actually, you were telling mayor Morano – he was still mayor – and I was there. It was just after you'd decided to fight in the election and I was thinking that was all I needed: replacing a wine-grower with an olive-grower... Why?'

'Did I say how I was getting it organised?'

'You mentioned EU grants for trees, and you'd got somebody – was it Portelli? – to plant them, in return for oil when they were harvested.'

'Nothing secret about it, then?'

'Secret? You were boasting about it.'

He asked whether they knew about his purchase of a plot of land.

'I did,' said Francesca. 'I did the paperwork for that, for Alessandra. The deal was that Portelli was buying it from the council and selling some of it on to you because you had this conscience thing that the mayor shouldn't buy directly from the council.'

'Who else knew about it?'

'Everybody knew. There are no secrets on this island.'

Concerned and confused by the line of questioning the two secretaries knelt beside his lounger, both putting a hand on his body – Francesca's on his chest; Sophia's on his thigh.

'Is something the matter?' Sophia asked.

'Nothing. I just might be asked about them, that's all.'

'Well, if there's nothing to worry about,' Francesca told him, 'let's have another drink.'

He poured more sparkling wine, went back to get the second bottle from the fridge and sat with them, making small talk. The girls didn't use their sun-loungers but knelt beside him on their beach towels. Four coral pink nipples pointed directly at him.

Even in the shade it was baking hot. 'I'm going for a swim,' he said.

'We'll come too.'

In the water they swam playfully around him, diving between his legs – always touching the front of his swimming shorts on the way through – and somehow contriving, each time they surfaced, to rub their breasts against him. When he ducked his head to refresh it he found two thongs bobbing in front of his face.

'Let's get the mayor's shorts off!'

'And the magistrate's!'

It seemed pointless to resist and he had no intention of resisting. When he clung to the edge of the pool to catch his breath, the girls on either side of him, Francesca said: 'I'm going to schnorkel.' And she disappeared beneath the surface.

Distracted, Horatio didn't hear the garden gate opening. But he eventually became aware that someone was coughing, or attempting to simulate coughing; it was Johnny, endeavouring to appear as discreet as it was possible for a *carabiniere* to be.

The water hid their nakedness, so Horatio shouted: 'Hi, Johnny!'

'Hi, boss. Er… just changing shifts. Alfio is here. See you tomorrow.'

When they heard the gate close Sophia said: 'The water's too hot. Let's go inside, to the air-conditioning. It'll also be more comfortable.'

Horatio didn't think there could be much that was more comfortable than being buoyant in water while exploring different orifices, but he agreed that the air-conditioning would be pleasant.

Flat on his back on the bed with a head on either side of his chest and small hands stroking the middle of his body, he told them: 'Before we had television in England, and when the only form of entertainment at home was radio – this was before either of you was born, I suppose – there was a popular show featuring two pianists called Rawicz and Landauer. The programme was known as Four Hands On One Piano…'

'Aren't I the privileged one?' asked the countess of Ciampino. 'Entertaining, and being entertained by, the two most prominent gentlemen on the island. The head of the Roman Catholic Church on Montebello…'

The bishop bowed his head, affecting embarrassed modesty.

'Actually,' interrupted Horatio, quickly but quietly, 'I thought the Pope was the head of the church on Montebello. And everywhere else.'

'Of course he is,' said the bishop, a little gruffly.

The countess corrected herself. '…His excellency, the pastor of our tiny flock on Montebello, and his honour the mayor of the island, who is himself the recipient of no fewer than two papal medals.'

The bishop appeared concerned. 'What's that? I hadn't heard about that. It can't be…'

'Oh, your excellency… You didn't know that, on this little rock, there was a member of the *commune* to whom His Holiness had personally awarded two medals. You surprise me. Horatio, tell his excellency how you came to receive them.'

'It wasn't much,' he started…

'Not much?' asked the bishop. 'Two papal medals? Two? Not much?'

'Not many people know it, but it wasn't the Church of England, nor even the Queen, and certainly not the Catholic church, that invited the Pope to the United Kingdom in 1982. It was the press, Fleet Street, where I used to work. And when he accepted the invitation I was invited to lunch with his ambassador – the *papal nuncio* – who I'd met a couple of times before.'

The *nuncio* had offered Horatio a drink and asked: 'Now you've persuaded him to come, what are we going to do with him when he's here?' And the two of them had sat side by side at a huge refectory table and sketched out a provisional programme for the visit.

162

'You wouldn't know the guy,' said Horatio. 'He's a cardinal. Anyway, he'd told JP2 that he knew I would be helpful, so the Pope had said, in that case, I deserved a medal for assisting in making his visit the success he knew that it would obviously become.'

'But –' said the bishop.

'Yes; there's always a but. The Vatican had done its homework and they knew I wasn't Catholic. Their intelligence is absolutely amazing, eh? But they also knew that my daughters were Catholic. So the Pope said that, since he couldn't give me a medal in my own right, the cardinal should present me with two, one for each daughter, to honour their father on His Holiness's behalf. A neatly diplomatic solution, don't you think?'

'So, actually, the Holy Father didn't recognise you, after all,' the bishop said.

'He recognised my work. For him personally, and for his church… Your church. Good enough for me.'

'Good enough for all of us, I'd say,' said the countess, smiling.

The bishop changed the subject. They were meeting over this splendid repast, he said – the countess was serving *pesce san pietro*, lightly pan-fried in butter with just a squeeze of lemon – to discuss the opera. The editor of *La Gazzetta* had never supported it personally, but the mayor had a responsibility to do so.

And so the mayor would, Horatio confirmed. But he suggested changes in the programme. His proposal was to hold the usual opera, inviting top soloists from New York Metropolitan, Covent Garden or Milan, as always, but to follow it with a concert, a week later, on a general operatic theme.

Most operas, he said, had only one main aria or chorus, and those were the tunes the people knew and liked. What he had in mind was a concert featuring a selection of the most popular music from a number of operas, a week after the main event. And during the week in between, a festival of different types of music – rock, jazz, choirs, orchestras, village bands and chamber music, possibly an evening of sacred music in the cathedral with the organ and choir, and with visiting performers if possible, alongside the local talent.

'A week-long music festival, featuring a variety of styles, could become an international event,' he said. 'It should then attract more tourists, which this island desperately needs.'

The bishop wasn't overly enthusiastic – probably, thought Horatio, because it hadn't been his idea; but he supported the suggestion of a big – he'd already decided that it would be big – performance of sacred music in his cathedral. The countess, seeing herself as being in charge of a large-scale international event, described the idea as brilliant.

Excusing himself on the grounds of an early mass the following morning, the bishop took his leave immediately after licking the last remnants of *tiramisu* from his spoon.

'Now he's gone, I can open some decent wine,' said the countess, taking Horatio's arm. 'Let me show you our cellars.'

She led him down the stone steps of the castle that – Horatio knew, even if most of the native population didn't – had been built in the fifteenth century by a king of Spain as a wedding present for a favourite niece.

'He walked right into the thing about head of the Roman Catholic church, the pompous fool. And did you see his expression when I mentioned your medals? The look on his face said, Oh shit! And I loved it when you said, You wouldn't know him, he's a cardinal…'

'How did you know about the medals?'

'Your father told me, years ago. I think he was quite proud, and he also probably thought it was very amusing.'

The cellar was packed with both rare and popular vintages. Horatio picked up a bottle. 'Frescobaldi,' he said approvingly. 'Best Chianti in the world.' Teresa had told him that.

She crouched beside him, holding his leg for support as she examined some of the lower shelves. 'There may be better years down here. Can you see?'

What he saw, beyond the scoop neckline, was her cleavage and the tiny jewelled strap connecting the half-cups of her brassiere.

'Do you see anything that you like? Anything you'd like to have rolling around in your mouth?'

They chose a couple of bottles of different vintages to compare and Horatio carried them up into the comfort of the drawing room. She indicated a sofa so he sat down and she perched on the arm, leaning over him, displaying the upper crescents of her breasts as he tried to concentrate on the bottles.

'My husband, the count, is away, in Rome. And he won't be coming back.'

'Tonight, you mean?'

'I mean: not ever.'

'Oh dear,' said Horatio, assuming that she'd been deserted.

'He was unfaithful to me, with my best friend – isn't that always the way? She told me. He didn't. We were talking about friendship and she said she was such a good friend to me that she even sucked my husband's cock because she knew, she said, that I didn't like that sort of thing.'

Horatio busied himself with the corkscrew.

'And that was crazy – he obviously lied to her if he'd actually said that – because in fact I love doing that. I really love it!'

As he poured a sample, sniffed it, then filled two glasses, she looked pensive, as if trying to weigh up two options.

'Is your driver sitting patiently outside? Why not tell him to go home and come back for you in the morning? Then we can have a real tasting session.'

The following day, sitting again on a deckchair among his olives, he decided that birthdays weren't necessarily all bad. Three gorgeous women in one day had to amount to something of a record, even among the excesses of old Fleet Street hands.

# Twenty-five

At the end of summer Horatio thought he should get his sex life – now that he appeared to have one again – in order, much as he was trying, and seemingly succeeding, with his professional lives. He considered himself a totally free agent, not committed to, and certainly not in love with, anybody.

The two secretaries, individually or as a pair – sexy in itself – were clearly available, or 'up for it', in the current jargon. 'When you're feeling horny on a summer afternoon,' Francesca had told him, 'whichever office you happen to be in, remember that one of us is just outside the door.' The beautiful contessa had also made it obvious that he only need ask, in order to continue that relationship. But, all things considered, he preferred the sexual companionship of Alessandra, his legal director: the girl the police referred to as The Body. And they had contrived a series of lunchtime trysts, which Horatio described to himself as 'lunchtime quickies', along with what the French called *cinq-a-sept*… fairly regular sexual encounters between daily office work and evening engagements.

They were in her bed, enjoying that type of late afternoon diversion, when the telephone rang.

Alessandra answered the phone.

She put her hand over the mouthpiece and whispered: 'It's your friend Cesare. He says it's urgent. How did he know…?'

'There's a police car, parked outside your house. Remember?'

'I'm sorry to interrupt your pleasure. I hope I didn't get you on the short strokes. But we have a situation. Two shootings. You're needed now. Meet me at the harbour.' The urgency was implicit.

'On my way.'

He sat on the edge of the bed, searching for his socks. She reached round his body and held him. 'Isn't there time for…?'

'No time,' he told her. 'Got to go. Two shootings.'

'Will you be coming back?'

'Very much doubt it.'

'In that case, I'll have to finish off, myself.'

In the car Johnny switched on the siren and took the flashing light from underneath his seat to put on the car roof and part the traffic. As he drove past a section of road cordoned off with police tape, all he said was: 'Two shootings. Looks like we've got the motorcyclist.'

The Sicily ferry, long after its scheduled departure time, remained tied up to the quay, still packed with passengers who were standing hopelessly on the upper decks trying to see what was going on beneath them. The harbour was awash with policemen but their car was recognised and waved through the police cordon into the embarkation area. Horatio found Cesare directing his team. Some were taking statements from civilians, others with tapes were checking measurements and logging information on clipboards; plain-clothes officers, some in white forensic coveralls with brushes and powder, were collecting fingerprints or moving around the car deck of the ferry with metal detectors, or taking photographs.

'Two shootings, both fatal. The first, on the main road to the harbour; that guy's on his way to the morgue. The second, here on the car deck of the ferry: a shoot-out. One officer slightly injured. But we got him. The shooter's body is over there on the ambulance trolley. No rush. He's not going anywhere, now.'

Horatio had called Aldo from the car. He saw his reporter arrive and produce his notebook to start interviewing people.

From information gathered so far, Cesare told Horatio, the motor-cyclist had overtaken a red Fiat with Rome number plates and forced it to stop. The biker dismounted and walked back to the car. When the driver wound down his window the motorcyclist shot him, then walked – quite calmly and deliberately, the eye-witnesses said – to the nearside passenger door and removed a briefcase. Then he got back on his motorbike and rode off to the harbour.

But there had also been a *carabinieri* motor-cyclist nearby. He pursued the gunman while calling for back-up and followed him into the car deck of the ferry. Cornered, the man tried to shoot it out, said Cesare. 'We had more fire power and eventually we got him.'

The briefcase was still being fingerprinted. They had no identity, yet, for the driver of the Fiat.

'This looks like the guy who shot the lawyer, though. One of the later eye-witnesses to that one eventually decided that the gunman's bike had Palermo plates. So does this one. Anyway, we'll see what forensics turns up, when we compare the rounds.'

There wasn't anything for Horatio to do, but the police preferred to have a magistrate present at any major crime scene in case of complications later. And this crime scene was as major as they came.

He went to talk to Aldo, who told him: 'Gunfight at the OK ferry corral. High speed police chase. Dozens of shots fired inside the car deck. Drivers and pedestrians in panic all over the place. Cars shot up. That ferry's going nowhere tonight. The cars will need to come off it. The passengers will be looking for overnight accommodation: chaos all round.'

'There was a first shooting, on the main road. You'd better call the office and get somebody on to that. You can say police suspect a link with the Piscopo shooting. Looks very much like our professional hitman again.'

'Mafia?'

'You can say police are looking into it, but I'd say yes.'


He was in his own bed the following morning when Cesare telephoned. 'You're down for court this morning. Any chance that you can get out of it, or postpone it?'

If there was a good reason, he could get Vincenzo to reassign his list to other magistrates, Horatio told him.

'It's a good reason. You have this friend who works in oil fields, a geologist, an Englishman: is he currently on the island?'

'He's actually Welsh.' Cesare didn't recognise a distinction. 'And yes, I am pretty sure he's still here, on leave.'

'We need his help. Can we meet him in your office? Would nine o'clock be reasonable? And would you also fire up your computer?'

The police chief arrived at the *municipio* carrying a briefcase, still bearing traces of grey fingerprint powder on the mottled leather. Introduced to Elwyn Morris, the geologist, he told him: 'This belonged to a man who was shot yesterday. From his documents he appears to be a field geologist for an oil company, like yourself. We are trying to find out more, starting with what he was doing here. The only clue to why he was shot might be on the disks in this attaché case. We need to know what they show.'

Morris took the disks. 'These would be the property of the oil company,' he said. 'Do you know his name, or who he worked for?'

'His ID card shows him as Daniele Greco, from Rome. But there are no business cards, no headed notepaper, nothing to suggest who his employers might be – so we can't deliver the disks until we know something.'

The disks were numbered and the geologist fed them into Horatio's computer in sequence. He reached across the desk for a blank sheet of paper, took a pen bearing the Exxon logo from his shirt pocket and started making notes and copying formulae.

'These are soil tests,' he said. When he had removed the final disk he re-entered the first one, studying it closely and taking more notes, occasionally correcting what he had previously written.

Cesare and Horatio watched all this, a little impatiently. They called for coffee and were on the second round before the geologist put down his pen and leaned back in Horatio's chair.

'Basically,' he said, 'these are tests for hydrocarbons. We do it all the time. It gives a good clue – usually very accurate – about the quality of the material beneath the surface. There are different ways of doing it. One is quite primitive, but effective; we used to do it on field trips when I was at Nottingham. You put a handful of soil in a litre of water, shake it about to mix it well, then allow it to settle. If hydrocarbons are present it will produce a smear on the surface that looks like oil, what we call a rainbow effect. Or you can examine soil samples under a blacklight and microscope. If hydrocarbons are present, they will fluoresce under blacklight.'

Cesare asked him what hydrocarbons actually were.

'Put simply, hydrocarbons are organic compounds of carbon and hydrogen, hence the name. In liquid form they are petroleum or crude oil.'

Morris looked at the readings again. 'But this chap wasn't doing the simple test. He had a portable machine that interpreted the samples for him. That's why these findings are so accurate. Did your people find an analyzer, a penetrometer, with him – about the size of a computer hard drive, maybe in the boot of his car?'

Cesare said they didn't.

'In that case, he must have lodgings, or a hotel room, somewhere, and he's left it there. And he was probably going to his employers to report his findings in person and present the evidence. It's like police work in a way. The man who does this job is called the witness. Somewhere there's a very high quality piece of kit, calibrated to provide exact measurements of the quantitative amounts of specific petroleum products. I mean, the equipment he was using will distinguish between Brent crude, diesel fuel, leaded and unleaded petrol, lubricating oil and weathered gasoline. That's how precise it is.'

'And... if you're not a geologist,' asked Horatio, 'what does it all mean?'

'I'd say he's found oil... on Montebello You should open a bottle of Champagne.' He nodded towards the mayor's refrigerator. 'Is there anything in there to drink?'

Horatio opened the fridge and produced a bottle of white wine. He showed the label to the geologist who raised his hands to indicate that anything cold, liquid and alcoholic would suffice. He filled three glasses while Cesare was on the telephone to his office instructing people to make inquiries and establish where the man called Daniele Greco had been staying on his temporary visit to the island.

The police chief sipped his drink, then asked whether the readings provided any clue as to where the samples had been taken. The geologist said he could probably make a reasonable guess if he could look at a soil map, or a geological map, of the island, so Horatio buzzed Sophia and sent her to the council engineer's department to collect one.

But Horatio already knew in his heart what the findings were going to show. In all the time he had spent on Montebello – indeed, on all his travels to anywhere in the world – he had only once seen a soil scientist at work…

'As we know,' said Elwyn Morris, his fingers tracing the contours and strata lines of the map, 'what we basically have on this island is limestone. Lower coralline here… all the way to upper coralline, here… with globigerina, blue clay and greensand in between. There are a couple of beds of phosphorite pebbles… and here,' he jabbed his forefinger, 'is where I'd guess your man found hydrocarbons.'

He produced a pair of reading glasses from his pocket. 'It isn't easy to make out the name of it. Oh yes… *Zarafa*… that's an Arabic word. It means…'

'Distant beauty… I saw a man doing soil tests there, more than a month ago, around the time of Santa Maria *festa*,' said Horatio. 'How long does this testing usually take?'

'It depends on quite a few factors. Basically, you do tests and, if they're interesting, you go back to do more. If they're still interesting, you do them again. You keep going until you're fairly confident that you have – or, of course, that you don't have – commercially viable oil down there.'

'Now,' said Cesare, 'tell your friend here who actually owns that piece of land.'

'I do,' said Horatio. 'In partnership with the contractor, Portelli.'

'And… remind me… whose idea was it to buy it, originally?'

'Oh, it was his idea. I hadn't even heard of the place.'

The police chief said he needed to use the mayor's phone again. He rang headquarters and told them to pick up Portelli, and take him to headquarters for interview in connection with a murder investigation.

He collected the disks, replaced them in the briefcase and left for his office.

'Now,' said Elwyn Morris to Horatio, 'my suggestion is that we both write off the rest of the day and go in search of some real Champagne. The drinks will be on you. It isn't every day that you become a millionaire.'

# Twenty-six

Aldo tracked down the two friends at Giosetta's restaurant. Horatio was eating pork belly in an effort to soak up some of the day's alcohol intake; Elwyn Morris was cutting into an inch-thick imported Irish rib-eye. The reporter appeared excited, so Horatio told him to pull up a chair and asked a waitress for a menu, but he said he had already eaten, at his desk.

'In that case, grab a glass and do me a favour by drinking some of this stuff. I'm nearly drowning in it.'

'They arrested Portelli – not the plant-hire bloke, his son the contractor – but then they let him go home. But there is a mafia connection. The problem is I'm not sure yet how to go about writing it. It involves the capo, Don Salvatore.'

'Tell me the story and we'll worry later about how you write it.'

Somehow, said Aldo, pouring wine into a Champagne flute, the mafia had discovered that there was a possibility of oil on the north side of Montebello. 'Nobody's sure how they learnt this, but Portelli's belief is that it must have been his own soil expert, who was making random tests, and then sold the information and it got to the mafia, as these things do. Anyway, the police brought him in, too, Portelli's soil man, and they're keeping him in, according to my source at headquarters.'

There was a long stretch of land, he said, part owned by the church and part by the council, but it was all waste land, and outside the development area. Don Salvatore came over himself, to try to negotiate to buy the property from the church, hence the involvement of the monsignor. Portelli – the old man – was brought in because the Don knew him from way back, and also possibly because he thought the deal might go through more easily, and even more cheaply, if a local man was buying it. It was cheap in any case because nobody could build on it.

However, Aldo continued, the church became suspicious about anybody, especially a Sicilian mainlander, even one with local contacts, wanting to buy what was ostensibly useless land. They somehow got the idea that, once sold, building permission might be granted and then the place would be worth far more than they sold it for and they'd lose out on the deal. So they wanted to hold on to it. In any case, they prevaricated too long and Don Salvatore was arrested.

In the meantime, Portelli – the son – learnt about it from his father and thought that if there were problems with buying from the church the next best thing was to buy the land beside it that the council owned. 'Apparently it doesn't make much odds with drilling – once you're underground you can just go sideways,' he said.

'That's right,' said Morris. 'You can quite easily go a mile or more, sideways in any direction.'

'But can you just go off at an angle and tap into somebody else's oil?' Horatio asked.

'It isn't somebody else's oil,' said the geologist. 'The meek may inherit the earth, but not the mineral rights. It's the government's oil. The valuable bit is the land that they drill from, where they position the rig.'

After he had bought the land, and before Horatio paid him for half of it, Portelli passed the soil report to an oil company and sold them an option to explore it, said Aldo.

'That fits,' Horatio told him. 'Elwyn made some phone calls this afternoon. Field geologists are a small fraternity and most of them know each other, or know somebody who knows them. The Fiat driver, Greco, was a freelance and the oil company commissioned him to check out the site. When he finally concluded that there was oil down there he was obviously in a hurry to present his findings to them, in person.'

'And the obvious conclusion is that the mafia didn't want anybody to learn about it until they could somehow get their hands on the land,' said Aldo. 'So they put a hit on him before he could tell anybody.'

'My problem now,' said Horatio, 'is that I need to speak to Portelli and find out what game he thought he was playing with me as a partner. I suppose he thinks that I, so to speak, oiled the wheels for his purchase. Maybe he was going to tell me that the land, after all, wasn't suitable for growing olives and buy my share back from me.'

'I'd say that's unlikely,' said Morris. 'He – or the oil company who applies for the licence to drill on the land – will still need the back-up and whole-hearted support of the council. There are lots of other considerations to come, like access to the land, building heavy duty roads, storage, accommodation, amenities… things he can't do without your compliance. You could still screw up the deal for him, if you felt so inclined. No: in my view he's made you a gift; and made you a very rich man.'

'Well, that's my problem,' said Horatio. 'Your problem,' he told Aldo,' is writing the story without mentioning oil. Say it was believed to be over a land deal, if you like, but leave the victim as a businessman from Rome, and by all means run the mafia connection. Leave Portelli out of it, for now. There's plenty to write about, without going into too much detail.'

Aldo told him that the office linage pool had already sold a story to the Fleet Street papers. One of the eye witnesses to the shooting of the Fiat driver had been a former Page Three model, one of the originals, a still-attractive blonde from Newcastle upon Tyne who had been a passenger with her boyfriend on an open-deck tourist bus. She had seen everything. She'd told reporters: 'I will never get that image out of my mind, of the man with a bullet hole in the middle of his forehead. But apart from that incident it's been the best holiday we've ever had.'

# Twenty-seven

Portelli telephoned the *municipio* and asked for a meeting. He could explain everything, he told Horatio, just as he had explained everything to the satisfaction of the police, including the *antimafia* commission. But the mayor had a court case with no fewer than 17 defendants that he expected to take all day and possibly even longer. Since the police were no longer interested in Portelli, he decided there would be no harm in meeting him over dinner, so he asked Sophia to book his usual alcove table.

The hearing was the last on the list of long-delayed cases that had been outstanding when he had taken over as chief magistrate. The crime – Horatio had to discipline his mind to think of it only as an alleged crime, at this stage – had come to light after a convent schoolgirl wrote an essay about what she had done during the summer holidays. She described how a gang of youths aged between 15 and 19 systematically kidnapped, tortured and raped or defiled at least 15 teenage girls and another aged under twelve, plus the gang rape of a disabled teenager by six males.

Her teacher, a nun, had seriously chastised her and threatened her with expulsion for writing what she interpreted as imaginative filth. Then the following summer another girl at the same school had presented an almost exactly similar essay. The headmistress summoned the parents of both pupils to the convent and reported to them what she considered to be the girls' wickedness.

The parents, however, believed their daughters who produced some of their friends to substantiate their accounts, and the police were called in; intensive inquiries followed and the youths were arrested. Nothing had happened after that.

Alessandra's diligent research produced a chart akin to a family tree, detailing how the boys were 'connected' – they had started using that expression – and related to parents or people on the island in positions of power. She had even tracked down who had spoken to whom, with the intention of delaying court proceedings, presumably in the hope that they would eventually be forgotten about. One of the accused was the son of a magistrate, two others were the nephews of different magistrates, several were related to directors of government departments, and one was the son of a senior policeman.

All 17 defendants now intended to plead not guilty, necessitating a trial. Horatio's role was simply to hear the basic evidence and, assuming there was what he considered to be a *prima facie* case, commit them to a hearing in Sicily before a panel of professional judges.

Not all the victims were willing to testify, but most of them were. He decided to rely chiefly on the two written contemporaneous accounts, plus the supporting evidence of two other girls. By early evening he had decided that there was sufficient information for the accused to be remanded in custody, pending transfer to Sicily.

When Portelli pulled out a chair to sit opposite him at the table, Horatio was not in his usual good humour. 'It'd better be a good story,' he said. 'You have seriously dropped me in the shit.'

The developer started by relating what Horatio already knew, or had surmised. His own soil expert had been carrying out routine explorations on unused or undeveloped land. He had a government licence to do that; it also required the consent of the landowner but that, he said, was always forthcoming because people were naturally interested in knowing whether the wasteland that they owned had any practical use or value. When he'd examined samples of earth on an empty site owned by the church, he had discovered the likely presence of oil deposits and decided, as Portelli put it, to go into business on his own.

'Effectively, he sold the information to the mafia. Not directly, but it appears that he knew what he was doing. Don Salvatore came over here to negotiate the deal and he involved my father in the transaction.'

'It was just fortuitous, was it, that the *capo* happened to know your father? That appears to be a remarkable coincidence.'

Portelli said he would come back to that part, later.

When the don had been arrested, and the deal fell through, the Portellis – father and son – had discussed the secret nature of it. That was when Portelli junior, studying a survey map of the island, had spotted the parcel of land immediately adjacent to the church property: the area of wasteland owned by the *commune* and known as Zarafa. He had fired his soil expert for disloyalty, employed another, and instructed him to concentrate on compiling a detailed report on the area. The findings showed sufficient elements of hydrocarbons to suggest the likelihood of petroleum, deep beneath the surface.

'I wanted to buy it. But I thought that if I made the request for a patch of useless land, it would raise eyebrows. Your land valuer might be suspicious and even order a soil survey himself. That's when I decided that the simple way was to involve you. If I told you there was a possibility of oil down there, your famous conscience would have got in the way. So I invented the story about growing olives on it. And I came up with this idea about a joint purchase done, so to speak, through the back door, in a roundabout way, because I knew that, even then, you wouldn't do it in secret and would let a few people in on what was actually happening, so your valuer knew that you were somehow involved, and didn't make any waves to affect the purchase.'

'But you lied to me. You cheated me.'

'I don't think I actually lied. I said we could plant trees on it, which we can, and I said we could produce oil. What I didn't say was that I had a different sort of oil in mind. *Madonna!* You can't complain: look what you have ended up with. And without any mafia involvement, either.'

'I don't know about that. There's still your father's involvement. There are some people who believe he is the godfather on this island. I think that possibly even includes the cops. After all, he owns most of the construction equipment; the government hires from him, even your competition needs to hire from him. In effect there's hardly any development happening that doesn't involve a cut for him in some way or another.'

There was also the unforgettable fact that Portelli senior was somehow connected to Don Salvatore…

'I asked him about that, after you raised it last time. He told me a story. We'll order another bottle and I'll tell it to you, then you can decide for yourself.'

According to his father's account (which may well, he said, have some basis in fact) in the humid early morning mist in July 1943 – a few days after Horatio's father's 'timely' forced landing on Montebello – a US Army Air Corps reconnaissance aircraft took off from the tiny Maltese island of Gozo and flew unnoticed across the Sicilian Channel over what was German-occupied territory. As it approached the small hillside town of Villalba, a subsistence farming area in north central Sicily, residents who had left their homes in response to the aircraft's unfamiliar drone reportedly noticed a square yellow patch stuck to either side of the fuselage, each with a large black *L* painted on it. Flying low and slowing almost to stalling speed, the pilot dropped an object into the main street then regained altitude and velocity and returned to base.

The parish priest, a certain Fr Salvatore, appeared from his fine baroque church in Piazza Madrice, the square at the end of Villalba's main street, and took the package from a family employee who had picked it up. He delivered it to his brother, Don Calogero Vizzini, local mafia boss and one of the most powerful of *capi*, a long-term fugitive with 39 murders already to his credit and who had controlled sulphur mines, farms, shops – and crime – for the past 45 years. While theoretically being sought by the authorities, said Portelli, the *capo* had represented the sulphur industry at top-level meetings in Rome and London to discuss governmental subsidies and international tariffs.

Inside the jettisoned canvas envelope was a yellow silk handkerchief, embroidered with another capital *L* – the trademark of New York gang boss 'Lucky' Luciano who had been born Salvatore Lucania 46 years earlier in Lercara Friddi, a few miles to the north-west along the road from Palermo. There was no evidence that the two men had communicated previously, and Luciano had been only nine years old when his family emigrated, but from his American prison cell 3,000 miles away he had identified Don Calo as the most influential contact on the island. And he had been promised a reduced sentence if he co-operated with what the Americans called *Operation Husky*: the invasion of Sicily.

Part of the folkloric anecdotage of Luciano's colourful life was that he had once, in order to authenticate the credentials of an emissary, sent one of his yellow silk pocket handkerchiefs along with the message, and the tradition had started in that way. On such stuff, said Portelli, legends were made.

The don may, possibly, have seen similar handkerchiefs before; Luciano had, in the past, given them to Sicilians returning to their homeland, with the implied message: 'This is a friend of ours. Look after him.' Portelli explained the syntax to Horatio: 'Friend of mine', implied a personal friend; 'friend of ours' meant a friend of the *cosa nostra*.

The message to Don Calo was equally simple to interpret: the Americans, who had landed in Sicily four days earlier, were coming and the Sicilians should support them.

'When Luciano spoke the other gang bosses listened. Now he was speaking, through a handkerchief, to Sicily…

'In any case, it seems to be an undisputed fact that after being handed the air-dropped package Don Calo immediately despatched horsemen with messages to his confederates in the surrounding area. Italian servicemen were advised to desert, being promised support and civilian clothing if they did so – and being threatened with reprisals, later, if they declined. It was an offer they found difficult to refuse. Two of the soldiers who defected together happened to be my father and a certain Salvatore Barracato.

Comrades in arms, nothing more sinister than that. In fact at that time Barracato was not a *mafioso*. But friendships formed in that way tend to endure.'

Portelli poured Horatio more wine, then refilled his own glass.

'So, the American government conspired with Luciano, who was famously the boss of bosses in the United States. And General Patton used Don Calo and his chums in Sicily.... But do I hear you, or your friend Cesare, or the *antimafia* commission accusing them of co-operating with the mafia? Were my father and his comrades consorting with the mafia when they defected from the army...? I don't think so.'

'If you put it like that...' began Horatio. But he couldn't think how to finish the sentence.

# Twenty-eight

The Americans, continued Portelli, had another job for Don Calo: having captured the island of Sicily they needed to secure it. They organised a public ceremony at which they declared him mayor of Villalba, and the newly appointed civic leader responded by holding his first official reception at which his new friends, the American army, and some old friends, all the neighbouring *capi* that he had been able to round up for the occasion, were his personal guests.

To the invasion officers he made the introduction of the 'men of honour', all of whom, as he reasonably and rightly described them, were victims of Mussolini's fascism, many of them released from jail only in the past few days. It would be helpful, he now explained to the conquerors, if firearms certificates could be restored to these people 'to help prevent any possibility of a new fascist coup' (Don Calo failed to mention that, because he had found it expedient to do so, he had joined the fascist party himself) and further, since his friends were men of high esteem in their communities, it would seem logical to install them all as mayors, too.

The Americans considered Don Calo's suggestions to be perfectly acceptable and within the week dozens of towns and villages found themselves with newly appointed civic leaders who had only recently been in jail for murder, kidnapping, extortion, banditry and bank-robbery.

The army also presented the village of Villalba with a number of captured Italian army trucks (which would immediately form the basis of a big black-market operation) and of equipment including tractors and construction machinery (which could be hired out to contractors repairing bomb and shell damage). Grateful citizens and other *capi* who benefited from Don Calo's personal preferment or patronage also paid homage and showered him with other gifts – cheeses, pasta, jewellery… and stolen military equipment.

As the invasion forces left Sicily in an apparently peaceful and controlled state to press forward into Italy, Don Calo became the nearest thing the mafia had seen, or was likely to see, to a Hollywood-style *capo di tutti capi*, or 'boss of all the bosses'.

He had proved his personal power with contacts at the highest level. He had appointed friends to positions of honour. He had shown them respect. They were all, individually and collectively, in his debt. The respect was reciprocated.

'Now,' said Portelli, 'after 20 years of fascism, after living in the shadows and often in the Ucciardone prison, the *mafiosi* were once again the rulers of Sicily – and this time it was official. While Mussolini had come close to achieving the demise of the mafia, the Americans had recreated it at a stroke.'

He told Horatio: 'I am deeply grateful to you for prompting me to speak to my father, which is how I learnt all that. He got the idea of hiring out construction machinery from watching Don Calo's operation – and decided to set up in that business when he returned to Montebello. I wouldn't have known anything about it, if it hadn't been for you.'

And now, he added, Horatio knew all about the post-war connection between the Sicilian mafia and the majority of Sicilian mayors.

'None of this affected Montebello, though.'

'Of course not; we had a British governor, your esteemed father. So we just developed our own style of mafia, quietly, but nevertheless indirectly connected to what became known as the syndicate on the mainland. Think what you like, but we are still part of Sicily, here.'

'No,' said Horatio, firmly. 'We don't have a mafia here. The sole reason for the presence of the *carabinieri* is to prevent it spreading its tentacles onto this island. We have no organised crime, here.'

'Don't we? Haven't you heard the saying that the mafia comes to Montebello to learn? The mafia has changed measurably over the years. It is big business – it always was – but in many ways it is legitimate business, now. It even owns and runs hospitals, and it controls service industries that are simply a system of collecting their *pizzi* in a different way. That's what they learnt from Montebello.'

'If that's true, how does it work here? I know there's all sorts of minor corruption and nepotism and small-scale bribes and deals between friends and friends-of-friends. God knows, I have been trying to put a stop to all or most of that. But where do you think the mafia is, if you say it is here on Montebello?'

'Think about it. Who has a finger in every pie? Who gets a rake-off, directly or indirectly, from virtually everything that happens on this island?'

Horatio said he had no idea. Maybe the wine was slowing down his thought processes, but he couldn't think of anything or anybody that fitted the scenario Portelli was describing.

'Sleep on it,' said the developer. 'And think about this… There was a rumour – no more than that, but there was a certain amount of logic to it – that when you were famously shot at in Palermo the bullet wasn't intended for you, but for that girl who was your bodyguard. Apart from you, who knew that she was going to be there?'

'Her boss Cesare, naturally. And her colleague, Johnny. And my secretary and I suppose Manuel, the clerk. I don't know about anybody else.'

'That why I'm telling you to sleep on it. Maybe somebody else knew. It's just possible, don't you think, that somebody told somebody on Sicily, somebody who nursed a grievance against her, that she was going to be there?'

In the meantime, said Portelli, there was other business that he described as being more pressing: the future of their joint investment in the plot of land called Zarafa, and the potential of becoming seriously rich from the discovery of oil. Before going home they arranged another meeting, in the mayor's office for the following afternoon.

They decided that common sense dictated the involvement of Elwyn Morris, the only man on the island who knew anything about the oil industry. Morris said that contracts were not a part of his expertise, so Horatio asked Alessandra to attend the meeting. 'I can advise you, at this stage, as a friend,' she said. 'But I can't become involved. Conflict of interest; I will be advising the *commune* in the oil venture. As for the mayor... well, any time that oil is mentioned in a council meeting the mayor will need to declare his interest; you can speak, but you can't vote.'

She congratulated Portelli on the wording of the option he had sold to an oil company. 'This gives them first rights to explore, and first rights to bid for development. They have done the exploration, now they can bid for it. But you can offer similar rights to exploration, or do the exploration yourselves, and publish your own findings, and invite other bids for the property.'

'Our findings, if we did them, would be the same,' said Morris. 'The man was an expert, I have checked him out. If he says there's oil there, there is oil there. We could just replicate his findings, maybe with a few discreet alterations, but the result would be the same.'

'So,' said Alessandra, 'you can now hawk them around and seek competitive bids for the highest tender. But that is only for use of the land. The oil, and the licences to produce it, will be down to the Italian government. That won't be a problem; they will be delighted to discover that there is oil here.'

'What normally happens,' said Morris, 'is that the oil company puts in its investment – that will be many millions, hundreds of millions – and hopes to recoup it in the first five years. And I am talking dollars, not worthless Italian liri. After that, the profits are shared with the government. The land owner, meanwhile, just gets rent from use of the land. The cost of drilling can be many millions of dollars per day. But the land to do it on is crucial.'

'So who do we approach?' asked Portelli. 'More importantly, who can you approach on our behalf, as our broker?'

The major companies, Morris said, were household names. He reeled off some of them: Exxon-Mobil, BP, Royal Dutch Shell, Chevron, Total, ENI, Conoco… 'And that's not counting the Arabs or the Africans. I can contact all of them. For some of them, it will be fairly small beer. Bear in mind that companies like Exxon have a bigger budget and turnover than many countries. But the ones who are interested will send people to investigate and to negotiate. You can, however, ask them for a down-payment as a sign of their interest and goodwill. Say a million dollars – that's less than the cost of a day's drilling – for the geologist's report and the right to bid. The unsuccessful bidders get their million back.'

Alessandra said she thought she could draw up a contract on that basis, and Morris told her he could probably find a template, from other earlier deals, to help her with the format of it.

'Let's go for it, then,' said Horatio.

'Let's go for a bottle of Champagne, first,' suggested Morris. 'I find I work better and quicker when I don't have to wrestle with a thirst.'

'I had better form you a company, right away,' said Alessandra. 'Zarafa Oil Company sound all right?'

'To be known as Zoco,' said Elwyn Morris.

# Twenty-nine

The bishop telephoned to ask for an appointment to visit the mayor. He made the call personally – no chaplains or secretaries involved – thus convincing Horatio that the matter was important, at least to the church. He replied that he would see him immediately, and ten minutes later was opening a bottle of Sicilian red when the bishop, sweating in his hurry, was ushered into the office.

He came straight to the point. The church owned land on the coast that was not currently scheduled for development but which, it was generally thought, would one day get planning permission. The problem was that title to the area had been disputed for generations: the church actually possessed the deeds but the Camilleri family   one of the Camilleri families – claimed that their ancestors had bought the land without the paperwork having been passed to them. Over the years the dispute had been in and out of court without ever getting resolved.

Suddenly – in fact earlier that day – it had been in court again and this time the argument had been adjudicated upon... with judgment being made against the church.

'It's absolutely scandalous,' declared the bishop. 'Wrong, illegal, immoral, and totally corrupt.'

Horatio said he honestly didn't know anything about it. 'But that's the way these things are normally settled. When there's a quarrel that can't be resolved in any other way, it's usually left to the court to decide the truth of it. That's generally considered to be the fairest possible course.'

'Generally, as you say, and I would probably agree... generally. But not in this case. Your magistrate was Ferra, and Ferra is related, on his mother's side, to the Camilleri family. The disputatious Camilleri is the son of Ferra's mother's cousin.'

'That's the problem with small islands, isn't it? Go back far enough and everybody on the island is related to everybody else.'

'Distantly related, yes, if you go back far enough. After all, there was a time when nobody left the island at all. That necessitated quite a lot of inter-marriage, although usually the church endeavoured to confirm that there were sufficient degrees of separation for such relationships to be practical and acceptable. In this case, however…'

He paused to take a sip of wine, and also for dramatic effect.

'Tell me.'

'Magistrate Ferra's wife's brother is also the lawyer for the litigious Camilleri.'

Horatio said that, on that additional basis, he would certainly look into it, and report back to the bishop who, in the meantime, could appeal against the adjudication – if he had not already done so.

'No,' said the bishop, clearly not a man who was used to having active responses to his requests delayed. 'It would be greatly appreciated if you would do it immediately, and then you can overturn the ruling. I have all the necessary paperwork, here.'

Horatio believed that, pompous and annoying though he was, the bishop was no less entitled to justice than any other citizen. He buzzed and asked Sophia to find Alessandra, then opened the cleric's envelope and studied the literature. He paid particular attention to the map; the disputed territory was slightly more than two miles away from his own property at Zarafa.

While they waited he said: 'With no planning permission pending, nor even likely in the foreseeable future, it can't be worth much, can it?'

The bishop said it was rented to a couple of hunters, although litigation over the years had almost certainly cost more than the site was actually worth, or earned in letting. 'Nevertheless, we are an island. There is a finite amount of land and one day it is more than likely that the shortage of space would mean that development permission would be finally granted.'

'That could be a very long way into the future.'

'The Mother Church has been in existence for two millennia. We are not in a hurry.'

When Alessandra arrived she said she had no idea that magistrate Ferra was related, even remotely, to the plaintiff Camilleri. 'I didn't go into people's mothers' cousins,' she said. Nor had she been aware of the relationship between the magistrate and the lawyer representing one of the litigants appearing in front of him; that, she said, was more directly a matter for Vincenzo, the court clerk but, in fairness to him, magistrates were supposedly aware of the rules and at the end of the day it was Ferra's responsibility to avoid potential conflicts of interest, especially of family interests.

'So what can we do about it, now?'

'On the face of it,' she said, 'as chief magistrate you can overturn the adjudication, arbitrarily. It doesn't need to be appealed. In any case, all dealings concerning church land are subject to ratification by the council. As mayor, you can simply veto the transaction.'

The bishop, all signs of pomposity withdrawn, looked at Horatio pleadingly.

'I can do all that. It still doesn't resolve the basic problem of the ownership of the land.'

'It's been going on since before the war,' said Alessandra, leafing through the documents. 'The plain facts are that nobody knows the truth of it. There will be no living witnesses and presumably there is no written evidence to support either side. The best anybody can do is guess. I can think of one solution: that is for the *commune* to buy it. That would involve getting it valued at a fair price and buying it from the church, because it's the church that is in possession of the physical title, the deeds. And that would be the end of the matter. The Camilleri people would have no claim because it would be council land, and the *commune* would then own the deeds, having paid for them. End of argument. Plus a kick in the... erm...' she remembered that she was in the presence of a bishop: '...in the teeth for magistrate Ferra and his brother-in-law.'

'Does that sound like a solution to you?'

'It sounds more than fair,' replied the bishop.

'I'll get the valuer on to it right away,' said Alessandra. She grinned wickedly as she departed. 'The mayor will probably want to plant olive trees on it.'

'A truly splendid girl, you have there. Delightful, in so many ways...'

'Intelligent,' said Horatio, 'and also beautiful.'

The bishop sighed, nodding. 'Beautiful... And, in case you are wondering, just because I am on a diet, it doesn't mean I can't look at the menu.'

Horatio thought the bishop might be human, after all.

The chaplain telephoned a couple of hours later, also requesting an interview. 'His excellency wants to organise your belated blessing as mayor,' he said. 'Can I come to discuss the arrangements?'

'We've had this conversation before. Blessing what, or whom, exactly?'

'You, personally, Don *Orazio*, on your appointment as mayor of Montebello, of this diocese. After all, if His Holiness himself can recognise your work for our church...'

Tony Peagam, his sometime drinking companion in the Fleet Street era, arrived on the island for a three-day visit with his friend Brian, the would-be entrepreneur. Horatio asked his secretary to collect a folder of information about grants and tax breaks from the department of development and asked her to accompany the visitors and give them a tour around the island. 'Show them everything,' he said. '...Except your holiday photographs.'

He had booked them in to sea-view rooms at the Porto Hotel and on their first evening took them out for dinner, inviting his other public relations chum, Franco di Giorgio, to accompany them, confident that as promoter of tourism and with a new portfolio to attract overseas investment, he was the right man to extol the island's virtues.

Horatio was right about that. Franco worked a brilliant PR pitch, explaining the expertise that some local workers had with perfectly moulding glass-reinforced fibre for making fishing and sports boats, and also mentioning that, in the past, there had even been a small industry on the island assembling Triumph Herald cars from parts supplied from the UK.

'What appeals to me,' said Tony, 'is that you could have your E-type replica built here, come out to collect it, have a short holiday in the sunshine, and drive it home to England via the Italian *autostradas* and the French *autoroutes*. That would be an amazing first drive in your new Jag. You just drive it on to the ferry, here, and when you disembark at the other end it would be motorway virtually all the way home.'

'Even on Sicily there are some really good roads,' agreed Horatio. 'You just need to check the map because some of the roads don't go anywhere; some of the bridges go only halfway across a valley. That's because the sainted European Union has this – or had this – tendency to pay in full for new roads and bridges before they were finished. So they never were. But the majority of roads there are good.

'I was at a conference in Palermo recently, a seminar organised by the EU,' said Franco, 'where they explained about all the grants that were available.'

'That's where you got shot?' Tony, interrupting, asked Horatio.

'Well, somebody fired a shot in my direction, and I was slightly injured, yes.'

'A delegate at the conference,' Franco continued, 'told the story of a mayor from Sicily who had visited a town hall in France and asked where the funding had come from to provide what was virtually a palace – marble walls and floors and chandeliers all over the place. His French counterpart said that the town had received a grant from Brussels to build a two-lane bridge, but they had built it only single-lane, with traffic lights at either end, and had used the rest of the cash on their *hôtel de ville*...'

He paused, applying a match to his cigar. His audience thought that was the end of the story but, satisfied that his Havana was burning evenly, he continued:

'Sometime later the French mayor paid a visit to Sicily and this time it was his turn to admire the even greater and more elaborate extravagance of his friend's *municipio*. He naturally asked how it had been funded and the Sicilian took the Frenchman to the window and said: "See that bridge…?" And the Frenchman replied: "What bridge?"…'

Laughing, Brian said: 'Montebello is certainly an attractive proposition. My only concern would be that, well… it is Sicily. What about the mafia?'

'We don't have mafia here,' said Horatio. 'Okay, we have Sicilian attitudes and many shared traditions, but the mafia isn't one of them. The islanders have their own loyalties, basically to family, friends, village and island – more or less in that order. But in the main they are also loyal to their employers. I mean… sometimes, apparently, their bosses even tell them which way to vote, in the elections.'

'There's nothing here like protection money that you might have heard about on Sicily in the old days, if that's the sort of thing that worries you,' added Franco.

The Englishmen appeared to be becoming convinced by the island's potential. Sophia had shown them a ready-built factory that was partly equipped and available for immediate occupation. They had already been impressed by the friendliness and helpfulness of the local population, and also by the financial inducements offered to new businesses. They intended to visit a boatyard the following day to watch craftsmen working in glass fibre.

'If you decide to go ahead, my company can help facilitate all the arrangements,' Franco told them. 'And obviously Horatio here will ensure that everything goes smoothly. We can also assist with local recruitment, and my real-estate division will find you property to buy for your home on the island. And then, if you need it, we can obviously support you with your PR, marketing and advertising, which after all is our core business.'

Horatio was about to say that, yes, indeed, his friend Franco was effectively a one-stop shop with contacts and influence in every aspect of life on the island. But he managed to stop himself. Instead he became silent, deep in thought.

He had suddenly remembered Franco offering to share transport to the Palermo conference, but having to turn him down on the grounds that he was required to travel in the small police helicopter with his bodyguard, Teresa.

Then Tony actually said it: 'That sounds really helpful, Franco. You certainly appear to have a finger in every pie.'

It was an expression that struck a chord with Horatio; he had heard it most recently, in exactly that form, from Portelli.

# PART FOUR

# *Thirty*

They were impressed by the speed with which Elwyn Morris's oil industry contacts responded but, as the geologist explained, 'When you're dealing in hundreds of millions of dollars, rather than in Italian lire, time is money.'

From among the interested parties – and all the major players had expressed serious interest – he had recommended a second-level company: not one of the biggest, but one that was cash-rich. 'They would all pay more or less the same,' he said. 'But a slightly smaller oilfield developer will pay more attention to it, and appreciate it more, than the big boys, for whom it would be just another bunch of wells in the Med.'

He negotiated a deal, $60million between the two land owners for the initial lease, and three million a year (with phased increases dependant on output) in rent. Horatio found the sums incredible, and confessed that he kept looking at his bank statement and counting, then recounting, the noughts. The two new millionaires decided to pay Morris ten per cent, as commission for handling the negotiation.

Licensing then became a matter for the central government – organising rates of payments of royalties and taxes on the oil that was expected to be produced. The announcement of the discovery was made at a ministerial press conference in Rome; that suited Horatio, who felt he should distance himself as much as possible from the project, and didn't want nosey European journalists visiting Montebello and making enquiries about the ownership of the actual land.

It was all sorted out, with work preparing to start, within a matter of weeks.

Suddenly, Montebello started to enjoy full employment, and even to create vacancies for overseas workers. Lots of overpaid and underworked government employees, who had been shuffling half-heartedly towards their pensions, immediately realised the benefit of more than doubling their pay by transferring to relatively menial tasks on the oilfield. The hours were much longer – mainly 12-hour, 7-day, shifts – but they worked only on alternate months, allowing plenty of time for fishing, farming, and working as self-employed plumbers, electricians, painters and decorators and carpenters.

There were new access roads to build, and old roads to be reinforced to take heavy traffic, a perimeter to secure, plus accommodation and catering blocks, offices, laboratories and finally a pipeline to the coast. The *commune* sold – more accurately, arranged a lease – of the recently acquired church land on which the oil company was given permission to build a working harbour from which to ship the crude oil to a refinery in Sicily.

Zoco, the Zarafa Oil Company, was in business, with two joint presidents and with Elwyn Morris (on commission plus twice his previous salary) installed as director of operations, even before the first drilling rig was installed.

Not for the first time, Horatio realised that there were not sufficient hours in his day. He seriously needed to reorganise his life.

With his newly acquired wealth he bought the ownership of *La Gazzetta* from his friend Hannibal Spiteri, assuming the titles of publisher and editor in chief, and installing Dino, the chief sub, as editor with day-to-day responsibility and with himself more or less in the background, as a consultant. 'You can criticise the council as much as you want,' he said, shaking hands as the deal was done. 'Only don't forget who's paying your salary at the end of the day.'

He appointed a joint-deputy mayor – coincidentally another Labour member – to assist *vicesindaco* Marco Bonnici, and promoted Alessandra from head of legal affairs to chief executive of the council. Effectively, he would assume a consultant's role as mayor, too, presiding only over the monthly assembly and the more important committee or departmental meetings and functions. He would, he decided, make time to continue to sit as the chief magistrate, at least one day each week.

Now, when he looked at his diary, it appeared refreshingly light. He could also play a full part in the administration of his new oil venture – although Elwyn Morris told him that the oil company would do almost everything that was required, and to a large extent an oilfield ran itself.

He had one more task. He took Franco di Giorgio out for another dinner and eventually convinced him – for a sum he thought was slightly more than its value – to part with 50 per cent of his PR company, Campanello, along with all of its subsidiary interests.

Even with those responsibilities, he reckoned, he would finally be able to make time to become close enough to what he'd always wanted to be: a gentleman of leisure.

He was also still 'seeing' – his ex-wife's one-time euphemism for having sex with – both Alessandra and the contessa, typically each of them on a weekly basis. And on summer Saturdays, and sometimes on public holidays, his two secretaries would often turn up uninvited to cavort in his pool, and then in his bedroom. It was what he described to himself as 'recreational' sex: no attachments, no commitments on any side, no responsibility and no serious relationship. But, *Madonna!* It was fun.

Life, he thought, was looking good.

# Thirty-one

Horatio may not have received recognition from Rome's government for bringing oil wealth to Montebello, but he was given all the credit for it by the bishop when the service of civic blessing was eventually held in the cathedral of Santa Maria. The son of 'the man who had rescued the island from fascism and prevented its bombing during the invasion of our island nation'… had now secured Montebello's economic security. The bishop even included a reference to the rarity of an Englishman – he didn't mention the word protestant – having received no fewer than two medals from His Holiness the Pope for his work for Mother Church… 'work that the new mayor of Montebello continues to do', he said.

The bishop's ringing endorsement of the new civic leader was not based wholly on economic stability, nor was his enthusiasm simply on the grounds that the mayor had settled a long-running argument in favour – and in financial favour – of the church. In fact, when the *commune* leased the former church land for development by the oil company as a harbour, his initial thought had been that the church had lost out badly on the deal. Then he realised – Horatio had pointed out the fact to him – that all the property around the coastal plot also belonged to the church. There would have to be a road to the harbour; and if there was a road, there could and would be building – houses, shops and factories and all the sorts of properties that went naturally with the creation of a harbour, even with a predominantly industrial harbour. He had somehow got it into his head that the mayor, obviously knowing in advance about the likely coastal development, had planned it all, well ahead, and to the church's benefit. There was already talk of attaching a marina to the harbour and possibly even building a hotel; there was no shortage of interest in development of the adjoining property, nor any doubt that planning permission, when applied for, would now be granted.

At the civic reception – paid for by the council – that followed the service Cesare, dressed for the occasion in his number one uniform, quipped: 'Don Orazio today… Saint Orazio tomorrow. You make best friends in the unlikeliest places.'

'Oh, one likes to do one's bit for the Mother Church.'

The contessa approached and, instead of offering her cheek as most of the women had been doing, held out her hand as if to shake it then, holding Horatio's hand in hers, bent her long neck and reached down to kiss it.

'See… *baciamano*,' said Cesare, nodding. Smirking, he told the contessa: 'He doesn't have a ring to kiss… yet.'

She gave the police chief a look as if to signify that she, alone, understood the correct etiquette for such an occasion.

Alessandra joined the small group, linked her arm through Horatio's and kissed his cheek, saying 'Congratulations, *caro mio*.'

The contessa moved round and linked through his other arm. There were no secrets on Montebello.

Cesare beckoned a waiter and handed the mayor a glass of sparkling wine and a small plate of finger food. Horatio was forced to release both women in order to take them from him. Cesare then touched him in the small of his back to steer him away.

Walking him towards a large window overlooking the gold-hued buildings of the *piazza*, he said: 'More good news for you today. At least, I hope you'll think it's good news. Your old travelling companion, Teresa, is being posted back to Montebello next month, newly and deservedly promoted. She came out top of her class.'

'She wrote, telling me about her promotion. She didn't mention that she was coming back to the island.'

'She also learnt about that posting only today. She's going to take charge of the *antimafia* department.'

'I'm delighted, and looking forward very much to seeing her again.'

'I know that you became close…'

'Close? The girl saved my life!'

'No, she didn't.'

'Well, that's what she thought she was doing. It amounts to the same thing.'

'You must take her out to dinner to celebrate her promotion, and her return. But this time she won't be the one driving you to the restaurant.'

Early on the following Sunday morning Cesare telephoned Horatio at home and asked whether he was alone. He was. Cesare knew that he was; he was simply being polite.

'You have so many jobs these days, you wear so many hats, that I never know which hat you're wearing when I call. You are going to need two of them. You'd better put on your magistrate's hat first: we have a sudden death...'

'Who... where...?'

'Far side of the island. On some land owned by the church and rented out for hunting. In fact I think it's a place we were talking about last week. Anyway, it's a hunter. He's been shot, and he's dead. You'd better come and examine the scene.'

'I am getting dressed while you speak. Do we know who it is?'

'Yes. You need a different hat for this bit. I have to inform you, with regret, that the dead hunter is your partner, or one of your partners, Franco di Giorgio.'

The police chief told him that the driver had been given the precise location and would already be outside his door. Horatio took a pair of field boots from under his bed and ran downstairs, carrying them, to the car.

Closing the door on Horatio and climbing in behind the wheel, Johnny said: 'Bad news, boss. Your friend... blown the back of his head off.'

'Sounds horrible.'

'These hunters, they have no discipline with firearms.'

Cesare pulled back the tarpaulin and raised his eyebrows towards Horatio. He didn't need to ask, and probably wasn't even asking the question, but Horatio formally confirmed: 'Yes, that's Franco.'

'Shot in the back of the head while hunting quail – there are a couple in his bag. Now, how does that happen?'

The body was dressed in a disruptive-pattern smock and trousers and had a bandolier of cartridges across its chest.

'You don't normally dress like that, for quail. It's the birds that have the camouflage.'

'Mediterranean macho,' said Cesare. 'Put a shotgun in their hand and they all think they're Rambo, and dress like that.'

Horatio looked around the field. Not bad for quail, he thought. Lightly wooded with sparse grass – the little birds couldn't cope with thick vegetation – but plenty of seeds for them to peck at.

'He was on his own?'

'No sign that anybody else was present, so how…?'

'Did he have a dog?'

'Not found one. Why…?'

'Well, it would be very long odds, but he owns one and it has been known for a dog to step on the trigger of a gun. Do you have a time of death?'

'Not precisely. But only a few hours ago.'

'You usually shoot quail just after sunrise. Although, in England at least, you tend to shoot them at the end of the season, rather than at the beginning.

'You know about these things.' It wasn't a question.

'I used to do a bit, but many years ago. Can I see the gun?'

The police chief took it from the boot of his white Range Rover and handed it to the chief magistrate. It was an expensive weapon, a Benelli 12-gauge side-by-side with a satin walnut stock, hand-engraved on one side with a pair of pheasants in flight and on the other with a scene of rising woodcock.

There was no sign of forensic powder to suggest that the weapon had been dusted for fingerprints. Admiring it, Horatio opened the gun.

'One cartridge fired, and the empty case removed by us; one still in the barrel,' confirmed Cesare.

'You should extract the remaining one, for transporting.'

'Sure,' agreed Cesare. 'Take it out. Here's an evidence bag.' Horatio shook out the red plastic cartridge and, holding it by the brass rim, placed it in a transparent pouch which he handed to a sergeant who sealed it and marked the label with a felt-tip pen.

Horatio released the safety button and pulled both triggers on empty chambers. 'See how light they are? They should be firm.'

Holding the shotgun by the barrel, he asked: 'May I...?' And Cesare shrugged to indicate that he could do anything he wished.

'See this?' He showed the policeman the end of the stock, finely checkered to hold the weapon in position against the shoulder during recoil. There was a slight indentation on one corner, to which his finger was pointing.

Horatio cocked the gun again and dropped it onto the ground, stock first. Nothing happened. He dropped it again, this time onto a rock, and there was a click as one of the triggers was released.

'If there'd been a cartridge in there... I've heard about that happening, but never actually seen it, personally. My guess – maybe your lab will be able to tell you – is that Franco played about with the trigger mechanism at some time, maybe to make it lighter, and he buggered it up, with the unintentional result that the trigger could go off if you banged it or dropped it. Otherwise, with a gun of this excellent quality of craftsmanship, certainly in the condition it would have left the gunsmiths, it could never happen.'

'I think it seems that you have solved the case,' said Cesare. 'So if we assume that he had it over his shoulder, and dropped it from that sort of height, and it fell on a rock or hard ground, it would have gone off?'

'Looks like it. We've just seen it happen.'

'And by some fluke all the pellets hit him in the back of the head.'

'They could have gone anywhere. They have to go somewhere.'

'And if somebody had shot him...?'

'I wouldn't think so. If it had been intentional it would have been a *tiro fortunato* – a pure fluke – for all the shot to go to the head, rather than in, say, the middle of his back. Hunters are not usually so accurate with shotguns… A tragedy, eh?'

'Accidental death is always a tragedy, I think. Okay, thanks, Horatio. My report will be on your desk tomorrow.'

As Horatio walked away, Cesare rushed to catch up with him. 'Oh… just a formality… but, as you were the partner of the deceased… I ought to ask… just, as I say, a formality, no more than that, but where were you, early this morning?'

'Ask your driver. I went for dinner last night with the contessa, at the *castello*. She would obviously confirm that, discreetly of course. Your man brought me back, very early – well, quite late – this morning. He must already have told you that, because you knew where I was when you were calling me.'

'Don't you usually stay the night, when you visit the *castello*?'

'Not last night. I had reading to catch up with this morning. The driver waited for me – as you doubtless also already know.'

'Then he went home. You didn't go out again, after that?'

Horatio didn't reply.

'No…' said Cesare, answering his own question with a shake of his shiny head: 'You wouldn't have had the energy.'

# Thirty-two

Flags on the rooftops were flying at half-mast, and Horatio went to work in a black suit and tie on the morning following Franco di Giorgio's death. There was already a black beribboned wreath hanging on the front door of the *municipio*. Manuel must have telephoned maintenance to tell them to put it there. Fair enough: he wasn't only a prominent citizen, big businessman and sponsor of the arts, he was also a major government contractor, partly responsible, through advertising, for the island's tourism image abroad and more recently having become involved in helping to attract overseas investment. He had a finger in every pie.

Most of the staff murmured their condolences as the mayor entered the building, knowing that he was both a friend and a business partner.

He called Vincenzo at the court offices and told him to put a magistrate on stand-by for an inquest, probably in the afternoon. 'It looks like an open-and-shut case,' he told the clerk. 'The police said it looked like accidental death, so it shouldn't take more than a couple of minutes to reach a formal verdict, and we don't want to delay the funeral, which is scheduled for tomorrow.' In the Mediterranean funerals were usually held quickly, unless there was a postponement to await the attendance of a family member who lived abroad, but all the di Giorgio family members were currently on the island, so that wouldn't be necessary. He told Sophia to rearrange any diary appointments already scheduled for Tuesday, and keep the day clear.

He had an early meeting with the director of planning, who wanted to go over some applications – mainly for road access to the oil field and from there to the proposed harbour, as well as a draft outline of plans for the port that was being built. If Horatio approved them, they would go through the full meeting of council; there'd be some argument – there always was because members felt that they ought to make their presence felt – but they'd be accepted and agreed, in the end.

The director said there would also be competition to develop the land alongside the roads, with shops, houses and offices.

'We have only two competent major contractors,' Horatio told him. 'We'll examine the proposals and the tenders, as usual. But my feeling is that one of them should get the road in, and the other the road out. As for the buildings, we might give one of them the north side of one of the roads, and the south side of the other. Toss a coin for which of them gets which; can't be fairer than that.'

Alessandra, in a black trouser suit and black silk polo-neck shirt that somehow emphasised her cleavage, came to see him. Despite her recent promotion she maintained an overview of what she described as the morals and ethics of the magistrature. A witness in a court case had reported overhearing a defendant in the courthouse corridor say that he was confident that his case, when it came up before magistrate Ferra, would be dismissed because he had made him a gift of two freshly shot rabbits the previous week.

'There's too much of this with Ferra,' she said. 'Remember the birthday present left for him at La Spada? It's totally blatant. You need to do something about him.'

'Have we ever fired a magistrate?'

'Not to my knowledge; but the mayor giveth, so the mayor can take away. When the mayor appoints a magistrate, it has to be ratified by the full council with a two-thirds majority. Dismissal works the same way: it needs a two-thirds majority.'

'I can appreciate that it would be a salutary lesson for the rest of them – and for the entire government establishment – but I don't really want to debate corruption in the public forum of a full council meeting. For a start, it's relatively small scale. Two rabbits or a bottle of bubbly don't actually amount to very much, bad though it might appear, and corrupt though it might be. There is no evidence, anywhere, of any actual money changing hands, and this is, after all, a Sicilian island; it's all considered pretty normal.'

'It's true that we don't know about any bribes in cash. But if you can influence a magistrate with a brace of rabbits, he's patently equally open to receiving brown envelopes stuffed with *lire*. My view is that you should nip it in the bud while, so far as we know, it is all low key. Ferra wouldn't want his conduct to be debated in the council meeting, either. My guess is that if you threatened him he'd resign to save face.'

'Let me think about it,' said Horatio. 'Meanwhile, tell Vincenzo to assign him to nothing more important than parking tickets.'

'We're not getting so many of those, these days.'

'True, but these days the *commune* doesn't need the money.'

The council's exchequer was close to bursting with cash. The oil drilling company was flooding the place with financing for roads and buildings, developing the oilfield and investing in the new harbour. Speculators were buying or leasing land to benefit from the mineral exploitation and islanders who were already making money were buying new cars and, in some extreme cases, luxurious motor cruisers or racing yachts.

The *commune* couldn't spend its own income, which came from taxes, licences and national government grants, fast enough. It could hardly spend it at all.

There were constant calls for proposals for grants from an endless variety of EU funding opportunities. These were then evaluated in Palermo or Rome, and Italy's own EU funds office approved them. Whether it was a plan to improve a farm track, repair a wall, or embellish a beach or public park, a request went in and 85% of the total cost was instantly provided, as if by magic. There was nothing on the island, it seemed, that the European commissioners were not desperate to improve or 'rehabilitate'. The process involved a lot of paperwork – the *commune* had its own EU directorate to handle that – but no apparent obstacles. The only requirement was that the council had sufficient funds of its own to pay 15% of the cost of each project – and there was no problem, there.

Horatio, who had voted against the proposal for Britain to join the European community – 'I'm with the *Daily Express,* on this one' – quietly told friends he sometimes felt guilty that the taxpayers of Manchester, Munich and Marseille were picking up the tab for his island without ever being likely to visit it. On the other hand, he consoled himself philosophically, it was there for them if they wanted to come.

Now, all the projects that Horatio had envisaged during his election campaign – without knowing where the money would come from –were gradually reaching fruition. The *commune* was building a new sports stadium that could double as an arena for concerts and for the annual music festival; pavements and footpaths were being widened to become more user-friendly for push-chairs and wheelchairs; electricity cables that had previously been strung loosely and untidily between buildings were being buried underground; a pre-school day centre was in process of construction and the *liceo* was being extended to house an IT centre and a language laboratory; a new oil-field ring road would reduce and maybe eliminate heavy traffic in the city centre. The island's bus service, which previously had not run to some communities after dark (or, in some isolated cases, after lunch) now operated an all-day service to every village. He had even arranged for the *piazza duomo* to be repaved, to the delight of the bishop. New wealth had encouraged bigger and better shops and supermarkets with a greater choice of goods for sale, and there were new banks and cash machines all over the island. He had personally – and publicly – presented a large cheque to the contessa for new seating, curtains, backstage facilities and a bar at the opera house, and she had expressed her gratitude privately, in the usual manner.

A *carabiniere* messenger arrived with the police report and Sophia handed it, unopened, to Horatio. She also placed a cup of *macchiato* on his desk, and stayed watching as he tore open the envelope, extracted the papers, and leaned back in his chair to begin reading…

On the evening prior to his death Franco Salvatore di Giorgio, aged 55, described as a company director, had informed his family that he planned to go hunting early the following morning. His wife and three children had still been in bed when he left the house, driving his Land Rover Discovery to a field that he rented from the church for occasional hunting. He had not said that he would be meeting or hunting with any friends, and often would go on his own.

He had shot two quail which he had placed in his hunting bag, along with two used cartridges.

Another tenant, one Silvio Rossi, who also had shooting rights on the land, had been driven there by his wife, arriving about 7am. He had noticed di Giorgio's car and then seen the body lying in the field. He ran over and saw that di Giorgio appeared to be dead. He returned to the car and his wife drove him to the nearest building, a farmhouse, from where he used the phone to call the police. All this, including the approximate timings, was confirmed by Rossi's wife and the local farmer whose telephone they had used, and by the emergency services log at *carabinieri* headquarters.

Police had arrived at 0720 and confirmed that the man was dead. His shotgun, a Benelli Executive Grade I, 12-gauge side-by-side model, was on the ground beside the body. One cartridge had been spent and was still inside the barrel, as was an unused cartridge. The safety lock was not applied.

Forensic enquiries showed no fingerprints on the weapon, other than those of the deceased himself, and of the police chief, the evidence officer and the senior magistrate (who had been officially summoned to the scene as a matter of routine) and which were all post-incident.

The ground was too hard to establish whether there were any other footprints at the scene, even including those of the witness Rossi.

However, in the laboratory, forensics did establish that the mechanism of the gun had been adjusted at some stage – presumably to make the trigger action lighter in use. This was totally contrary to the gunsmith's instructions and would have automatically invalidated any guarantee.

Further, experimentation in the police laboratory showed that, in its altered state, the weapon could fire spontaneously if dropped on to a hard surface. There was a slight abrasion in one corner on the pattern of the stock that suggested this might have happened and could consequently have been what caused the trigger, with the safety catch off, to fire if mishandled or dropped.

A second possibility, considered to be remote, was that if di Giorgio had placed his shotgun on the ground – possibly while placing the quail in his hunting bag – his dog might have accidentally trodden on the trigger, causing it to go off. This theory, however, could probably be discounted because there was no dog-hair or paw-print on the weapon; also, it was not compatible with the angle of the shot. It was not even known whether the deceased had taken the animal with him (although he usually did), but the dog was at the deceased's home when the police arrived to inform the family. Although it was possible that the dog, an Irish retriever, had made its own way home, the dog-handling unit was of the opinion that its natural inclination would have been to stay with the body.

The police and forensic conclusion, therefore, was that the deceased had been carrying the gun over his shoulder, and accidentally dropped it behind him, releasing the trigger mechanism and causing it, with the barrels still pointing upwards, to discharge shot into the back of his skull. There were no other pellet wounds to his back or shoulders.

The shot caused extensive head injuries (the medical examiner's report was attached) from which death would have been instantaneous.

The last sentence of the typed report was the investigators' recommendation: NO SUSPICIOUS CIRCUMSTANCES; ACCIDENTAL DEATH.

There was a dotted line at the bottom where Horatio added his initials before handing it back to Sophia. He had no interest in reading the lurid details of the pathologist's autopsy report.

He took a draught of cool coffee. 'Accidental death,' he told her. 'Get this over to Vincenzo, will you? Ask him to get it processed as a matter of urgency. And tell him to suggest a warning against hunters tampering with the mechanism of their shotguns.'

# Thirty-three

'You read the report?' Cesare asked. 'Of course you did; you signed it. Did you know? Were your surprised?'

'It was very comprehensive, I thought. Maybe too comprehensive. I thought the dog theory might have been clutching at straws. I know I suggested it, as a long shot, but...'

'You know my methods, Watson: cover all contingencies. Actually I meant the pathologist's report.'

They were smoking cigarettes on the terrace of the di Giorgio family's villa, after the funeral. It had been a massively attended ceremony. Anticipating a large congregation, the service had been held in the cathedral with the bishop – never one to miss an opportunity to take centre stage – officiating, accompanied by no fewer than five priests.

The family had occupied the front pews with the civic dignitaries, mayor, police chief, *commune* directors and government officials, behind them and hundreds of local businessmen who were di Giorgio's clients packing into the other seats.

The bishop had drawn attention to the size of the congregation, pointing out that there was no aspect of life on the island that had been untouched by Franco di Giorgio. 'He sponsored the baby-wear fair... and also represented our funeral directors. It could therefore be said that he looked after our community from the cradle to the grave.'

Every member of the congregation had been handed a bookmark-size memorial card, bearing a colour head-and-shoulders photograph of the deceased.

'It must be unique,' Cesare had whispered to Horatio: 'the only picture in existence of the guy without a cigar in his mouth.'

'It's in his right hand,' said Horatio.

'You can't see his hand.'

'You can see the smoke curling up at the side.'

Cesare put on his reading glasses and checked. 'You're right. You should have been a detective,' he said.

When family, clergy, and honoured guests moved on from the cathedral to the villa, the two friends collected drinks and went out from the curtained gloom into the sunshine.

Cesare was saying that he hadn't been referring to the forensic details; he was asking whether Horatio had read the autopsy report.

'I never read the medical stuff. I think that, basically, I'm too squeamish.'

'You should at least have scanned it. It turns out he was riddled with cancer. He would have had three months to live, at most.'

Horatio paused in thought. 'Perhaps that makes his death even more of a tragedy. On the other hand, maybe it saved him from suffering a lot of pain.'

'Another view might be that it may, after all, have been a very cleverly contrived suicide. That was the thought that occurred to me.'

Whatever the real truth of the matter – 'and I suppose we will now never know the real truth' – a verdict of accidental death was the most suitable and satisfactory from all points of view, said the police chief.

But, he asked Horatio, had he noticed the bishop's reference to 'from the cradle to the grave'?

Horatio said he had.

'And you've heard that expression before, perhaps?'

'It sounded familiar. Isn't that what they say in Sicily about the mafia?'

'It is; it made me wonder whether the bishop was also aware of the saying.'

Portelli joined them, bearing fresh glasses. When they took theirs from him, he raised his. 'From the cradle to the grave,' he said, as if proposing a toast.

'As a client... well, everybody here is a client... I was wondering...'

'I wasn't a client,' said Horatio.

'As mayor, you were a client,' corrected Portelli. 'He handled the marketing for tourism and development. As editor, his company – your company too, I know – does the newspaper's promotions and competitions. As joint president of Zoco, it does your recruitment advertising, your real estate for new employees, your public relations...'

'I suppose...'

'I'm not a client,' said Cesare.

'Except that he sponsored the corps annual athletics meeting, and also the police band. As the bishop said, he had everything covered. So, I was wondering, as a client myself, what happens now, to Campanello.'

Horatio said that under the terms of the partnership, the shares could be transferred only between the partners; in the event of the death of one, the other bought his shares and recompensed the heirs of the deceased.

'So it's all yours now.' Horatio confirmed that it was, or would be, as soon as the paperwork was completed. Business would continue as usual, he said.

A waiter appeared with a tray bearing fresh drinks. As he moved away to serve another group of smokers on the terrace, Portelli told Horatio: 'You have done remarkably well, my friend. Within only a couple of years you have become mayor and chief magistrate of Montebello... you are the owner and publisher of the only newspaper on the island... as mayor you are the biggest single employer of labour, and as joint owner of Zoco you run what is rapidly becoming the second biggest... you represent, with marketing, advertising and public relations, every business on the island... anybody who wants funding or grants or sponsorship has to come to you...'

Cesare raised an eyebrow, inclined his head and nodded, as if contemplating that list of achievements for the first time. 'The entire island population covered, as one might say, from the cradle to the grave.' Horatio studied his business partner's face, he wasn't sure whether he was smiling.

'So,' asked Portelli: 'You asked me the question some time ago… And my father asked me the question this morning – he wasn't meaning to be offensive, I assure you -- who would you now say is the godfather of Montebello?'

Horatio shuffled his feet a bit, clearly embarrassed by the question. None of it had been planned; every single aspect of his recent career movement had been happenstance. He hadn't wanted to become mayor – in fact he had originally described the idea as being crazy. The chief magistrate position had been an incidental effect, out of his control, that came with the mayor's job. The joint ownership of the oil company had been virtually forced upon him, through Portelli's own conniving. His purchase of the newspaper, and of the Campanello company, were off-shoot benefits of his newly found wealth from the oil field – the plot of land where he'd thought he would be planting olive trees. He was as surprised as anybody by the route his life had taken.

'…And he controls the only source of news and information on the island, and through his boys at *La Gazzetta* also any news that goes abroad about the island,' added Cesare. 'It's like Russia, or China.' Horatio noted with relief that his friend was smiling, as he spoke.

'Well, okay,' said Horatio. 'But if I am the godfather – and obviously I don't see it like that – I must be the only one who has been elected by the majority of the population. And almost certainly the only godfather who got the job on an anti-corruption ticket.'

# Thirty-four

Horatio had offered to meet Teresa at the airport but Cesare told him no; there was such a thing as protocol. She would be picked up by members of the *antimafia* commission and driven straight to their offices, where she would immediately start work by being given a briefing on the current situation. Then she would be driven to her new quarters, to unpack and move in.

'Tonight she can be all yours, but this afternoon she will be working.'

She had obviously told Cesare that they had already arranged a dinner date. There were no secrets on Montebello, and few even in the *carabinieri*.

Anticipating her return to the island had helped him concentrate his mind on what he had started to think of as his sex life.

It occurred to him that his recent course of relationships with women – some of them not much more than girls, hardly older than his daughters – had run almost along parallel lines with his new career changes. Certainly the liaisons with his secretaries, and with Alessandra, had been direct results of his election as mayor, and even Teresa had been an unexpected bi-product of that appointment. Only the contessa had been known to him before he was anything more than editor of the local paper, but during that time she had apparently been happily married and therefore, to his mind, off limits, sexually alluring though she undoubtedly was.

On the nights he'd spent alone in his own bed he had sometimes fallen asleep while comparing and contrasting their different attributes and attractions.

The secretaries, Sophia and Francesca, were, he had to admit, great joy, jointly and individually – although they had never visited him socially except as a twosome. A twosome, becoming a threesome with him, was in itself incredibly and excitingly sexy, he thought. They asked for nothing apart from the opportunity to frolic, usually on high days and holidays, with their boss, first in his pool and then in his bedroom. Moreover, on an island overburdened by gossip and rumour, they appeared to be amazingly tactful about their relationship with the mayor-cum-magistrate; there were never any knowing looks, no murmurings from other members of staff, even other secretaries, whenever he was in the presence of either of them. They seemingly enjoyed the companionship of a man twice their age; perhaps they thought that there was no inherent risk in such involvement. But most important was that they, all three of them, enjoyed a lot of harmless pleasure together.

Perhaps even more important was the fact that their adventures in no way affected their professional association. And they were both damned good secretaries.

Horatio reckoned that they would eventually mature, find boyfriends, settle down and marry and produce children, and probably become fat in the process of contentment, as most of the island's women seemed to do. They might even buy brassieres.

Alessandra, in terms of looks and possibly also in terms of intelligence, was simply the most desirable single woman on the island. Not for nothing did the cops refer to the female lawyer as The Body. It was difficult, well nigh impossible, for him or for any man in her presence to avert their eyes from her tits or her bum and she knew it. She was, however – as she frequently reminded him when she invited him into her bed and issued directions for foreplay – sexually self-sufficient. She didn't actually need a man at all.

It was, Horatio felt, something of an honour to be chosen as her partner from all the men in Montebello, but he was never sure that she saw him as an essential part of the proceedings.

The contessa also had her own sexual preference which, happily for him, revolved mainly around providing pleasure for her male partner. Those full heavy breasts, the by now familiar back of that long noble neck, her middle fingers teasing the rim of his anus, that vigorous tongue… Her invitations to dinner, with sex guaranteed as dessert, were frequent but not reliably regular. Horatio thought that perhaps she called him only when she didn't have a better offer, but whether her alternative preferences were for social or for sexual intercourse he had never quite managed to determine.

None of them, he coolly calculated, meant any more to him than his summer reunion meeting with his childhood sweetheart Jessica. And that, he thought, had been merely a diversion, just something that he thought he had needed to do, after hearing from her following a gap of so many years. But worthwhile, and fun, nevertheless. And he had to confess that, when he saw her off on her return flight, he'd wished she were staying longer.

On the other hand, there was Teresa…

She may not have had the Page Three or *Baywatch* curves of Alessandra, nor the voluptuousness and social confidence of the contessa, but she had a firm and shapely athlete's figure and was as fit, lively and agile as the two secretaries; she was bright, intelligent, well-read – and not only of police reports and training manuals; as a driver and as a dinner date she had been excellent company, sharing and joining in with Horatio's cynicism and sometimes off-the-wall sense of humour. She had also once been an enthusiastic partner in the bedroom, and a good friend in every other location.

But most of all, she had put her slender body between Horatio and a potential bullet. Greater love… And when they had both been suffering from the shock of that experience, they had sought and found beautiful solace and intimacy in each other's arms.

He arrived early at the restaurant that night and was sitting at the door sipping a bloody mary when she drove up. She went first to shake hands and talk briefly with Horatio's driver, Johnny, who was sitting patiently in the Alfa, as usual, outside. Then she saw Horatio and they both walked swiftly to greet each other. They kissed on the cheeks, then on the lips. A beaming Horatio put his arm round her shoulder; she put hers round his waist, and they walked into the dining room like the long-separated lovers that they were.

Settling her into a chair he found it difficult to take his eyes off hers. Groping blindly for his own seat he put his hand across the table towards her and she, smiling, placed her own small hand on top of it.

'I can't begin to tell you…'

'Don't,' she smiled happily, almost deliriously. 'Don't try. Enjoy the moment.'

'No,' he said. 'I *can* begin to tell you. I want to tell you. Many years ago I made a promise to myself that I would never say this again. But I think I am in love.'

Teresa squeezed his fingers silently, nodding and grinning at him, and mouthed: 'I know.'

The ever attentive Giosetta allowed them a few minutes alone and then glided up to their table, aware of the obvious electricity between them. Teresa stood to exchange cheek kisses as the restaurateur welcomed her back to the island.

'We don't want much to eat. Maybe just *antipasto* or a *primi piatti*… and a bottle of bubbly. Let's have some *Franciacorta*.'

'*Cuvee Annamaria Clementi*?' It was the queen of Italian sparkling wines, from the low-lying hills of Lombardy.

'Absolutely. Special occasion.'

'I understand. Leave it to me; I'll bring a small selection of *antipasti*. But the bottle first, right?'

It was difficult to eat and drink one-handed, but Teresa didn't release her hold. She traced circles and drew imaginary pictures on the back of his hand, or ran her pink-white unpainted nails along the length of his fingers.

'It's been such a long time. I don't know how I survived without you.'

'Oh, don't worry: I know how you survived; I have heard reports. But I don't mind about that in the slightest. A man needs to keep in shape, and in practice… so long as that all stops now, eh?'

Pushing aside the empty plate, standing and finishing his drink, Horatio said: 'Johnny's in for a surprise. He's never known me leave this place so early.'

'He won't be surprised at all. He's not there. I told him he could go home and take the rest of the night off.'

She opened the front passenger door for him: 'Don't try to play the gentleman; you are still under protection.' And she drove most of the way to his villa with her right hand resting on his thigh.

They went straight to his bedroom where she first unfastened the flap of her handbag and placed it on the bedside locker. There would be the little Beretta inside it, he knew; he was still under protection, her protection. She unbuttoned his shirt, and sat on the bed to unbuckle his belt and lower the zip of his flies, then grabbed his buttocks and pulled him towards her. She told him to get into bed and he obediently laid there, beneath the single sheet, watching her undress. Naked, she took his shirt from the back of a chair and put it on, buttoning it loosely. When she came close to the bed he reached for her through the lower buttons and this time she didn't move away.

They made love eagerly, frantically, then rested and did it again, slowly and gently, Horatio taking time to explore every inch of her firm body. Just before sunrise they were woken by his neighbour's poultry. 'Cock crow,' he said.

She reached down for him. 'Good name for it,' she said.

He went to the kitchen and made fresh coffee and squeezed orange juice and took it to her in bed. They fluffed up the pillows and reclined side by side, constantly touching and stroking.

'So what's on the agenda today? I have a committee meeting this afternoon but I could finish early.'

'More briefing and debriefing. A lot of reading to catch up. I want to go over the Franco di Giorgio shooting incident, then I should unpack my gear, properly.'

'The di Giorgio case is closed. There was an investigation, forensics, an autopsy and an inquest: accidental death.'

'I know. It's just that it was the strangest shooting, don't you think? It's okay. Cesare has told me it's closed. I just want to read it through, carefully. I'm the new sheriff in town, don't forget: I need to understand everything, thoroughly.'

Horatio refreshed their cups from the percolator.

'What I've never properly understood, although I have asked Cesare several times,' he told her, 'is why, when we famously have no mafia here – probably uniquely in the whole of Sicily – we actually need an *antimafia* commission or an *antimafia* department of any kind. I mean, I know that the first role of the *carabinieri* is to prevent organised crime coming to this island. Assuming that they are doing that job competently, which I am sure they are, where is the mafia to rationalise an *antimafia*? What are you supposed to do, to justify your existence?'

'There are different types of mafia, that's the explanation for it. It's the movement of money, it's investment, it may be bribes or protection money, or money laundering, or it may be commissions for services. It's really all about power.'

'If you look at it like that,' said Horatio, 'most of the so-called power on this island is right here, lying in bed beside you. I effectively control the council, and the courts; to a large extent I even control the news; I receive commissions for promoting businesses; I issue the licences... it was never intended that things should happen that way, but that's the way it went.'

'I know,' Teresa said, thoughtfully. 'It's going to make my job very easy, I think.'

The heavy silence that followed was broken by Teresa.

'You asked me once... what it felt like to shoot somebody. I said we never talked about it. Well, I think the reason we don't talk about it is that you don't feel anything, so there isn't an answer to the question.'

She sipped at her coffee, pensively.

'It doesn't keep you awake at night or give you nightmares. Somebody needs to be shot, for some reason, and you shoot them. It's almost a natural thing to do. It is justice. It is far more justifiable, in fact, than shooting an innocent bird in flight. If the person deserves it, there is no need to feel guilty about having done it. It's just something that needs to be done. And when it's done you don't feel anything at all.'

As she took the half-finished cup from his hand, Horatio kissed her forehead and said: 'I know…'

#

Lightning Source UK Ltd.
Milton Keynes UK
UKOW06f1827210116

266846UK00011B/165/P